No Right Way
to do a
Wrong Thing

by Janice M. Allen

Allen Creative Group
Ridgecrest, CA

Allen Creative Group
708.439.0541
janiceallen7519@gmail.com

This is a work of fiction. Names, characters, places, and incidents are products of the author's imagination or are used fictitiously and are not to be construed as real. Any resemblance to actual events, locales, organizations, or persons, living or dead, is entirely coincidental.

No Right Way to do a Wrong Thing © 2018 by Janice M. Allen
published by the Pernell Group (South Holland, IL) 2018
republished by Allen Creative Group (Ridgecrest, CA) 2021
ISBN (trade paperback): 978-0-9863149-1-9
ISBN (e-book): 978-0-9863149-0-2

Cover Design: J. L. Woodson ~ www.woodsoncreativestudio.com

Interior Book Design: Lissa Woodson ~ www.macrompg.com

Editorial Team: Lissa Woodson ~ www.macrompg.com

                             Valarie Prince ~ vp1editing@gmail.com

                             Katie Walsh Giannini ~ ktwedits@gmail.com

Manuscript Evaluation: Tanisha Pearson-Jones

Printed in the United States of America

Acknowledgements

All things are possible through God.

For that, I say, "Thank you, Lord Jesus, for all that You have done for me and for all that You are to me. Thank You for putting this gift of writing in me. Most of all, thank You for leading me to a great friend (Lissa Woodson), who saw my gift and helped me nurture it.

Thank you to my Mom (Mary McCoy) for always encouraging me, never doubting what I could accomplish and always being there for me. I love you more than you'll ever know.

Thank you to my cousins (Debbie Thomas, Raven Thomas, Dawanna Davis and Devon Walker). During the years that it took me to complete this book, they constantly asked when it was coming out because they read my sample chapters and couldn't wait to see what was going to happen next. Special thanks to my aunt (LaVerne Walker) and to my friends (Regina Martin, Mary Meyers, Lela Page and Pam McKenzie) for encouraging me along the way.

Thank you to my Macro Literary All-Star Angels (M- LAS): bestselling authors Naleighna Kai, Joyce Brown, Susan Peters, Valarie Prince, Martha Kennerson, Tanisha Pearson-Jones (rest in the arms of Jesus, Baby Diva), D. J. McLaurin, Lorna L.A. Lewis and J. L. Woodson. A special thanks to my Aunt Marie (Rose Grandberry) for her support. I discovered my gift of writing around the same time that she discovered her gift of poetry.

And a special thanks to Lissa Woodson, Valarie Prince and Katie Walsh Giannini for being the most awesome editors a girl could ever have!

Chapter 1

3:47 p.m. Saturday, July 16, 2011

"Let me get this straight," Val snapped at her husband. "You want me to abort my baby, but some other woman you swear up and down you *don't* love can walk around eight months pregnant with your child?"

"You're *not* having that baby," Kurt growled, his bronze skin ablaze with anger.

He took two steps forward. Val instinctively backed away, her heart performing an erratic drum solo. Two years of marriage and she'd never seen this side of him. She scanned the kitchen, calculating an escape route out the back door, but there was no way her moist palms would allow her to get a firm grip on the doorknob. He was closer to the car keys on the table anyway.

Thunderous banging against the outside security door made both of them snap their heads toward the front entrance.

"Police! Open up," ordered a deep, authoritative voice.

Val marveled at how quickly Kurt transformed, pasting a phony smile on his face before marching to the living room and cracking the wooden door. "May I help you, officers?" he asked through the thick glass security door. His tone was sickeningly sweet.

"We got a call about a disturbance coming from this address," a female voice stated.

"You alone in there?" Judging from this resonant voice, Val pictured the man outside the door to be the size of Dwayne 'The Rock' Johnson. She couldn't tell for sure. Kurt had positioned his muscular frame so she couldn't see out, which meant the cops couldn't see in either.

"There's been some type of mistake, officers. I'm here by my—"

"Quit lying, Kurt," Val shouted. His head whipped in her direction, lightning flashing in his eyes. She returned his glare. Evidently he was banking on her being afraid to speak up while he played Mr. Nice Guy for the police.

One of the officers jiggled the knob on the locked security door. A female officer demanded, "Open up—right now!"

"Everything's fine," Kurt said as he closed the wooden door, leaving just enough of a crack to peek out of. "We don't need your help."

"If we have to tell you one more time to let us in, I'm going to shoot this lock off," the baritone voice outside impatiently roared.

Val moved in, shoved Kurt out of the way and turned the deadbolt on the heavy glass door. She swung it wide open and stepped back, feeling Kurt's heated gaze on her the whole time as the officers marched in. A statuesque cop with bleached-blonde hair peeking from her hat moved immediately to Val, conducting a quick assessment of her from head to toe. Val had no illusions about her own wrecked appearance. She finger-combed her shoulder-length spiral curls into place.

"What's your name, ma'am?" the female cop asked. She guided Val by the elbow to the suede sofa. "Are you all right?"

Val balanced her curvy frame on the arm of the couch, staring at Kurt. She studied his face for any sign of regret. What she found was a murderous glare that almost made her wither.

Almost.

She closed her eyes and weighed her options. It would be better to talk to the police and incur her husband's wrath now than to keep quiet and continue the argument alone later.

"My name is Valencia Timmons, and that's my husband Kurt. We were arguing about my pregnancy, and then he threatened me."

"No, I didn't!"

"Shut it!" the burly officer standing next to Kurt snapped. "You already lied about being in here by yourself."

"We don't need you here," Kurt protested, his rigid shoulders heaving in an effort to remain calm.

The giant officer stepped in front of Kurt and pulled a set of handcuffs from his duty belt. "If I have to put you in the back of my squad car to give Officer Buchanan a chance to take your wife's statement, that's what I'll do." The cuffs clanked against each other as they dangled on his fingertip in front of Kurt's face. Kurt folded his arms across his chest and angrily slammed his back against the wall.

Officer Buchanan was now standing in front of Val, holding a pen and notepad. "Go ahead, ma'am. What happened tonight?"

Val looked down at the officer's spit-shined shoes, heaved a deep breath, then looked up at her ivory face. "Like I was saying, we were arguing about my pregnancy."

The officer frowned, jotting something on her notepad. "Why would your pregnancy be an issue?"

Val wrapped her arms tightly around her midsection. Three years of being unable to conceive in her first marriage, followed by the unexpected death of her first husband Hunter during a medical mission in Indonesia, had embalmed her heart and given it a closed-casket funeral. She met Kurt eight years later. Many men had tried to date her after she was widowed. But Kurt was different. He understood the anguish she'd been through, and he wanted to come into her world to fulfill all her dreams. Or so she thought.

"Kurt surprised me with this house a month before our wedding," she said, gesturing like she was a game show host and the house was the next prize up for grabs. "He said he wanted plenty of room for our family." That promise had resuscitated her heart back then. She tilted her head back and closed her eyes, trying to remember that moment of happiness. "So I sold my house and we moved here after the wedding. But as soon as we got back from our honeymoon, he sang a different tune." Val shot an accusatory glare at him. "That's when he told me that his business was struggling and he wanted to put off having children until he was sure he could support our family by himself."

"That doesn't sound like an unreasonable request," the handsome, beefy policeman piped in.

Kurt clenched his fists at his sides. "Finally somebody's starting to see my side of this mess." His eyes lowered to the man's name badge. "Officer Dell, when I met my wife, her psychiatric practice was growing and the medical office building she owned was almost at full occupancy. All of her profit was going into her business, and I was fine with that because I wasn't some gigolo looking to sponge off of a woman."

"That's not the point," Val said, jumping to her feet but sitting back down after Officer Buchanan shot a warning glance at her. "You made a promise, knowing full well that you weren't going to go through with it." Finding out about his business struggles before they married would not have made her leave him at the altar. She loved the man he was when they met; she would have stuck by that Kurt. She couldn't say the same about the man Kurt had become in the last two years.

"I was doing what was best for us," Kurt said, raising his hands as if to say "I give up."

"Totally disregarding my needs is what's best for us?" she pointed out. Settling a hand on her knee didn't stop the nervous energy that made it shake. She turned to Officer Buchanan and said in a low voice, "I agreed to wait to have children, though." Breathing deeply, she concentrated on not bursting into tears. She'd shed enough already. "Then about seven months ago, his stepfather gave us more than enough money to put his business on solid ground, and Kurt still wanted me to wait!" Her mouth twisted into a contemptuous frown. "Then just a few hours ago, up pops a mistress I never knew he had."

Officer Buchanan stopped taking notes and tossed a furious gaze at Kurt like she was ready to tear his head off.

Val flashed eight fingers in the air. "She. Was. Eight. Months.

Pregnant!" Each word was more shrill than the previous one. Thrusting an index finger toward her husband, she yelled, "With his child!"

"Yeah, but she got pregnant by mistake," Kurt shot back from the other side of the room.

The officers shared a speaking glance and frowned.

"You got pregnant on purpose," Kurt snarled with disdain.

Val's rage propelled her off the arm of the sofa. "Oh, so it's okay for you to have an affair and *accidentally* get your lover pregnant, but it's not okay for your *wife* to carry your seed?!" Hands on her hips, she dared him to say something.

Kurt pushed himself off the wall. The muscle-bound cop put his hand on Kurt's chest to keep him in place. "Look, what you two got going on is way above my pay grade. You need marital counseling or something. But for now, you'll both need to steer clear of each other and cool down."

Kurt's nostrils flared. "What? You taking me to jail?"

"Nope. But you can't stay here tonight." The officer nodded toward the back of the house. "I'll give you five minutes to pack up a few things and come with me."

"You didn't even ask *me* what happened," Kurt complained.

"I think we've heard enough from both of you."

"So you're just going to take her side?" Kurt turned his nose up at the officers. "I figured that drug dealers and politicians had cops on the payroll, but I didn't think the average Jane Doe could pimp the department too."

Fast as lightning, Officer Buchanan whipped out her billy club and streaked across the room to Kurt. He stumbled back into the wall, anticipating a blow that never came. An insolent look darkened his face like he was ready to do something that would land him on the evening news. The female officer didn't seem the least bit rattled. She stood in front of him, smacking the club against her open palm.

"You've got five minutes to pack for the night," the stocky officer instructed again, pulling his sleeve up to look at an enormous watch strapped to his hairy wrist.

"No, better yet," Officer Buchanan amended, "let's make that two nights."

Stomping into the dining room with the other officer in tow, Kurt grabbed both sets of keys off of the table, then flung Val's key ring onto the floor. "I don't need anything. I'll crash at my mother's house." As he passed Val, he announced, "I'll be back Monday afternoon. We'll talk then."

Both police officers filed behind him as he stepped out of the front door. "If we have to come back here," Officer Dell said to Kurt's back, "somebody *will* be going to jail."

A minute later, Kurt fishtailed his 2011 GMC Yukon down the street. The moment the squad car pulled away, Val hurried from the window and double-checked the locks on the front door. She scurried to the kitchen too, securing the deadbolt and latch on the door that led to the garage. Her heart felt an instant of relief—until she heard something hard crashing to the floor in the bedroom.

Calf muscles tight and shoulders hunched, Val tipped up the stairs. She let out a pent-up breath when she realized that her cell phone had vibrated itself right over the edge of the dresser and onto the hardwood floor. What she saw when she picked the phone up and turned it over made the veins in her head feel like tiny straws with a raging river surging through them.

An earlier text from a blocked number had caused her and Kurt to be at each other's throats in the first place. Now Whitley, the woman Val now knew to be her husband's mistress, had re-sent the message, for the third time that day.

It simply said, "How well do you know your man?"

Chapter 2

"Whitley, we don't have a *relationship*! We have a *situation*!" Kurt barked into the Bluetooth as he merged his SUV from I-57 to I-80.

"You low-down, lying bastard." Whitley spoke in a whisper, but the viciousness she spewed couldn't have been louder if it came through a megaphone. Her tirade was interrupted by muffled voices in the background, then he heard, "Take this hallway to the east elevator, then two floors up."

Calling Whitley while she was working at the hospital's information desk hadn't been the smartest move, but Kurt was too troubled to wait for a more appropriate time. She certainly hadn't been concerned about what was appropriate when she showed up at his house a half hour ago.

She turned her attention and menacing voice to him again. "I don't know who the hell you think you are, calling here and going off on me." Before he could reply, she ordered him to hold on. He could tell her hand was over the mouthpiece this time, but he snatched bits and pieces of the conversation. "Nell ... outside ... this fool." Whoever Nell was, she must not have liked what she was being told because Whitley came back with a loud, "Girl, I'll be back before your funky little nicotine break."

Kurt checked his speed, eased off the gas and bore left to get on the I-294 Tollway. The ride from his Matteson, Illinois home to his mother's house in Burr Ridge would take about another twenty-five minutes. He set the cruise control to sixty since being distracted by Whitley might have him speeding again before he knew it.

"Okay, I'm back," she hollered over some clunker with a bad muffler that nearly drowned her out.

When the noise faded into the background and he was sure she could hear him, Kurt started with, "Whitley, you need to listen to—"

"No, you listen to me," she snarled. "You lied to me."

"How many times do I have to tell you I'm not leaving my wife for you? I made that clear from the beginning." His head was so tight that black and white polka dots were dancing around in his peripheral vision.

Her voice faded in and out. "... should've known ... sorry ass ..."

Kurt's finger itched to end the call. None of this was anything that he hadn't repeatedly heard since learning that she was pregnant. Unable to curb his hostility, he cut into her ranting. "Four months ago when you said you were four months pregnant with my baby, I told you we were done and I wasn't leaving my wife. Then you go and threaten to take me to child support court even though I gave you all that money?" For all he knew, the child wasn't even his, but going before a judge to prove otherwise would surely have gotten back to his wife and made his crumbling marriage self-destruct.

"But I didn't take you to court, did I?" she cried. "You know why? Because I love you."

"You love money," he shot back. The stack of hundreds tattooed on her left shoulder was a testament to that. "Why else would you sign an agreement promising to get out of my life in exchange for a hundred fifty thousand dollars?"

She may never have demanded that money had he not mentioned his cut of his stepfather's lottery winnings. Good sex had made him share way too much pillow talk with Whitley.

"I only signed it because I thought I could walk away from you," she countered, her voice both sensual and poisonous. "But my feelings changed."

"Yeah? Well, words on paper don't change," he growled, giving a what-are-you-looking-at glare to a wide-eyed child who stared at him from the back seat of a passing car. "We had a contract. And now you think I'm just supposed to magically change my life around to make a happy little family with you?"

"That's exactly what I think!" she screamed.

"News flash—that's never gonna happen. So you can just stop calling my wife."

"I didn't call," Whitley defended. "I texted because she needed to know."

"This mess is between you and me. You should've left her out of it." The windows seemed to vibrate with the force of his words. As best he could figure, Whitley had gotten Val's number through a careless mistake on his part. While driving Whitley back to work after a noontime quickie, she nagged him to death about being hungry and not having enough time to eat when she clocked in at the hospital. He foolishly left his unlocked phone in the SUV while he dashed into a convenience store to get a giant slice of pizza to shut her up.

Still fuming, he said to Whitley, "Look, we need to talk about this some other time."

"I need to get back to work anyway. But you can best believe that we *will* talk."

Whitley hung up. Kurt boiled. He pulled down the sun visor hard enough to make several CDs tumble out of the holder strapped to it. As he stuffed them back in, a Temptations anthology slid out. He loaded both volumes into the CD player, then pressed the Bluetooth button on his steering wheel before the music started.

"Call Mom," he commanded when an automated voice said, "Ready." After a few moments, the call connected to a warm voice.

"Hi, son." His mother always sounded so glad to hear from him.

"Hey," he said. "You busy?"

"Never too busy for you, baby," she said in a soothing tone. "What do you need?"

"To come by and talk."

"I made meatloaf last night," she offered. "I'll heat up a plate for you."

Kurt's stomach turned at the thought of food. "Not hungry, Ma. But thanks."

She was silent, then said, "You must have something really important on your mind if you're turning down a meal."

"Yes, ma'am."

"Then I'll be waiting for you."

Kurt ended the call and turned up the volume on the CD. He snorted as the Temptations sang "Ball of Confusion." *Story of my life.*

If anybody could give him some sound advice about his marriage, it was his mother. Lord knows his stepfather wouldn't. Since the day Foster Timmons learned that Val's mother had been in prison almost all of Val's life, he repeatedly warned Kurt that Val was going to go down that same road. "You need to go on and get a divorce now." Foster was forever dictating what everyone else should be doing. But the woman Foster saw wasn't the Val that Kurt knew. Val was loving, honest and kind—even if she was ready to kill him right about now.

Funny, those three qualities are what Val says drew her to him.

Kurt opened the sunroof, letting the afternoon light fill the cabin of the SUV. The CD had segued to Eddie Kendricks' smooth falsetto in "Just My Imagination," making Kurt wish that everything happening to him right now was only in his mind.

Maybe he shouldn't have insisted that they put off having children. It had overloaded the circuitry of his marriage and caused it to go up in flames. The conversations were always the same. She'd cry and say, "I'm thirty-seven years old. How much longer am I supposed to wait?" His comeback was always along the lines of, "So! I'm forty-three. If I can wait a little longer, you can too."

When Kurt still stuck with that excuse after getting two hundred fifty thousand dollars from his stepfather's lottery winnings, Val became impossible to live with. And now this.

He snapped back from his thoughts and merged right to exit the

Stevenson Expressway. Coming up the ramp, he switched to track five on the CD. While the bass line from "My Girl" poured through the speakers, it occurred to him that the lyrics echoed everything that he had felt for Val. Until recently.

In less than forty-eight hours, he'd be going back home. He had to make her do the right thing—no matter how much it hurt.

Chapter 3

Val pressed the Home button on her iPhone for a couple of seconds, causing a voice-control prompt to appear on the screen. "Call Dwayne," she commanded, rubbing the taut muscles along the back of her neck.

She waited to be connected, thinking back to the text message that started the chaos. Against her better judgment, Kurt's heated denial had led her to thinly accept that maybe she was over-reacting to that first "how well do you know your man?" text message. Then a second one had come—a selfie some brunette took of herself nuzzling up against Kurt's cheek. Timestamp 2:01 p.m. The caption at the bottom had read, "This is what real love looks like."

Val had exploded into their home office. "Kurt!"

He had been on the cordless phone and typing on his laptop.

"I guess this is a wrong number too, huh?" she had shrieked, thrusting her iPhone into his face with enough force that it would have bloodied his nose had he not pulled his head back as quickly as he did.

"What the?!?" He had grabbed her wrist, yanked the cell phone from her hand and stared at the screen. An annoyed expression had flickered first; then his bronze skin went gray. He had put the cordless phone back up to his ear and said, "I have an emergency here. I need to call you back."

Anger had clouded his chiseled face. Val didn't know if he was mad at himself for getting caught, mad at the woman for aiding in his capture or mad at his wife for catching him. Whatever the case, Val wasn't backing down.

For the next thirty minutes, a hailstorm of curses and accusations had ensued. Less than an hour later, a tornado named Whitley had touched down on Val's front porch.

Now Val had just forty-eight hours to decide whether to try to rebuild from the ruins of her marriage or to simply call in a wrecking crew to haul away the debris.

Her brother answered the phone, out of breath. "Hey, Val. What's up?"

"Nothing," she lied. His feet were pounding away, but it didn't sound like his shoes were slapping against pavement. "You're on the treadmill?"

"Yeah, but that's not what you called about, li'l sis. Something's wrong. I can hear it in your voice."

A couple of beeps, followed by the slower patter of footsteps, alerted her that he'd turned off the machine.

He huffed and puffed a few times more. "Give me a minute." The line was silent except for the drone of a newscaster in the background. A moment later, Dwayne was back on the line. "Okay, I'm ready," he said. "What's up?"

"It's Kurt," Val answered.

"Is he okay?"

She switched to speaker mode and placed the phone on the island in the center of her kitchen. "Can you come over? I really need to talk. I'm ... I'm going to be a mother."

Dwayne whooped it up. "Finally!"

"And a stepmother."

Silence, then he choked out, "What?!"

Thinking about it made her feel faint. If Hunter were still alive, he would never have done anything like that to her. That man loved her more than magnets love metal. And she returned his love a hundredfold. So how had she hit the jackpot the first time around in love, then landed a losing scratch-off ticket the second time?

She propped herself against the refrigerator. "It's too complicated to tell you over the phone. How soon can you get here?"

"As soon as I pick up Uncle Bubba. He's at the park around the corner helping coach the church's little league team."

"Oh, Lord," she exclaimed. "Is that little Robinson boy still running the bases backward?"

"Yep. No matter how many times Uncle Bubba reminds him, he still runs to third base when he gets lucky enough to hit the ball." They shared a bit of nervous laughter. "I'll see you in an hour-and-a-half, li'l sis."

Although Dwayne was ten minutes younger than his twin sister, he'd been calling her li'l sis since the tenth grade, when his legs had doubled in length and he suddenly towered over her and nearly everyone else in the family.

"Just get here," she said, thinking *forty-eight hours*.

₪ ₪ ₪

Uncle Bubba parroted the lyrics of Will Smith's "Summertime" as he and Dwayne pulled into Val's driveway. At sixty-five, Uncle Bubba was a Will Smith fanatic. He watched the multi-talented entertainer's movies and re-runs of his TV series to exhaustion and knew the words to every rap the superstar had ever recorded.

He got out of Dwayne's Dodge Charger, cane in hand, and walked up the driveway. The onset of Parkinson's Disease sometimes caused him to lose his balance when his leg movements became jerky. But even with the cane, he strolled toward the house with the confident swagger of a man forty years his junior. "This cane ain't holdin' me up; I'm holdin' it up," he had often quipped. "If I let go of it, I can still stand—but it can't."

The front door opened before he rang the bell. Val stepped out and spread her arms for a hug. He pulled her to him, then took a step back to examine her red, puffy eyes. "I'm glad to see you, girl. But you look awfully sad." His gentle squeeze to the tip of her nose was a show of affection they'd shared since she was a child. She tweaked his nose in return.

When he moved away, Dwayne stepped up and held his sister an extra-long time. He draped a finger across her cheek where tracks of tears had probably been not too long ago and leaned in to hug her once again.

"Uncle Bubba," she said as they all walked into the house and past the living room. "You want a Mountain Dew?"

He waved her question away with a weathered brown hand and made himself comfortable on a high-back vinyl stool at the island in the kitchen. "I'd better not. I'm headed to the doctor's office Monday, and if I get all that caffeine in me now, he'll be fussin' 'bout my blood pressure bein' too high or my heart beatin' too fast or some foolishness like that."

Val climbed on a stool across from him. Dwayne helped himself to a Coke from the fridge, took down a glass from the cabinet and noisily filled it with ice before he sat down next to Val.

"Now what's this talk about a baby, sis?" He fished a small ice cube out of his glass and tossed it in his mouth.

"Babies. Plural," she corrected.

Uncle Bubba didn't miss that slight quiver in her voice. She covered her face with her hands. Fresh tears seeped between her fingers and dripped down her wrist.

He wagged an arthritic finger at Dwayne. "Go get the girl a Kleenex or somethin'."

Dwayne snatched a paper towel from the rack by the sink.

"Boy, that's too rough," Uncle Bubba fussed.

Dwayne hurried to the bathroom while Uncle Bubba slid off the stool and stood next to Val. He was still rubbing her back when Dwayne returned with a wad of Kleenex in one hand and the paper towel in the other. She took the tissue and delicately patted under her eyes and wiped her nose.

"Now, what's going on around here?" Dwayne asked.

"The police—"

"*What* police?!?" Dwayne and Uncle Bubba chorused like two angry bulls.

"The neighbors called the police because Kurt and I were arguing."

"Did he put his hands on you?" Dwayne asked, taking a step back and scanning her frame from head to toe.

She shook her head. "He didn't."

"And he never will if he knows what's good for him," Uncle Bubba said, giving her a sideways glance.

"Where is he?" Dwayne asked, craning his head toward the steps leading upstairs.

"The police told him to leave," she said.

Dwayne's shoulders relaxed a little as he took the seat beside her and poured his can of Coke into the glass of ice.

"But he'll be back in two days," she added.

Dwayne's arm twitched, causing the last few drops to spill on the counter.

"Back. For. What?" Uncle Bubba shouted, banging his cane against the porcelain tile floor with each word.

"To talk," she whispered.

Dwayne laid the paper towel over the mess he'd made. "What were you arguing about in the first place that made the neighbor have to call the police?"

"Yeah, you were sayin' somethin' 'bout a baby." Uncle Bubba walked to the other side of the island and slid back onto his stool, hanging his cane on the back of the stool next to him.

"Babies!" she amended again. Tears began to roll down her cheek and she blurted, "I'm pregnant."

"But that's a good thing, ain't it? Why you cryin'?" Uncle Bubba always expected tears of joy when the day finally came that she could say those words. Instead, her pained look told him that the supposedly-joyous announcement had blasted shrapnel into her heart.

She wiped her face with her hands. "Kurt doesn't want me to have the baby."

Both Dwayne's and Uncle Bubba's mouths dropped to the floor. "Be-caussse?" Dwayne prodded, his gaze narrowing on her.

"Because he's a damn fool, that's why," Uncle Bubba answered.

"You haven't heard the worst part," Val explained, and they both snapped to attention. "He wants me to get rid of *our* baby, but his mistress gets to keep *her* baby."

Uncle Bubba almost toppled off of his stool. "Well, I do declare."

They knew about the couple's arguments over money and starting a family. Val had shared it, hoping that getting male insight from these two men that she had trusted all of her life would help her find a solution that would make her and her husband happy.

Val propped her chin in her hands. "When Kurt's step-dad gave us that money last year, Kurt started acting real strange."

Uncle Bubba cocked his head to the side and frowned, a move that matched Dwayne's.

"Even with my fertility problems, he kept trying to talk me into taking the pill," she explained. "I refused to do it, but it did let me know that he was going to renege on his promise again."

She sniffled, and Uncle Bubba's heart melted. But at the same time, his eagle-eyes picked up on the shamefaced expression in her delicate features. "I helped raise you, child, and I know when you're not tellin' the whole story. Whatcha leavin' out?"

"Well I got desperate ... and I uh ... got some fertility drugs."

Dwayne's left eyebrow shot up. "Where'd you get a prescription from?"

"I didn't." Val averted her gaze. "I surfed the Web and found sites where I could get the pills without one." She hoped they couldn't see through her lie. Misrepresenting the truth wasn't her forte.

Dwayne smacked his palm against his forehead. "Girl, have you lost your mind? You don't know what's in the bottles you get from places like that."

Uncle Bubba toyed with his cane. "Even I know you shouldn't giggle that kind of thing."

"Google, Uncle Bubba. I Googled it." She smiled, a little.

"Giggle, Google, same thing," he shot with a dismissive wave of his hand. "How'd you know what to buy anyway?"

Sorrow replaced her smile. "I remembered the names of the meds the fertility specialist prescribed when I was with ..."

"Hunter," Uncle Bubba supplied, a stab of sadness in his own heart at his niece's loss. Hunter was a good man, filled with the kind of love, compassion and loyalty that made for the best kind of husband. Just a couple months after Val and Hunter's fourth fertility treatment yielded several good embryos, he had been killed on a medical expedition in Indonesia.

Not many people were blessed to find true love. Val had found the real deal with her first husband, and after grieving for him for eight years, she thought she was being given a second chance at happiness when Kurt came into her life. But not long before they tied the knot, Uncle Bubba developed a worrisome feeling that she had settled for second best. A man could see things about another man that a woman might miss. Now, it seemed that Kurt had done a serious Jekyll and Hyde number on her, as Uncle Bubba had expected.

Dwayne drained his tumbler, then gestured to her stomach. "So, how pregnant are you?"

"Three months." She locked gazes with them. "I'm pregnant. She's pregnant. What kind of madness is that?" Her lips quivered and she rubbed her stomach.

Dwayne set his tumbler down and folded his sister into his arms while she cried.

"I'll getcha some water, child," Uncle Bubba said, ambling toward the refrigerator. "I don't know what to say 'bout Kurt. When I first met him, he acted like that real estate business of his was keepin' him busier than a one-eyed cat watchin' two mouse holes. But all the while, he wasn't doin' nothin' but runnin' 'round here pornicatin'."

"I think you mean fornicating," Dwayne said.

"You know I know the word," Uncle Bubba defended as he pulled out a pitcher of ice water. "I'm just tryin' to dry up my little girl's tears."

"Thanks for wanting to make me feel better," Val said. "But it may be awhile before that happens."

"So who's this other hussy who's having his baby?" the old man asked.

"Some woman named Whitley," she said, taking the half-full glass he offered. "She brought her crazy behind over here today."

Uncle Bubba was just about to sit back down but froze mid-air before his overalls made contact with the stool. "She did *what*?" he shrieked.

Dwayne grumbled, "That slick son of a—"

"Humph, forget callin' the police. Yo' neighbors shoulda had to call the ambulance." Uncle Bubba waggled a finger in her direction. "I hope you kicked her tail from here to Timbuktu." He settled onto the stool. "When did you say Kurt's comin' back?"

"In forty-eight hours," she replied, her furrowed eyebrows registering alarm at his grave tone. She narrowed her eyes at him. "Why?"

He pulled an old flip phone out of the chest pocket on his overalls and held it at arm's length as he punched the big buttons and connected with someone on the other end. "Hello, this is Paul Burgess. I need to leave a message for Dr. Pratt's office to cancel my Monday 'pointment." After a short pause, he added, "Naw, I'll call him back when I'm ready." Returning the phone to his pocket, Uncle Bubba grabbed his cane. "Come on, Dwayne."

"Where're we going?" his nephew asked, abandoning his spot by his sister and digging for his car keys.

"Home to get some clothes, my medicine and my shotgun. We're gonna be right here when Mr. Man comes back."

Chapter 4

Kurt pulled up in front of the three-car garage at his parents' Burr Ridge estate. They moved into the two-story, castle-like home after Foster cashed in on the lottery. As soon as those millions hit the bank, Foster not only quit the grocery store job where he'd worked all his adult life, but he also ran right out and bought one of the most expensive homes in the same suburb where the wealthy owner of that chain of grocery stores resided.

The center garage door went up slowly, revealing Melva Timmons bit by bit, from her slightly bowed legs all the way up to her radiant smile. Kurt rolled down his window, and she stuck her head inside the truck for a quick peck on the cheek. "Hey, son."

"Hey, Mom."

He parked and hopped out as Melva brought down the door. They slipped their arms around each other's waist and walked to the patio. Kurt opened a gigantic striped umbrella in the center of a round glass table as he asked, "*He's* not inside, is he?"

Melva brushed a butterfly off of one of the lawn chairs and sat down. "No. Your father's downtown."

"Stepfather," Kurt corrected, laying his keys on the table and taking a seat next to her. "Doing what?"

"Probably getting on the bank teller's last nerve." Deep dimples poked holes in her cheeks when she laughed. "When he leaves there, he's supposed to be meeting a neighbor for a round of golf. So he'll be gone another couple of hours or more."

"Golf?" Kurt could only shake his head.

"He doesn't know the first thing about it, but he's been breaking his neck trying to do all the things he thinks these"—she crooked her fingers as quotes—"'rich white people' do."

The way Kurt saw it, Foster was an obnoxious jerk on a good day. Money had made him an even bigger fool. He half expected his stepfather to become cross-eyed as much as he now looked down his nose at the people he used to live and work around.

Maybe he was just destined to be that way. Born to a black father who had rejected him and a white mother whose family had disowned him, Foster Timmons had spent a lifetime chasing after acceptance. When that eluded him, he lusted after status, ever crowing about how he was going to climb the ladder of success. An apparent fear of heights had kept him stuck on the same rung he was on when he met Kurt's mother over forty years ago. But racking up fifty-five million in a lottery pool last fall changed all that.

A soft breeze made rustling noises in the garden behind Kurt. He turned to look at his mother's handiwork. "You planted tomatoes this year?"

"Bell peppers and collards too. Of course, Foster threw a fit." In a deep, gravelly voice, she imitated her husband talking around the huge wet cigar that was always glued to his bottom lip. "That stuff will make our neighbors think we're country with a capital 'C'."

Kurt gave a dry laugh.

Melva's eyebrows furrowed. "You sure I can't get you anything, not even a cool drink?" She pulled his hand to hers. "You're more troubled than I think I've ever seen. Talk to mama."

With his free hand, Kurt tugged at his chin. "I need to spend a couple of nights here."

"You know you're always welcome," she said, her gaze instantly narrowing on him. "But why?"

Kurt looked away. Melva caught his chin with her tiny hand and redirected his gaze. He drew in a deep breath and confessed. "Mom, I messed up big time. The police had to come to the house."

Her sharp gasp caused him to shut his eyes and lower his head in shame. She released his chin, and he scrubbed his hands down his face. "They told me I had to leave the house for a couple of days."

A lawnmower sputtered to life next door, and Kurt waited until the noisy machine was pushed away from the wooden privacy fence before adding, "I don't think me and Val are gonna make it."

He heard the hollow thumping of his mother slapping her hand against her chest in shock. "Are you sure, son?"

"Yes, ma'am."

When Kurt raised his head, Melva's light brown eyes probed his for understanding. Rubbing the crown of his head, he said, "I have two babies on the way."

"Val's pregnant? With twins?" She clasped her hands and lifted her head heavenward. "Thank you, Lord," she cheered. "Son, I've been praying for so long that you two would be able to see eye-to-eye on that. You've got to find a way to make your marriage work now." She cradled her arms as if an infant were already in them. "Two grandbabies," she mused. "How far along is she?"

Kurt rubbed his temples, disturbed that she felt such enthusiasm when he could generate none. "She's three months, but Mom, you don't understand."

Melva's deep-set eyes showed both delight and confusion.

"Two babies, but Val is only carrying one," he said, holding up an index finger.

There was more silence in that backyard than there was in most libraries. Even the lawnmower noise had stopped.

"My God," she whispered. Standing and taking his hand, she said, "Let's go inside and have a drink."

"I need something stronger than lemonade," he warned.

"You and me both, honey."

As they left the backyard, self-pity ate at Kurt. In the eyes of Val and her family, he had to look like the sorriest man alive compared to her first husband. Hunter would forever be a saint because he gave his life in Indonesia trying to save someone else's.

Chapter 5

Jungles of Papua, Indonesia
July 2011

Matius was neck deep in a critical situation. Village elder Toma, a wise, petite woman with delightful crinkly black eyes, was clutching her fragile chest in agony as she crumpled to the ground.

"Toma!" Matius yelled as he rushed to her side and rolled her onto her back. Her breathing was weak and erratic. Suddenly she stopped breathing altogether. "Hold on, Toma! Hold on!" Everything in him was demanding that he save this sweet, gentle woman who eleven years ago had been the reason why he was alive.

He pressed the heel of his hand down into Toma's chest several times, then stopped for a few seconds, watching for her chest to rise back up on its own.

"She still does not breathe," a panicky voice to his right cried out.

Matius tilted Toma's head back, pinched her nostrils together, clamped his mouth over her open mouth and forced air into her lungs. He wasn't sure what made him do it—he had not learned it from anyone in the village—but his every instinct screamed not to stop.

A five-year-old fell to the ground beside Toma, sobbing into the old woman's hand. "Don't go. Don't die. Don't leave." His wailing was joined by others in the common grounds of the tiny jungle village. "Don't let her die, Matius," the little boy pleaded.

"Kyo." Matius' deep, steady voice wrapped around the small child. "Keep holding her hand; keep talking to her. Let Toma know that this world still needs her loving presence."

With more urgency, Matius pumped his hands into the old woman's chest then breathed into her mouth. The frantic people surrounding them crowded in more when Toma gasped, coughed, exhaled heavily and then slowly began to catch her breath. Matius gently pulled her up to a sitting position.

Pressing his head to her chest, he listened to the thumping inside. The irregular heartbeat slowly leveled out. When he raised his head, her terrified eyes sought his, and he smiled to ease her fears. "You almost died."

She placed her aged and worn palm to Matius' chest and he settled his palm on hers. It was a practice of the people of the village, symbolic of sharing one life force to strengthen another.

Reaching up to caress Matius' strong cocoa jaw with her other hand, she whispered, "A life for a life."

נ נ נ

Matius checked in on Toma after the women had gotten her comfortably settled in her grass hut. She meant so much to the people in the tight-knit Berani tribe. When he was brought to the remote village eleven years earlier, she had been a dynamic bridge for him to cross over into the culture of her people. In their first encounter, she had said some words that were foreign to him, then pointed to herself and said, "Toma." When she pointed at him, her inquisitive dark brown eyes asked what his name was. He had pointed back to her and said, "Toma," wishing he could remember his own name—or anything else about himself—to share with her. Not having any success in finding out who he was, she had finally pointed at him and said, "Matius." He came to know later that the name she had given him meant 'gift from the gods'.

During his first year in the village, Toma had picked up a rudimentary understanding of the language Matius spoke, while teaching him the basic verbiage of her people. Eleven years later, both of them had fluid command of each other's native tongue, and about ninety percent of the villagers spoke some make-shift version of Matius' language.

He now rubbed Toma's delicate hand as he sat cross-legged on the floor beside the mat made of woven palm leaves that she lay on. She smelled of sweet orchids, the abundant jungle flower picked by Berani women and crushed into a paste that they used to decorate their arms and legs.

"Your mind is heavy, my child," she said, pulling him from his private thoughts.

Being on the high side of ninety, Toma had seen more happiness, horrors and survival than a person with five lifetimes. So it didn't surprise Matius that she could sense the internal battle brewing inside of him. He gave a small smile and cleared his throat. "Kepala has been to see you again?" he asked. When she nodded, he said, "He has not changed his mind?"

"No. He has received the approval of the elders' council. When Kepala rises to the sky, you, Matius, will become chief." Although Matius was a muscular giant—a solid six-feet-five-inches in height—the quiet confirmation in her tone made him cringe like a boy frightened by sounds in the jungle at night. He loved these people. They had become his family. But …

He gazed at her beseeching raven eyes. "This is not what I want, Toma. I cannot become chief. It is not my path. Without my memory, I am only a piece of a man. It would not be fair to the people for me to lead them."

"Child." Toma gave her small white-haired head a shake. "The will of the gods and the will of the people sometimes align and become one." She reached up and stroked his strained face. "If you are meant to be our next chief, the way will be made clear to you."

Matius gave her hand a gentle squeeze. "I will not contest the decision, but I am not thrilled about it. And there will be opponents to Kepala's choice."

"Yes," she agreed. "There are always others who covet. But do not weigh your heart down with thoughts of it. Kepala is still of strong mind and good health. It could be years before you have to take his place. Until then, be content, child." Amusement lit her eyes. "Marry Madra. Give her babies who will be strong warrior grandsons and healthy granddaughters to secure Kepala's line of chiefs."

The process of the elders' council appointing a successor chief was slow and meticulous. After the process was through, Matius and Madra, the exotically-beautiful daughter of the chief, would be wed.

He held Toma's gaze.

She cocked her head. "Madra is not to your liking?"

"She is to my liking, Toma." Even as he offered a slight smile and a soft chuckle, he knew it would not disguise the conflict he felt in his heart.

"Your eyes." She lifted her head and shoulders off of the mat, using her elbows to rest in a semi-reclining position. "They reveal too much of your mind, child."

He looked away.

"The shadow woman—she comes more now in your dreams at night?" she asked.

He looked up at the thatched roof and sighed. "I can almost see her, Toma. If only I could remember who she was. If only I could remember who I am. Eleven years without knowing is enough."

Toma patted his hand. "Time, child. Give it time. You have lived many lives, and each one struggles to have its story told."

"You and most everyone else in the village believe I am a prince from a past life who has been sent here to save this and many other villages from that rogue tribe of killers that has been wiping out nearly all the men." Tapping on his broad, bare chest, he added, "But from the pit of my soul, I feel like I have just this one life, and I once lived it in a place far, far away from here."

"The place of the shadow woman?" She gingerly laid back on the mat. Grasping his hand, she said, "I am an old woman, but I still remember the ways of a man in love. And you"—she pointed to him and gave a knowing smile—"you are in love. But you do not know what to do, for Madra and the shadow woman are warring for your heart."

Chapter 6

Burr Ridge, Illinois

Melva led the way into the family room. Not counting the gaudy psychedelic black light painting his stepfather had insisted on mounting over the mantle, the room was tastefully decorated in shades of gold and midnight blue.

Making his way toward the well-stocked wet bar in the corner, Kurt said, "What are you having?"

His mother settled into a plush recliner near the fireplace and answered, "Rum. And lots of it." Kurt looked back at her with wide eyes, and she gave him a wink. "I didn't stutter," she added, squeezing two fingers together to show him how much to pour.

He found a bottle of Bacardi behind the bar, splashed just a drop into a glass then topped it off with ice and half a can of Coke. He poured a shot of rum in another glass, got some napkins and joined his mother.

"Thanks, son," she said and accepted her drink. She took a sip of the weak concoction, smacked her lips and let her eyes roll up in her head. "Now that's good."

A smile tried to creep across Kurt's lips, but the seriousness of his problem vetoed it. In one long swallow, he drained the dark liquid from his glass, wincing as it scorched his throat.

As he sat down in the matching recliner next to his mother, he placed two napkins on the small glass table between them. Melva sat her glass on one of the napkins and gave Kurt her undivided attention. Under that relentless stare, Kurt wrung his hands and busted out with, "I got another woman pregnant." He wordlessly pleaded for forgiveness and understanding, but his mother remained silent. Kurt could feel the wheels of judgment churning slowly in her mind. "It just happened."

"Boy, don't 'it just happened' me!" she spat. "Your father and I have been together forty-two years, and sometimes we couldn't stand each other. But you best believe neither one of us ever went running around with somebody else!"

She gestured to his wedding ring. "You made a vow, young man. A vow to Valencia and a vow to God. I don't know who or what could make you forget that." Melva crossed her arms over her chest and tapped her foot on the floor, waiting.

Kurt was too embarrassed to admit that his stepfather had something to do with him being in this situation. Foster Timmons had given Kurt's half-sister Shannon a quarter-million dollars of his lottery winnings and the promise of another million-and-a-half in one year, no strings attached. He called it an 'inheritance,' stressing that there would be no more handouts after that. Kurt received the same deal, except his payout came with one big string attached. He had to divorce Val in a year's time in order to collect his other million-and-a-half. Kurt hadn't told Val about the other money because of the stipulation attached to it. But the memory of conceding to Foster still burned in his ears.

"You'd better not go running to Melva about this either," Foster had warned, looking at Kurt with contempt. "Damn mama's boy. I know how much you want to be her perfect son, but I'll tell her about you and that tramp you been romping around with."

"Like you didn't keep pushing me to find someone else," Kurt retorted.

"And you listened to me? So who's the fool?" Foster's thick lips had spread into a sly grin. *"Keep trying me and I'll tell your mama about that cocaine habit you've been hiding from everybody—well, from everybody but me."*

Kurt had agreed to take the extra money, telling himself he had three hundred sixty-five days to devise a double-cross, a way to keep the money and at the same time keep his marriage intact. He would teach Foster how to really play the game. Unfortunately, Kurt's marriage had imploded before that could happen.

His mother snapped her fingers at him. "Are you listening to me, Kurt?"

"Yes, ma'am," he mumbled, not sure if he had missed something.

"I asked you if Val knows about this other baby."

Kurt dug his nails into the arm of the chair and whispered, "Whitley— that's the other woman's name—she came to our house today."

Amazement, shock, disbelief and full-on outrage rippled across Melva's face.

He lowered his gaze to the carpet. "The doorbell rang," he said in a low tone. "I opened it without checking because I had just seen a Fed Ex truck pull up across the street. I figured he was delivering some exercise equipment I ordered. But it was Whitley. And she went ballistic the minute she saw my face."

Kurt left the chair and began pacing in front of the fireplace. "I never told her where I lived."

"She probably followed you home," his mother offered, shaking her head. "Or maybe she just looked you up. I mean, your number is listed."

He picked up the poker and jabbed at the brick inside the fireplace. "I tried to make Whitley leave, but she just got louder and louder about us having a baby." Putting the poker back in its stand, he squatted beside the fireplace, twisting his wedding ring around on his finger. "That's what made Val come to the door."

"Oh, I'll bet things turned ugly then," she said dryly. "Did Val handle that witch?"

"She did, but in the middle of them screaming at each other, Val hollered out that she was pregnant too."

In his mind, he could see Whitley's dumbstruck expression. She hadn't been prepared for that bombshell. Neither had he. In shock, Whitley had tucked tail and waddled back to her yellow Corvette—quick, fast and in a hurry.

His mother picked up her glass and swirled the drink around before taking a long sip. "How could you have missed seeing that this Whitley person was pregnant anyway?"

Kurt perched on the ledge of the fireplace, with his head against the cool stone wall, staring blankly ahead. "I found out about four months ago. After that, she became so possessive and demanding, always wanting to know when I was leaving Val. So I paid her off to leave me alone and we stopped seeing each other. I thought it was a wrap."

"It was a wrap all right—right around your neck." Melva traced a finger over the rim of her glass. "How bad was your argument with Val?"

A moan escaped through Kurt's tightly clamped lips. He leaned forward and used the back of his hands to wipe away the tears that were on the verge of spilling down his cheeks. "Bad." That one word was riddled with regret.

Kurt squeezed his eyes tight. "I thought Val was making up a lie about being pregnant just to shut Whitley up. I followed her back into the house and told her how much I loved her for taking up for me. And she came at me like a wild woman, screaming that she really was pregnant." He dropped his head, humiliation filling him all over again. "I guess I had that coming."

"Ya *think*?" his mother cracked.

"But I snapped." He barely could get the words out.

Perfectly arched eyebrows shot up.

Every breath weakened his ability to hold it together. "I cursed Val out harder than I'd cursed at Whitley. I told her how selfish she was. I even accused her of sleeping with other men."

Melva's stoic, cold look of disappointment stabbed at his heart worse than any words she could have said.

"I was trying to throw the blame off of me and onto her." He gave a bitter chuckle. "I love Val, but I don't know how we can fix this one."

Kurt's head whipped around at the sound of the garage door coming to life. He and his mother simultaneously glanced overhead at the clock on the wall. "I thought you said he'd be gone another couple hours," Kurt complained.

"Guess I was wrong. But we can still talk if you want."

"Not with him around," he said, cutting his eyes toward the door. When Kurt rose, his mother extended her hand so he could pull her out of the recliner.

She reached up and stroked her son's neat beard. Sorrow filled her eyes.

Foster made his presence known by unceremoniously dropping what sounded like a heavy golf bag on the floor of the mudroom. "Melva, you in there? Kurt's truck is in the garage."

"We're in the family room, Foster," she replied.

Footsteps clicked on the marble tile in the kitchen. Melva yelled, "I know you're not walking inside my house in those golf shoes, Foster Timmons."

"Shoot, Melva." He clomped back to the mudroom, thumped his body against the wall and dropped his shoes with a thud.

Kurt kissed his mother on the cheek when Foster's feet padded toward the family room. "I'll be upstairs for a while."

"Okay, baby."

The two men met in the wide family room doorway. No words were exchanged between them other than a reciprocal, "Hey."

Foster frowned at Melva. "What's he doing here?"

Kurt captured his mother's attention for just a moment by shooting her a pointed look.

"Nothing, Foster," she said as she turned her focus back to her husband. "He just wants to stay for a day or two."

The man's beady-eyed gaze shifted to Kurt. "Why? Don't he have his own house?"

"You go on in the kitchen and I'll fix you something to eat while you tell me about your meeting and your golf game."

Foster gifted Kurt with a wry smile and stepped away. Kurt grabbed his mother by the arm as she passed by. "I need you to ride back to my house with me," he whispered in a low tone.

"Kurt, if you go there now, Val will call the police on you."

He nervously looked over his shoulder. "But not if you're with me."

She put her hands on her hips. "What's so important that you'll risk having the police haul your butt off to jail? And what am I supposed to tell your father?"

"Stepfather," Kurt corrected.

She tilted her head in the direction of the kitchen when a chair was pulled from under the table. "He's waiting for me."

"Mom, you have to go with me. I can't afford to neglect my business for two whole days. I need to get my laptop."

Drawing in a deep breath, she shook her head and said, "Kurt, I don't like this."

"Please." He folded his hands together. "I promise I'll just run in and come right out."

Melva called out to Foster, "Baby, me and Kurt need to make a quick run."

The chair scraped across the floor again. "Aw, Melva, I thought you wanted to hear about my day," he whined. "And I'm hungry."

"Can we go after I feed him?" she mouthed to Kurt.

He dropped a grateful kiss on her head and shot upstairs to the guest room.

Chapter 7

7:30 p.m.

"I know you're not walking around in broad daylight with a shotgun," Val gasped.

Uncle Bubba stopped on the porch and leaned on his cane, holding the gun out just as calmly as he might hold out a piece of candy to a starry-eyed child. "It ain't real, Val."

She caught his arm and yanked him inside the house, scanning the area to see if any neighbors were nearby. "It's real enough to get you shot if the police see you with it."

"And it's real enough to keep that husband of yours in line if he comes back here actin' a fool," Uncle Bubba replied. He laid it across the coffee table, letting the heavy metal barrel clink a little too hard against the glass. "I used to respect that boy, but I swear I don't know what's gotten into him. I betcha if I put some lead in him though, that'll tighten him up real good. Get his head on straight."

Dwayne walked in the front door, arms loaded with overnight bags and a carry-out box that said Beggars Pizza.

"And you," Val scolded as Dwayne kicked the door closed. "Why'd you let Uncle Bubba come out of the house with that thing?" She tossed a cold glance at the shotgun.

"Take it in the other room if you don't want to see it," Uncle Bubba ordered.

"I'll keep a close eye on him," Dwayne promised. "He can't hurt anybody with it anyway unless he uses it to beat them over the head."

Uncle Bubba nodded. "Yeah, that gets my vote." He snickered as he eased down on the couch. "Dwayne, put that stuff down and get that *Bad Boys* DVD out of my bag." He patted the couch cushion. "Val, come watch it with me. You need to relax."

Dwayne sat the bags on the dining room table and brought the pizza into the living room. "Get a whiff of this," he said to Val as he opened the lid and fanned the steam toward her.

Val covered her nose and jerked her head the other way. "It's making me nauseous." She pushed the box away.

"I'm sorry, li'l sis. I guess I have to get used to you being pregnant." He took the box in the dining room and came back with the movie.

"You're not too sick to sit with me, are ya?" Uncle Bubba asked Val as Dwayne loaded the DVD player.

She laid a hand on her stomach, trying to settle the queasiness. "No, Uncle Bubba. That, I can do."

"I'm going to have some pizza," Dwayne said as he headed toward the kitchen.

Uncle Bubba scooted over, and Val curled up beside him. Her head settled on his shoulder and she prayed that peace would tiptoe into her soul.

בּ בּ בּ

Val awoke two hours later to a room that was completely dark except for the brightness of the screen on the sixty-inch plasma tv. She lifted her head from Uncle Bubba's shoulder and fluffed her hair where it had gotten flat while she slept.

"Told you that you needed to rest," he said, patting her gently on the arm. "You didn't slobber on me, did you?" He inspected his sleeve.

She gave him a playful nudge with her shoulder, then pried herself off of the sofa and stretched. Headlights in the driveway and the unmistakable hum of her husband's SUV made her whole body tense up. Suddenly she found it hard to breathe.

Kurt. Dwayne. Uncle Bubba. The shotgun.

Nothing but trouble waiting to happen.

Uncle Bubba called for Dwayne. "Come down here, boy, and pass me my piece."

Dwayne's footsteps clattered overhead, followed by him rushing down the stairs. "I thought you said forty-eight hours," he said to Val as he made it to the landing.

"*The police* said forty-eight hours," she corrected.

"Not only is the man unable to tell his wife from another woman, but he can't tell time either," Uncle Bubba grumbled as Dwayne rounded the corner. Dwayne went straight for the shotgun. Val went straight for the cordless phone in the kitchen.

"I'm calling the police," she said, scurrying back to the living room the moment Kurt's key slid in the first of the two locked doors.

Uncle Bubba grunted with the effort to get off of the couch. "Val, put the phone down," he said in a muffled tone. "We got this under control."

She shivered but relented, her hands shaking as she laid the phone on the love seat. "Uncle Bubba, that is just a toy gun, right?" she whispered back.

He didn't bother to answer.

Dwayne took up a position behind the door. Val stood frozen in place, praying that yellow crime scene tape wouldn't soon decorate her home.

The last lock clicked and Kurt tipped into the semi-dark house. "Now look, Val, I don't want any trouble," he said as he felt for the switch on the wall. "I just need to get my—"

Uncle Bubba cleared his throat as soon as the decorative ceiling light came on. Kurt's gaze traveled from the old man to the shotgun he held at his side. Dwayne stepped from behind the door. Kurt glared at the two men like they were bullies on the playground. "Did you have to get involved in our business?"

Dwayne positioned himself protectively in front of Val. "My sister *is* my business." He gestured to the rest of the house. "The police having to come to this camp *is* our business."

Peeking around Dwayne's sturdy body, Val asked, "Why are you here?"

Kurt's gaze remained locked on Dwayne.

"You heard the girl," Uncle Bubba prodded. "What do you want?"

"I just needed to get a few things," Kurt said, his gaze darting around the room, probably trying to find some object to protect himself with.

"Well, me and Dwayne here are gonna do you like the cops prob'ly did you," Uncle Bubba advised. "We gonna escort you through the house so you can grab what you need and get to steppin'."

Dwayne took a few steps forward and reached for Kurt's elbow. Kurt wrenched away. "Man, don't put your hands on me. This is *my* house," he said, clenching his teeth and thumping his chest with his index finger.

"You wait one cotton-pickin' minute," Uncle Bubba said, raising the stock of the shotgun to his shoulder and cocking the pump action.

All sound left the room.

Val's legs felt as though they were dissolving under her own weight. But she wouldn't give Kurt the satisfaction of seeing her blatant terror. She jutted her chin out and crossed her arms, matching Dwayne's stance.

A car door slammed outside. A few seconds later, the doorbell rang.

"Mama, I thought I told you to stay in the truck," Kurt answered without turning to face the door.

"She your bodyguard now?" Uncle Bubba taunted, the barrel still aimed at Kurt.

"Is everything all right, son?" Kurt's mother asked through the door. There was a slight, dull bump on the door as if she had pressed her head against it to listen in on what was happening inside.

"He'll be right out, Mama Melva," Val said loudly, motioning for Dwayne to hurry up and take Kurt to get his stuff so he could leave. A brisk burst of air swept over Val as the two men rushed past her. Uncle Bubba brought up the rear, his "phony" shotgun still trained on Kurt.

Mrs. Timmons' footsteps crossed the porch, clicked along the sidewalk, and then the SUV door opened and closed.

Three minutes later, Val's guardian angels were ushering Kurt to the front door. A laptop was in his left hand. With the other hand, he hung onto a pair of dress shoes with black socks stuffed in them. Two shirts and two pairs of slacks still on the hangers were draped over his right arm. The shaving kit, toothbrush and clean underwear sitting atop the pants and shirts were poised to slide to the floor. He jostled his belongings, trying to open the front door.

Dwayne opened it for him, saying "We're gonna be here for a hot minute, so don't think about coming back and starting some mess."

Looking like a ram ready to butt heads with a rival male, Kurt barged past his brother-in-law.

Having to have the last word, Uncle Bubba said, "You heard my nephew. Don't start none, won't be none!" As he closed the door, he crooned, "Bad boys, bad boys, whatcha gonna do? Whatcha gonna do when they come for you?"

Chapter 8

On the ride back to his parents' home, Kurt clutched the leather-covered steering wheel so hard that his fingertips burrowed into it and made deep indentations. It was a good thing Whitley wasn't sitting next to him right now, or else she'd have similar imprints around her neck. All of this was her fault.

His mother was cryptically silent, though the few disappointed looks he caught in his peripheral vision said plenty. When he worked up the courage to steal a full-on look, her pursed lips told him that if she did speak, he wouldn't like what she had to say.

Melva remained glued to the passenger door while Kurt alternately stomped on the gas and the brake pedal as they flew through the last few intersections before arriving in front of her home.

The tires screeched in the driveway when he brought the truck to an abrupt halt. His hand snaked out in front of his mother to hold her body, which strained against the seatbelt.

She huffed, then glared at him out of the corners of her eyes. "I'm not the one you're upset with. Tossing me around in this truck isn't going to undo the ugly stuff that happened today." She unlocked her seatbelt and pushed opened the door. "You need to get a handle on your problems, son, because right now they're handling you." She slammed the door and hurried inside.

When his mother's plump frame disappeared into the house, Kurt pounded his fist against the steering wheel.

He stretched across the seat and opened the glove compartment. A small black case lay underneath a flashlight and a mound of papers. Inside the case, there used to be a plastic bag filled with white powder. How many days had he dipped his pinkie in that bag, brought it to his nostril and let the white powder take his problems away?

Gulping down tears, he slammed the compartment shut and leaned back against the headrest. "God," he uttered, his voice cracking. "I don't want to go back to that. Please help me."

Trying to stay clean with just the help of a weekly support group had been one of the hardest things he'd ever done. Going to a professional therapist or in-house rehab was not an option. That was for weak people. Besides, it was hard enough to siphon off enough money from his business to feed his addiction. He would have to start robbing banks if he wanted to find additional money to fork over to a psychiatrist or psychologist—that is, if he could even find one who didn't know of his wife and her psychiatric practice.

When his cell phone rang from the cup holder in the center console, he looked down at it and grimaced. "Whitley," he grumbled. He hit the speaker button, asking himself why he hadn't blocked her number.

Whitley smacked her lips. "I've been waiting for your call since I got off work."

"Before you even get started," he snapped, "thanks to you, it's been a crazy day for me."

Her voice was loud and shrill. "For *you*? See, *that's* your problem. The only person you think about is yourself."

The veins in his temple throbbed. "I'm about to lose everything that matters to me."

"Oh, baby, you're not losing me," Whitley purred in a sultry tone that turned his stomach.

"*You* don't matter to me!" he shot back, adjusting his position in the seat. "I'm talking about my wife. *She's* the one that matters to me."

Whitley's sharp intake of breath gave him some small satisfaction. If his life was upside down and inside out, he was more than happy to infect Whitley with that misery.

"Oh, now you're saying you don't care about me?"

Kurt turned on the A/C to chase away the rage boiling inside of him. "No."

"Or the baby?"

"Hell no," he seethed. "I don't even know if it's mine."

"What's that supposed to mean?" Whitley screeched.

"What?!" he yelled loud enough for people three blocks over to hear. "We had sex the first day we met. Remember the day we met at that support group? I knew you, what, five, six hours maybe, before you gave it up."

"You're making me sound cheap," she balked.

"We had sex in a staged apartment in a vacant three-flat that had a for-sale sign out front!"

"Yeah, and you loved it. So what?"

Kurt pinched the bridge of his nose, trying to center his escalating fury. "You didn't even have enough self-respect to demand a hotel room." His skin felt like a pot of boiling water had been poured over it.

The property owner had gotten wind of their little rendezvous and accused Kurt of letting potential buyers slip through his fingers so he could use the building as a hump-house. Kurt quickly sold the property but had to relinquish his twenty grand commission to the owner because he threatened to take Kurt to court for low-balling the property's value.

"You talk like I'm the only bad one here," she vented in a fiery tone. "You're no saint in this either. I didn't just imagine our relationship and this baby didn't make itself."

The stream of air from the vent had finally cooled his face, but his tone was still blistering. "After what you did today, the last thing I want is to have anything to do with you or that baby."

Silence.

"Okay, that's the way you want to play it?" she said in a demented whisper. "You won't like me the next time you see me, Kurt. I guarantee that."

The call abruptly ended. He wiped the phone on his pant leg as if trying to erase the conversation from existence.

Though his marriage had become rocky, he had never crossed the line with another woman. That is, until Whitley Moore. Meeting her eight months ago in the support group had awakened his drowsy libido.

Whitley was a pretty woman. Her entire package was hard to miss—flawless cinnamon complexion, oval-shaped face with plump, come-hither lips that commanded attention. She had a confident air about herself, moving with sensual promise. You couldn't take the sexiness out of her any more than you could take the wetness out of water.

Val was that way once. Hell, in some ways she still was. But her desperate pursuit to conceive stripped all the spontaneity and passion out of their love-making. Sex had become a technicality—a function that had to be performed—instead of an expression of desire and an act of love to be enjoyed. He felt more like he was stealing something from her than sharing something with her.

Kurt had sizzled for Whitley—the same way he used to react to Val. Whitley was wild and ravenous in bed. She gave him some of the best sex of his life. And a nice parting gift—an STD. Then he landed a prize in the bonus round: an unwanted child. Actually, two of them.

Dropping the phone into his pocket, he checked his image in the rear-view mirror. Bloodshot eyes were like neon billboards advertising to the world just how badly life was kicking his butt.

His gaze shifted to the glove compartment. The call of that white powder was strong, but he pushed aside any thoughts of relapsing. Kurt turned off the engine, leaped from the truck and raced into the house and up to the guest room. To his relief, he didn't run into his mother or stepfather along the way. He closed the door behind him and tossed his belongings on the pillows near the headboard.

A jackhammer in his head was running on turbo boost. He went in the adjoining bathroom. He stared at the bottle of over-the-counter pain reliever and sighed because his painkiller of choice—cocaine—was no longer an option.

Kurt sagged over the sink, staring at his reflection again. It bore the strain of a man whose business was riddled with on-going issues—mechanic's liens, IRS levies and frozen bank accounts. He snapped the top off of the bottle, popped four pills in his mouth and washed them down with a fistful of tap water.

Dragging himself from the bathroom, he crashed onto the bed. Light footsteps echoed from down the hallway then paused outside his door. He held his breath, hoping there wouldn't be a knock. His mother hummed "Near the Cross" as her steps retreated down the stairs. Moments later, Kurt could hear her through the vents.

"Lord Jesus, watch over my child."

Mama wants to pray me into heaven; Uncle Bubba's trying to blast me into hell.

Chapter 9

Tension, fatigue and frustration were all ganging up on Val after Kurt's surprise visit. It didn't help that Dwayne and Uncle Bubba wouldn't allow her to sulk in her room. Every ten to fifteen minutes, one or both of them would shout up the stairs, "Come down and talk to us."

She would rather stay in her room, figuring out how life had thrown her this sharp curve when there should have been a straight path.

Her first husband Hunter had found a fertility specialist when they couldn't conceive on their own. After the first procedures didn't take, she thought her dream was coming true when their fourth effort yielded five viable embryos. But when duty called him away, she and Hunter chose to freeze the embryos, unaware that not only would her dream of motherhood be taken away from her, but so would the love of her life.

After forty-five minutes in her room, she was feeling no better, no calmer and certainly no happier. *This must be what a nervous breakdown feels like.* Val finally gave up on having that personal pity party and trudged back down to the living room.

Uncle Bubba tried to touch her shoulder, but she drew away. "Your brother and me, we was just doin' what we had to do," he said, stepping in front of her and seeking to hold her gaze. She turned her head.

"I think you made things worse," she chastised, putting some distance between them by flopping on the love seat and folding her legs under her.

Dwayne cupped a hand to his ear. "Come again? What did you expect us to do, invite Kurt to sit down for a game of Spades?"

She folded her arms over her tender breasts.

"You already forgot what that man did to you, child?" Uncle Bubba tossed back. "Plus, *you* the one called *us.*" His voice spiked an octave. "We didn't ask to be in this mess."

"Sure didn't," Dwayne agreed, furrowing his forehead.

She popped off of the love seat, flipped the switch to turn off the ceiling light and stormed toward a table lamp in the corner.

"Girl, what's wrong with you?" Uncle Bubba asked in a harsh tone.

"You," she retorted, eyeing both men. "You're what's wrong with me." She stuck her hand under the lamp shade and yanked on the chain hard enough to make the lamp teeter as the light flashed on. The metal string sounded like wind chimes as it clattered against the ceramic globe.

"Puh-leez," Uncle Bubba scoffed. "I know you ain't tryin' to throw attitude at us." Pointing to a wedding photo on a side table, he said, "Y'all jacked this up yo' damn selves." He looked ready to throw her across his knee.

"No, *Kurt* messed it all up," she countered, suddenly turning to make a hasty retreat back to her room.

Dwayne cut her off at the pass. "And you didn't have not even a small part in it?" he challenged.

"Shut it, Dwayne," she cautioned. Though tears rolled down her cheeks, she mustered a smirk before bending to slip under her brother's arm.

He corralled her with one arm around her midsection and she managed to wrestle free, the physical contact compromising her ability to stay in charge of the emotions churning inside. She shoved past Dwayne and hurried into the kitchen, wrenching the dishwasher open and slamming dirty dishes in the rack.

Dwayne cornered her and twirled her around. "Don't be taking this out on me and Uncle Bubba." Then he gave a side-eye to a plate. "Or the dishes either."

She threw her hands up, eyes filling with more tears. "You sound like you're taking Kurt's side."

His shoulders slumped. "I don't mean to hurt you, li'l sis. It's just that …" He grimaced and scratched the back of his neck. With his finger, he tilted her face to his. "I'm your brother and I've always looked out for you."

Stewing in anger, she looked away and blew out a heavy breath.

He brought his face around to her line of vision. His eyes went to her stomach. "What you did was wrong."

Val placed a hand on her stomach. "It wasn't wrong. I love my baby."

"And I love your baby, too, Val," he said softly. "But you went about this all wrong. You left your husband out of the equation."

She wriggled away, then slapped the dishwasher door closed. "He took me out of the equation when he kept forcing me to wait."

"And he was wrong for that too," Dwayne answered. "But you need to own up to your part in this." He moved a few steps away and leaned on the island, folding his arms over his chest and leveling her with a hard look. "I'm a man and I can tell you that no grown man ever likes having a baby forced on him."

She punched the dishwasher's start button so hard that she cracked a nail. "I had every right to do what I did!"

"Val, no matter how you justify it," he countered, "there's no right way to do a wrong thing."

Chewing on her tattered nail and looking up at the ceiling fan, her lips trembled as she tried not to cry—something she'd done more of in the last six-and-a-half hours than she had done at any other time since grieving the loss of Hunter Pierce, the man who was her soul mate. The man who was taken from her when she needed him most.

"Why are y'all turning on me?" She cast her eyes down, longing for yesteryear when she could sit at her grandmother's knee and talk things over with her. Mae Harper had gone through a decade of miscarriages before she birthed Val's mother Francesca. But neither woman was here for Val now. A heart attack had taken her grandmother when Val was five years old. As for Val's mother, drugs, prostitution and theft had kept her in and out of prison for most of Val's life. Recently released, she lived just twenty minutes away. But the emotional distance between them was larger than the distance between outer space and the ocean floor.

Dwayne gently pulled Val into an embrace.

"Was it so wrong to want a child before it was too late to have one?" she sobbed.

Even after she had no more tears, he didn't let go but held her in silence. "It's been a trying day, li'l sis," he eventually said. He kissed her forehead. "You're going to need to look at this from all angles so you can decide what to do. But for now, go upstairs and try to get some sleep."

She wiped her face and looked at the clock on the stove. It was twenty-five minutes after ten. Being assailed by one crisis after another had sucked every ounce of energy from her.

On the way upstairs, she glanced at Uncle Bubba. He refused to look her way. She lumbered up the stairs, hanging on to the banister to hoist herself up each step. In her room, she slid between the yellow percale sheets without taking off a stitch of clothing or doing her nightly bathing ritual.

Restlessness made it hard to get comfortable and fall asleep. Twice in one day, she had looked out of the living room window as her husband drove away from their lives. Is this what their marriage had become, one drama-filled scene after the next?

What did I do to make him run to somebody else?

"I wish you were here, Hunter," she whispered, images of her first husband blooming in her mind. Pulling a pillow over her head, she forced her angst out in one long, loud scream. "Why did you take Hunter away from me?" She demanded a response from God, as if He owed her an explanation for why her beloved first husband had to die. She would never love another man like she loved Hunter Jamal Pierce. And no man would ever love her the way he had.

A tinge of discomfort in her abdomen made her inhale sharply. She threw the covers off and gently pressed down around her navel. A heavy contraction shot through her midsection, nearly taking her breath away. A second spasm attacked, forcing the rest of the air out of her lungs.

The pain mirrored the kind of excruciating cramps that she had experienced once a month since the age of thirteen. It was the sensation of someone ripping out her uterine lining. She curled up into a ball and remained deathly still, distressed that the pain had begun and terrified that it might not end.

One minute passed, then two, then thirty, but the pain didn't surface again.

Her grandmother's favorite phrase came to her. "Have faith in God."

Val wasn't sure if it was faith or denial on her part, but she blocked out the menacing thought of miscarriage and refused to let it take root.

Chapter 10

Jungles of Papua, Indonesia
July, 2011

Matius was on the verge of accomplishing something no one before him had ever been able to do. For eons, each of the tribes in the jungle had been fiercely independent and self-reliant, sharing nothing more than the occasional trading of goods and services between each other. But they would be guaranteeing their own extinction if they continued to isolate themselves from each other this way. These people—his people—were being hunted.

Hardly half-a-season could pass without word that the band of bloodthirsty killers who called themselves the Setan—or the devil—had struck again. They were attacking any tribes they viewed as weaker or smaller, killing off all the men, then raping the females and leaving them to bury their dead and give birth to their enemy's children.

Matius had run into brick walls when he approached a few neighboring tribes about joining together to defend themselves against those onslaughts. Even Kepala, the chief of Matius' village, had initially joined the leaders from other villages in pushing back at the idea. Each thought it would be a show of weakness on their part to ask for help. It wasn't until two tribes were completely wiped out—every man, woman and child—that some of the chiefs finally began to see that making alliances and combining forces, resources and information was the only way to keep everyone alive and thriving.

₪ ₪ ₪

"Matius," Madra called out from across the grounds.

He turned to see her approaching, and his heart swelled. Rahmad, the son of her closest friend, was in her arms. Matius reached out and relieved Madra of the energetic four-year-old, stealing a hug from Madra as he did so.

"He wanted to see you," she said with a captivating smile.

Matius tossed the little guy in the air. Rahmad was crazy about Matius. The boy tried to follow him everywhere he went. Matius always joked that it had something to do with his height. There wasn't another male in the village who even came close to his physical stature. That trait was one of the things that had made some of the Berani tribe shun him in his first months among them, fearing that he might be one of the dreaded Setan they had only heard of.

After coming to know and love him over time as a man of goodwill, kindness, intelligence and strength, the villagers claimed him as their own. He had come with a knowledge of healing so unlike their own, which he readily shared with Toma in exchange for her teaching him their many herbal cures. He had also crafted inventions using resources found in the jungle and nearby lake to make some of the more mundane everyday tasks less tedious. The Berani learned from him and were thriving because of him.

Matius lifted Rahmad onto his shoulders then put an arm around Madra's waist. They began to walk, but she placed her soft palm on his forearm, slowing their approach to a central hut surrounded by a host of others. "This alliance will help keep us safe, yes?"

"I pray that it will."

"If this is favorable for us and stops the attacks, then we can start a family? Babies?"

Matius closed his eyes and weighed his thoughts. This conversation was edging too close to a hesitant feeling he had about children. He loved kids—wanted a bunch of them. Children took his breath away every time he laid eyes on them. But the desire to have a family troubled him because it felt like some echo from his past—a past he couldn't remember. Could it be that he adored children so much now because he already had children somewhere? Was the shadow woman a connection to these phantom children? Could she be their mother? His wife?

He opened his eyes and stared lovingly at Madra. She was an erotic beauty. Their love for each other was pure, but there was an element of uncertainty that held him back. Everyone in the village expected him to make her his life-mate once he was appointed to be the next chief. And when that came into play, she would want children immediately—lots of them. Slim, with abundant hips—Toma called them birthing hips—Madra was made to have babies. How he wanted to give her that joy of motherhood. But there were more pressing matters.

He cupped her face and dipped his head to brush his lips across hers. "My priority right now is the safety of the villages. Once we have a stronger footing there and God deems that I am appointed to be Kepala's successor, then I'll fill your belly with many babies."

She rose up on her toes and returned his kiss heatedly. "I love you, Matius."

"I love you too." And he meant it.

He took Rahmad off of his shoulders and Madra reached out for the tyke's hand. Smiling up at Matius, she said, "I will see him to his mother." Nodding toward the central hut, she added, "Papa and the elders' council are waiting for you."

Chapter 11

Burr Ridge, Illinois
8:45 a.m. Sunday, July 17, 2011

The smell of fresh coffee flirted with Kurt's nose. He peeled his heavy eyelids open and spotted two birds chirping noisily on the windowsill. "It's too early for all that noise, y'all," he said, rubbing his eyes.

He shed Saturday's wrinkled clothing and dashed into the adjoining bathroom. The half bar of soap from his shaving kit had melted down to mere slivers by the time he left the comfort the warm water provided.

The foul odor of his stepfather's cheap cigar drifted under the bathroom door.

"Hey." Foster rapped on the door. "Your mama wants to know if you're going to church with her this morning."

"Probably not." Kurt wrapped a towel around his waist and opened the door just enough to peer out. "Do you mind? I just got out of the shower."

Foster took the cigar out of his mouth and blew a ring of smoke in the air that almost caused Kurt to gag. "I'm just saying that you know she expects everybody in this house to go to church."

"I'm a grown man," Kurt said, waving the smoke away.

The old man planted the cigar back between his chapped lips and stuck his thumbs in his suspenders. "Well, *grown man*, she's not going to take too kindly to you staying home." Kurt started to close the door, but his stepfather stopped it with his foot, whispering, "What were you and your mother talking about when I came in yesterday?"

"Just getting caught up." Kurt coughed and cast his eyes on the cigar. "Why don't you get out of here before you give both of us cancer?"

Foster slid his hand in his pocket, then gave Kurt a scornful glare. "If I find out you told her about our deal, you'll be sorry."

Kurt flung the door wide open and stepped closer to him. "In a deal, both parties benefit. You and I," he said, pointing first to himself, then to his stepfather. "We didn't have a deal."

"Nobody strong-armed you."

He looked his stepfather up and down. "You didn't manipulate me?"

Foster grunted.

"You knew how much I needed that money." Kurt pounded a fist in his palm. "What would Mama think if she knew about the offer you made? She'd leave your decrepit old ass in a heartbeat."

In one smooth action, his stepfather whipped a switchblade out of his pocket and slammed Kurt against the wall. Not expecting the sixty-eight-year-old man to be able to move so swiftly or to carry a weapon inside his own home, Kurt was slow to move out of the man's reach. Foster had his forearm against Kurt's chest and the knife pricking at his jugular before Kurt could take his next breath.

"Watch your tone, young blood. I still have some hood in me," he cautioned. "And I'm still your father."

"*Step*father," Kurt spat.

"No matter." He looked Kurt squarely in the eye. "Just between me, you and the wiretappers, I wasn't planning on giving you *any* money. Not one dime." Breath that smelled like a sewer assaulted Kurt's nostrils as his stepfather added, "But your mama wouldn't let it go until I promised I'd give you and Shannon the same amount. You know how she doesn't want me treating my daughter better than I treat her son."

If Kurt's fists weren't clenched around the towel covering his naked body, he would have given the old man the beatdown he'd been begging for his entire life. Instead, Kurt shoved his stepfather off of him.

"Kurt? Foster?" Melva called out from downstairs. "Everything all right up there?"

"Yeah," Foster shouted back, straightening his out-of-date tie and smoothing his freshly-trimmed beard as he shot a malice-filled smile at Kurt. "You'd better get your church clothes on, *son*. Your mama will be heading out for the ten o'clock service in a half hour." He clicked the switchblade closed and strutted out of the room, slamming the door behind him.

The call of the white powder was a deafening roar inside Kurt's head.

Chapter 12

10:00 a.m.

If Kurt hadn't been raised better, he might have held his hands over his ears to drown out the tone-deaf man in the row behind him. The guy was belting out "Lord I Lift Your Name on High" with the choir. Singing off key, clapping off beat and messing up the lyrics, the man was getting his praise on nonetheless.

Kurt clapped his hands too. But his actions weren't because he was enjoying the service. When the person leading praise and worship had exclaimed in the microphone, "Come on, church. Clap those hands and say hallelujah," Kurt had mindlessly complied, like some kind of praise puppet.

Reverend Brownlee, a visiting minister, took the pulpit a few minutes later. In a solemn monotone voice that sounded like he was delivering a eulogy, he began a sermon on what he called TLC: truth, lies and consequences.

Forty-one minutes in, Kurt was checking his watch for the umpteenth time, along with the rest of the congregation. *I'll be glad when Pastor*

Phillips is back from vacation. He squirmed in his seat through the last half-hour of the tiresome message.

At the end, Reverend Brownlee said, "Turn with me if you will to the book of John, chapter eight and verse thirty-two." The words "And ye shall know the truth, and the truth shall make you free" were projected on a large screen hanging from the ceiling behind the pulpit. "I want everyone to read this scripture with me before we do the altar call."

While those around Kurt recited the words, Kurt remained mute, fanning the pages of his Bible with his thumb. When an usher came to his row, he thought she was about to chastise him for causing a distraction. Instead, she nudged Kurt's stepfather, who was nodding in the aisle seat. Foster shuddered, then looked to his left and to his right as though checking to see how many pairs of eyes had caught him catnapping.

The usher handed him a small folded slip of paper. Foster started to open the note, but the usher tipped her head toward Kurt and urgently pointed at him. Melva snatched the paper out of Foster's reluctant hand and laid it on Kurt's open Bible.

When he unfolded it, the six words on the page arrested his breathing. *Meet me in the vestibule. Now.*

Realization slammed into him. "Whitley," Kurt breathed, crushing the paper in his fist. He would know that handwriting anywhere. The day Whitley gave him her address, she had penned the letters just like the ones on the note he held. Her glittery inch-long nails kept her from holding a pen tight enough to make steady strokes.

She was here. At his church. During family time. In a supposedly safe place.

Anger poured out of him like steam from an overheated radiator. He dug a finger in between his collar and neck to create an entryway for cool air to rush in. Beads of sweat broke out across his forehead. Touching his thumb to one finger and then the next, Kurt inwardly listed all the personal things he had shared with Whitley—and some she might have dug up on her own—which she could now use against him. She knew what church he attended; his phone number; his address; and about the lottery money. Worst of all, he had told her about his problems with

Val—the fertility issues, the sex—everything.

If he didn't go out there and deal with Whitley before church let out, she wouldn't think twice about busting up in the sanctuary and acting a fool in front of the entire congregation. She certainly hadn't had any reservations about showing up at his home and dismantling his entire life.

Clutching the wadded up note and his Bible, Kurt stood. Several people in the choir stand applauded. Everyone around them joined in, and the visiting minister said, "That's right, young man. Come on down to the altar for prayer." He spread his arms wide toward the congregation. "Is there anyone else?"

Kurt looked toward the door behind him, then down into his mother's hopeful eyes. He edged past her, wingtip oxfords scraping against her two-inch pumps. His stepfather wouldn't move his stumpy outstretched legs. Kurt stepped over them and hurried to the back of the church.

A brown-skinned usher at the door looked poised to tackle anyone who dared to walk out during this most sacred portion of the service. Kurt gave an embarrassed grin. "I'm sorry, Brother Abrams, but I really have to leave," he said, squeezing past the linebacker.

Outside in the hallway, Whitley stood by the usher who'd passed Kurt the note. The lady frowned as she looked from Kurt to Whitley, then back.

Kurt took in Whitley's form-fitting blouse, unmistakably pregnant stomach, unnaturally high heels, and groaned.

The usher's sensible rubber-heeled shoes squeaked as she walked over, eyes narrowed to slits. "Brother Timmons, where's *the wife*?" she asked in a tone as sour as her expression.

Ignoring her, Kurt barreled down on Whitley. He grabbed her by the elbow and led her out of the building, with her protesting every inch of the way. She struggled to keep up with his pace.

Stopping about twenty feet outside of the front entrance, he gritted his teeth. "What the hell do you want?"

"I just thought you might want an update on our child," she said, flicking a speck of lint off of his lapel.

He fastened his eyes on the spot where she dared to touch him. "You thought wrong," he grumbled, gripping her elbow tighter. She resorted to the pout that used to move him, but the days when that persuaded him were long gone.

She drew her glossy red lips into a sneer. "Are you tired of me, boo?" she asked. "You can get me out of your hair for good if you're willing to give up a little more of that cash. Lottery winnings are meant for sharing."

Kurt worked to keep his jaw from twitching. "Do I need to remind you that you promised never to contact me again after I gave you that hundred-fifty thousand dollars? We have a signed contract."

She blessed him with a wicked smile. "We do, don't we?" Examining her candy-red nails, she added, "But people take contract disputes to court every day."

"Now, you're blackmailing me?" He gestured with a sweep of his hand. "Get in line."

Whitley held her hand like an imaginary phone and placed it near her ear. "Hello, Valencia," she said. "Yeah, this is Whitley and—"

"Cut the crap, Whitley!" Kurt snapped. "Val already knows about our affair and this baby you're carrying. You can't hurt her any more than she's already been hurt."

Whitley continued her imaginary phone call. "Yeah, girl it's me again." She shifted her predatory gaze squarely on Kurt. "I won't keep you, hon. Just checking with you to see how your husband's *drug rehab* is going." Whitley got dramatic and placed her hand on her face, feigning shock. "Oops. Girl, I thought you knew."

A stab of fear pricked Kurt's heart.

She giggled in mock surprise and placed a hand on her extended belly. "Oh, the man stays knee-deep in that white powder." She looked at Kurt and batted her lashes. "He's a coke-head, sugar. That's how we met, in a support group for recovering addicts."

Twirling a strand of auburn hair around her fingertip, she gave him another toothy grin. Whitley's eyes turned a darker shade of deadly as she ended the fake call. The creature standing before him now was nothing like the inviting, sexy woman he had met eight months ago. She was the devil incarnate. "You get me more money or else."

Kurt glared down at Whitley Moore, wondering what he ever saw in her in the first place.

She turned on her heels, her short flared skirt flouncing high above her thighs as she practically floated toward the parking lot.

Chapter 13

Dwayne did a double-take as he pointed the car toward the north side of the parking lot of Shiloh Baptist Church. "Isn't that Kurt over there?"

Val angled toward the back window. She screwed her face into a scowl when she saw Kurt standing in front of the church like a statue, gazing out toward the sea of parked cars. Wrenching her head back around, she stared out the windshield to see what he was looking at. Two or three car lengths ahead of Dwayne's vehicle, a woman sashayed past the parked cars. She dropped something and bent over to pick it up, brazenly allowing her skirt hem to creep up to her uncovered backside.

Val pivoted and looked out the back window again at Kurt. He stood in the exact same spot, his frozen stare aimed in the woman's direction and glued to her naked behind.

Dwayne maneuvered past the woman when she stopped in front of a sun-yellow Corvette parked on the right. As he drove by, Val saw her face—and her stomach.

"That's the heifer that Kurt got pregnant," she blurted.

Dwayne instantly hit the child safety lock on his control panel.

The mistress locked in on the people in the car, flipped Val the bird, then gestured for her to "come hither."

Val hated to be like so many others, attacking the other woman when a man is unfaithful. Her problem was strictly with her husband. He was the one who took vows, not the low-life he laid down with. But this skeezer kept popping up where she didn't belong. And now she was mocking Val too? Oh, no. Kurt wasn't the only one who needed a lesson.

Val unfastened her seatbelt and attempted to jump out of the car. "Unlock the door," she ordered, yanking on the handle.

Uncle Bubba reached back and grabbed her sleeve. "Girl, what you doin'? Get yo' tailbone back in here."

She hit the switch to lower the power window. "Stay away from my husband, tramp!"

Dwayne raised the window back up just before Whitley banged her fist against the glass. She turned her back to the car and pointed at her butt. "Kiss this," she goaded.

"Kurt brought this skank to church with him? *Our* church?" Val screamed, jerking on the door handle again.

Uncle Bubba smoothed out the brim of the hat perched on his knee. "We don't know what Kurt did or didn't do, Val," he said, the calmness in his voice riling her up even more.

Dwayne veered into a parking space at the end of the long aisle. Throwing his arm over his seat, he looked back at his sister. "I'm not popping these locks until I know you're not going to go out there and clown."

She rolled her eyes and gave a nod she knew was unconvincing. "I'm good."

Dwayne sighed and gave her a final once-over before releasing the locks and exiting the car. Val got out, then opened Uncle Bubba's door.

He looked at her and quipped, "Girl, you look mad enough to attack the fires of hell with a water gun."

She glared back at the spot where Whitley's car was still parked. The seductress stood beside it, her finger beckoning for Val to come to her.

"No you don't," Dwayne warned, running around the bumper to obstruct Val's path.

"Move, Dwayne, or you can get some of what I'm about to give her."

His powerful arms encircled her waist, lifting her from the ground as she thrashed around, yelling, "I'm going to strangle her with that cheap weave she's got on her head."

Val wasn't a brawler by nature, but her uncle and brother had taught her how to protect herself. Especially after two loudmouthed high school students who wore enough makeup to look like rodeo clowns tried to jump her in tenth grade. All because they were jealous of how boys were drawn to Val's velvety tan skin, naturally curly hair and shy ways. Well, she showed them a thing or two. Three missing teeth, two black eyes and a busted nose kept anyone else from ever thinking that they could terrorize little Valencia Harper.

Whitley slithered in their direction, grinning at Val.

Val scratched and pinched Dwayne's arms, forcing him to relax his grip. Wearing three-inch ankle strap pumps, she ran toward Whitley like a track star sporting a pair of Nikes. Whitley stepped out of her own heels and threw one in Val's direction. It whizzed past Val's head like a bullet and landed on the speed bump near Dwayne's car.

Dwayne made it to the women and sandwiched himself between them just as they came to blows. He took licks to the head and chest as the pregnant prizefighters reached around and across him to strike at each other.

Kurt appeared, jumping into the fray and pulling Whitley off of Dwayne. She fell back, but caught her balance and took on a defensive stance behind Kurt. Fists up, knees slightly bent, she was ready to battle all opponents. People walking to their cars inched closer to the fiasco instead of going to their intended destinations.

"Come on over here," Whitley taunted Val. "I gave your husband what he wanted, and I got something for you too."

Breathing like a lioness hot off of a chase, Val said, "You ain't ready for me, little girl." She snatched off her suit jacket and threw it to the ground. "If I'm going to jail behind this, I'm going to make it worth the bail money." This time it was Val who gave the come hither gesture. "Bring it on."

Kurt advanced on Val, but Uncle Bubba, who had just made it to the scene of the crime, held his cane midair in front of Kurt like a crossing gate at a railroad track. "Think, boy. Think before you act."

Kurt glared at Val. "You need to calm down," he warned, reaching down to pick her jacket up and chucking it onto the hood of the nearest car.

Val reared back and put her hands on her hips. "No you're not up in my face taking her side. She's at *my* church! She slept with *my* husband! She showed up at *my* house to tell me she's pregnant with *your* child. And you're taking up for her? For her?!" she screamed, poking him in the chest with an index finger. "You'd just better be glad the police took you away, because as of yesterday, sleeping in that house became hazardous to your health."

"What the hell does that mean?"

"You cut my heart out." She looked down at his crotch and quipped, "Maybe I'm ready to do some cutting of my own."

Kurt flinched as his eyes widened in shock.

More people gathered around.

"And this one"—Val shifted a dangerous glare at Whitley—"didn't even have the good sense to stay in a whore's place!"

"Who're you calling a whore?" Whitley screamed.

"You!" Val shot back. "You slept with a married man. That's the straight-up definition of a whore." She nodded toward the church and added, "You might want to step inside and learn how a Christian woman is supposed to act."

Whitley's lips spread into a smile. "Baby, your husband taught me everything I needed to learn."

Val stepped forward and thundered, "You came to my house to hurt me, and I hadn't done anything to you!" She lowered her voice and sneered, "Well, at least not *yet*."

Kurt's stepfather came trotting toward the group, a switchblade gleaming in his right hand. "You trying to jump on my boy?" he asked, eyes bucked at Dwayne and Uncle Bubba.

Uncle Bubba's cane whipped out toward Foster's ankles, making him tumble forward. Kurt caught him in a bear hug as he crashed into him.

"Go 'head, son. Let him go," Uncle Bubba prodded. "I'll beat some sense into that watermelon head of his."

Foster brandished his knife at Kurt, shouting, "I told you this gal ain't no good."

Dwayne had to hook his fists under Val's underarms to keep her from going after her father-in-law.

Whitley started to lunge at Val, but the tip of Uncle Bubba's cane pointing toward her midsection blocked her. "Look here, Witless."

"It's Whit-ley!" she screeched.

"Well, Witless, if you don't want more than you bargained for, I 'spect you better keep yo' hands to yo'self." He nodded toward a fuming Val and added, "I taught that one how to fight dirty. And if she could take down Big Bertha and Crazy Wanda in high school, you don't stand a chance."

"I ain't scared of her."

Cell phones whipped out, recording the exchange. Uncle Bubba held his hand up to block the one closest to him. "Let's go befo' we all end up on Do Tube."

"YouTube," Whitley corrected.

"YouTube, my tube, inner tube. You can stay out here if you want to, Witless. We leavin'."

A siren piercing the air had the effect of a boxing ring bell, causing bystanders to make hasty retreats to their corners. A police car drove past the church, then suddenly made a U-turn.

"Five or six of us out here fightin' and they just send one doggone officer," Uncle Bubba griped. He used his cane to retrieve Val's jacket from the hood of the car, then nodded to Dwayne, who whisked Val toward his car.

The squad car turned into the parking lot and drove up and down the aisles. Kurt aimed his stepfather in the direction of his 2010 Rolls Royce Ghost and gave him a shove to get him moving toward it.

Whitley slipped behind the wheel of her Corvette and flew out of the parking lot like a jet on a runway. As she skidded into oncoming traffic, a minivan slammed on brakes to keep from clipping the front of her car. The driver littered the air with a few choice curse words.

The police car zoomed up the aisle past Val, Dwayne and Uncle Bubba. Lights on and siren blaring, it took off down the street after Whitley. Val had lost track of her husband until she saw him jump in his truck and rocket toward the parking lot exit. He hit the street fast, turning in the direction of the police pursuit.

It felt like a python squeezed Val's heart.

Dwayne helped her into the back seat of his car, angling the side of her head to keep her from bumping it as she got in. She was so much like the walking dead at that point that she wouldn't have felt anything if it hit anyhow.

One thought swirled around in her head.

How had she ever fooled herself into believing that Kurt could give her the same kind of love she and Hunter once shared?

Chapter 14

After watching her husband run after another woman, Val went home and sat around like a corpse, present but unable to experience anything going on around her.

Functioning on autopilot, she went to her bedroom, removed her church clothes and pulled a nightgown over her head in the middle of Sunday afternoon.

It dawned on her that during the whole parking lot mêlée, not once had Kurt stepped up to protect her. Not when Whitley was trying to assault her; not when his renegade stepfather verbally attacked her. But he was quick as a thief in chasing after Whitley. Was he actually in love with that hood rat? Their marriage was in more trouble than she thought.

Val sighed, taking in the space of their bedroom. Kurt's presence permeated all of it. Black loafers and brown oxfords were lined up in the corner where he left them Saturday morning after shining them up with Griffin shoe polish. His Nautica Aqua Rush scent wafted up from the gown she wore. She remembered him embracing her Friday night, right after he'd showered, slathered himself with the woodsy cologne and left the house for a gathering with his co-workers.

'Gathering' my butt. He was probably with that woman.

The man with the benevolent smile in the photo on the dresser was nowhere near the same man she had encountered hours earlier. She slammed the photo face-down. "I hate you, Kurt," she cried, taking a pillow off the bed and beating her fist against it, wishing it were his face. "As much stuff as I put up with from you, how dare you take me through all of this. I'm the mother of your child!"

So is Whitley.

She held her hands out in front of her. They wouldn't stop shaking. She concentrated on taking deep cleansing breaths. Waving air toward her face, she pulled it into her lungs until they felt full enough to burst.

She expelled the air with force and inhaled deeply again and again, faster and faster, until lightheadedness slammed into her. The bed seemed to be moving. She stumbled toward it. Thinking she was close enough, she lurched forward and missed it by several inches, falling to her knees at the side of the bed.

"I guess this is your sign that I need to pray, huh, God?"

She pulled herself up and rubbed trembling hands over her sore knees. "You're right; I should pray. But I'm too mad and too hurt to do it." Her thumb brushed her stomach and she whimpered, "But I need You because I'm scared."

If only she could just stretch out on the bed, fall asleep and block all this out for a while, maybe she'd come up with some answers. But she was too tense to unwind. Maybe a hot, relaxing soak would help. She drew a bath, and when the tub was almost filled to the brim with the warmest water she could stand, she carefully stepped in. The water threatened to lap over the edge of the tub as she lowered herself into the steaming bath.

"Ahhh," she sighed. "Better."

Her hands rubbed her not-yet-visible baby bump, and she felt her lips pull into a smile. She had taken ten home pregnancy tests in the last two months just to see the plus sign in the window to continually confirm that she had finally conceived.

Giving in to the water's ebb and flow, she let her arms and feet float. When the water grew tepid, she let it drain out while she shaved her legs. As she dried off, she saw a minuscule smudge of blood dotting the white bath towel.

Dread covered her. She inspected her newly shaved legs for nicks. Nothing. She dabbed the towel between her thighs. It came back with another tiny stain. Panic ignited her body. Her tears felt like they were made of steam. She bit down on her sob to keep Dwayne and Uncle Bubba from hearing her.

Grabbing another towel, she wrapped herself in it and kept a protective grip on her lower belly, as if her arm could lock the embryo inside her body.

From the bedroom, she dialed her OB/GYN. A pleasant voice greeted her. "Dr. Farrow's answering service. How may I help you?"

Val cleared her throat. "I'm bleeding," she gasped.

"Yes, ma'am," the lady said in a reassuring tone in between a few clicks on a keyboard. "Your name please?"

"Valencia Timmons. I'm a patient of Dr. Farrow. A few minutes ago I started spotting."

"How far along are you, Mrs. Timmons?" the voice inquired.

"Three months," Val said.

There was brief silence and a few more clicks on the keyboard, then the lady replied, "Dr. Tobler is the doctor on call right now. I'll get a message to her right away. How can she reach you?"

While Val relayed the number, her hand went to her sore, swollen breasts. That part of her body still felt pregnant, but she was terrified of what may be taking place in her womb.

"Mrs. Timmons, stay by the phone. The doctor will call you back shortly."

Those few minutes of waiting on the bed for her doctor to call were nothing short of torture. All manner of second-guessing and condemnation went through Val's head. "Lord, please don't let anything happen to my baby." She turned her eyes heavenward. "I accepted all these years of infertility as my punishment for that abortion I had in college. If you're still angry, take it out on me. But please don't make my baby pay for what I did."

A small, still voice inside of her said, "My thoughts are not your thoughts, neither are your ways my ways." She didn't hear the words in her ear; she felt them in her heart. And there was more. "As far as the east is from the west, so far hath he removed our transgressions from us." She bowed her head in a moment of submission, thankful for God's assurance to her.

The shrill ring of the phone brought her spiritual moment to an end. The doctor listened to Val's concerns then said, "Some women spot through their entire pregnancy and still deliver healthy full-term babies. How heavy is the flow of blood?"

Val sat up and anchored her back on the headboard of the bed. "Not a flow really. Just a few drops."

"Any cramping?" Dr. Tobler questioned.

She hesitated, but the doctor needed to know exactly what was happening. "Last night, I had some bad cramping—but only for a few seconds. None today."

"From what I'm hearing, there's no need for alarm," the physician concluded. "But just to be on the safe side, get in to see your OB/GYN as soon as possible."

Val scrambled off of the bed and went to pull her planner out of her purse. "I already have an appointment for a check-up and ultrasound tomorrow." She set the calendar down. "Should I go to the emergency room today?"

"No," the doctor said in a thoughtful tone. "Just keep your appointment tomorrow. But call back if the spotting becomes a flow between now and then, or if you feel more pain."

"Thank you, doctor." Val exhaled, more relieved than words could say. After ending the call, she automatically dialed Kurt's number. Six digits in, she placed the phone back in its cradle. He wouldn't care. He'd probably be glad to hear she was having complications.

Val laid down, wondering how she could be so close to having everything she wanted, but still so far away.

Chapter 15

Jungles of Papua, Indonesia
July 2011

"As long as I'm alive, you, Matius, will never be chief!" Aboweh stabbed the earth with his spear. The red clay smeared from his cheekbones to his temples seemed washed out compared to the angry crimson blush spreading beneath his skin.

Matius gritted his teeth. This rival often expressed how incensed he was that Kepala favored Matius above all the other warriors of the tribe. It infuriated Aboweh even more that Madra had swatted away his advances at every turn. Everyone knew that Madra was meant for Matius, a reality the angry challenger refused to accept.

Aboweh pounded his chest as he glared at Matius. "I have been in this village all of my life. They dragged you out of the jungle and into the village like some wounded ape eleven years ago." He threw a snide look at the chief. "And now you, Kepala, cast me aside to offer my rightful place to him—an outcast."

Matius threw his spear into the water, then bent down and pulled the string attached to the spear, drawing a flopping fish to the bank. He knew that with Kepala having no sons, Aboweh had been sure that being the eldest son of the chief's closest friend in the elders' council guaranteed his rise to power. The fact was that succession was not automatically determined by bloodline. The chief and elders' council chose the next chief based on character. Only a strong, wise man who had a heart for the people and who had captured the heart of the people could fit the bill.

"I never asked to be chief," Matius said, not even bothering with the effort to turn his face toward Aboweh. "And it is not my fault that Kepala did not think you were man enough to be his successor." He heard footsteps rushing toward him and straightened up to his full six-foot-five stature, ready to take his foe to the ground.

The chief stepped in Aboweh's path, grabbing his wrist and locking eyes with him. "Is it not enough that our men are under attack from the wicked Setan? Will we help them by killing each other?" He looked down at the knife in Aboweh's hand and said something in a harsh whisper that made the younger man ease the blade into the cloth sheath around his waist. His thumb kneaded the handle of the knife.

"He is no chief. He is a coward." Aboweh's lip curled into a sneer as he picked Matius apart with his eyes. "Running away while his friends were killed."

That untruth rankled Matius' nerves as nothing else could. In the Berani tribe, no greater insult could be hurled at a man than the word "coward." Honor was something a man in this village would give his life to protect. Courage was rated even higher. Matius, in the eyes of everyone except Aboweh, displayed high quantities of both.

Eleven years ago, Matius and several other men with him were ambushed deep in the jungle. Matius had spent several days unconscious at the bottom of a deep hole, only to be found by people he couldn't identify as friend or foe. When they threw ropes down to him and hauled him out of the pit, the carnage that he saw on the ground made him begin to fight for his very life. Decapitated bodies lay strewn along a dirt path that led deep into the undergrowth of the jungle. The victims had been viciously killed, hacked by machetes from the looks of it. For all he knew, these "rescuers" were preparing to do the same to him.

It took a half-dozen men several minutes to subdue him. When they finally did, an old woman—who he later came to know as Toma—came forward and tried to communicate with him. Through her gestures and verbalizations, she seemed to be trying to tell him that he was safe among them. Something about her lively eyes, calming voice and guileless demeanor allowed him to believe it. He ceased his struggles.

Although grateful to be alive, Matius couldn't dredge up a single memory about who he was, who the dead men were or why he was in that jungle in the first place. As he and Toma learned to communicate in the weeks and months to come, he was told that he and the slaughtered men had been attacked by a group of rebel warriors called the Setan. Genocide of the Berani people and other tribes was a high priority to the Setan.

Kepala now narrowed his dark brown gaze at Aboweh. "Was not Matius found deep in the jungle at the bottom of the pit we dug to catch wild boars? The gods spoke to me, told me to heal him because he would heal our people. And they have never been more right." Gesturing to Matius, he said, "He offers wise and just words when we trade and join in peace with other tribes. He is as skilled as any warrior born to the tribe. You, Aboweh, do nothing but stomp around like a selfish child demanding what you have not yet earned," Kepala said with conviction. "Matius' actions and deeds are what caused him to be chosen as our next chief." He smiled up at Matius. "The gods believed him to be worthy and so do I."

"I do not believe in the gods," Aboweh grumbled, his milk chocolaty face flushed with anger.

Kepala scoffed, "You did when you thought they were going to ordain you to be chief after me."

"Aboweh," Matius interjected. "I find it odd that all you care about is that I could someday become chief, when the pressing matter at hand is the protection of the people." His rival shot deadly menace in his direction. Matius spoke again. "Not once since the attacks grew bolder have you offered to aid in any—"

"I offer aid with my skill as a fierce warrior. Something you know nothing about." He threw a hostile look at Kepala. "We should hunt these devils and kill them, not bow and scrape for the help of other tribes."

"That is enough!" Kepala yelled. Now it was his turn to get mean. "Your words are not that of a real chief. A *real* chief"—he glanced respectfully to Matius—"puts the safety of the people above his blood thirst for vengeance. Our people's survival must be the only concern right now. But since you are so set on proving your worthiness to be the next chief, you will travel with us to meet the Kahlo tribe. Show me that you are as skilled with words as you are with a spear. Show me that your hunger for peace can tame your greed for war."

Aboweh visibly blanched.

Kepala turned and headed back to the central hut, saying "We leave in two new moons."

Chapter 16

Park Forest, Illinois

Kurt laid his head against the steering wheel. Flashes of the debacle at church pinged around his head like metal balls from an old pinball machine. A palm slapped against his driver side door, making him jerk upright and turn toward the window.

"Get your butt out of there," Frederick George said, his voice strict and foreboding as he turned and headed toward the two-story office building near the place where Kurt was parked.

Kurt complied and met him at the front door of the beige brick structure. Frederick handed Kurt a plate covered in foil, freeing one of his hands up to unlock the door. Steam poured from underneath the foil and it caused Kurt to move the piping hot dish from one hand to the other. The smell of greens leaked out, but Kurt's stomach wasn't too happy about the intrusive odor. He held the plate at arm's length, immediately missing Val's good home cooking.

Keys in one hand and several file folders under the other arm, Frederick pushed the heavy oak door open with his backside and held it for Kurt, grumbling, "Got me missing out on time with my family, and for what?"

Kurt crept by him into a reception area with the words "George & Associates" stenciled in gold scripted letters along an ivory-colored back wall. At the end of a long corridor on the second floor, Kurt posted himself near a frosted-glass door. Frederick unlocked the door with an old-fashioned skeleton key, stepped into the office and flipped the light switch.

Kurt entered the room behind him and switched the lights back off. He hurried to the window, batting the draperies aside with his free hand and scoping out the street below.

"Man, is the Po-Po coming for you?" Frederick joked. "You're acting like a runaway slave dodging the Ku Klux Klan."

Kurt bristled, his teeth grinding together. "This ain't no laughing matter."

"Whatever this is, it had better be important," Frederick grumbled. "Dragging me away from Olivia's home-cooked Sunday meal."

Kurt would hate to be the one to tell his friend, but his wife's cooking tasted like she dragged something in to put on the table. Her culinary skills were more than a little suspect.

When Kurt turned around, Frederick was handing him a fork. "Eat up. She made this plate for you. I haven't even had mine yet."

Kurt laid the fork across the foil then sat the plate on top of a neat stack of boxes beside the window so he could get to the phone in his pocket.

"Man, don't fool around and drip juice on my files," Frederick warned, moving the plate to the top of a mini-fridge in the corner. "You want the courtroom smelling like a soul food restaurant when I pull my exhibits out at trial next week?" Taking his jacket off and hanging it on the back of the worn leather chair behind his desk, he sat down and motioned for Kurt to take a seat in one of two chairs in front of the desk.

Kurt thumbed his way to Whitley's latest text message. He walked over to Frederick and turned the screen to him.

"Order of protection," Frederick said, reading the words out loud.

"And?"

Kurt took a seat and placed the phone on the desk. "That message is from Whitley."

Frederick knitted his eyebrows. "Whitley?"

"The woman I told you about." Kurt's hands drew a curvaceous silhouette in the air.

Frederick's greenish eyes lit up. "Oh, the brick house." Leaning back in his chair, he propped his feet up and laughed. "Man, I told you to leave that broad alone."

"Well, now she's—" Kurt used one hand to draw an imaginary pregnant stomach in front of his body.

"Oh boy," Frederick said, putting his feet back on the floor and sitting up straight. "Even though you were reckless enough to sleep with her, why didn't you at least use protection?"

Kurt said nothing. Drug addicts don't usually think about what's safe. They're thinking of that next high; that next good feeling.

Frederick's eyes flicked to the cell phone. "A woman doesn't take out an order of protection because a man gets her pregnant. So what's really going on?"

Kurt placed his elbows on the arm of his chair and steepled his fingers in front of his mouth. "See, that's the thing," he said, studying his friend. "I don't know if she really got an order of protection or not."

Smoothing down his goatee like he always did when he was assessing the facts in a case, Frederick asked, "When's the last time you saw her? Because if she does have an order of protection, you damn sure don't want her to say that you've been around her."

"Well, we did get into it at church," Kurt answered. When Frederick cocked his head to the side, Kurt added, "Not *in* the church. *Outside* the church."

"Like that's any better," Frederick snapped, his voice dripping with sarcasm. "You two just had to have a *Jerry Springer* moment, huh?"

Kurt shook his head. "Oh, it gets even better. She got into it with Val in the parking lot, and Val's brother and uncle joined in. Then me and my stepdad got in it. The last I saw of Whitley, she was flying down the street and a police car was chasing her."

Squeaky wheels on a cart rolling past the door covered the temporary silence that filled the room. "That's just the cleaning service," Frederick explained. A vacuum cleaner came to life down the hall. "So why was she running from the police?"

"Someone must've called them when we were all out in the parking lot arguing."

"You mean out in the parking lot acting a fool."

"We weren't—" The vacuum cleaner now bumped against the floorboards of the adjoining office. Kurt leaped from his seat so fast that it tipped over backward. Charging over to the open door, he slammed it hard enough to make the plaques and degrees on the wall vibrate.

"Man, are you on crack or something?" Frederick asked in an alarmed voice. "Sit down somewhere. Nobody out there is trying to get in your business."

"Like I said, the argument ended the minute the cops arrived. Then Whitley almost hit another car. She didn't stop. That's why the cops went after her."

Pivoting back and forth between the overturned chair and the door, Kurt walked a groove in the plush carpet as he added, "I jumped in my car and chased her." Before Frederick could respond, Kurt shot up his hand. "Don't ask. I know it was stupid."

Frederick had stopped stroking his goatee and was staring at Kurt. "You left your *wife* standing in the parking lot while you chased after your *girlfriend*?"

"Something like that," Kurt mumbled, fists balled so tight that his short nails almost broke the skin in his palms.

When he had caught up to Whitley's car, it was pulled over to a curb. He had slowed down just enough to see that she was cuffed and standing in front of the police cruiser. With her arms behind her back, her belly had seemed twice as big. She had locked gazes with Kurt just as he sailed past as if he didn't know her.

"I guess my biggest problem is that I don't know if she really took out an order of protection or if she's just trying to rattle my cage." Kurt huffed, feeling frenzied enough to punch a hole in the wall.

He looked at Frederick, who sat silently twiddling his thumbs. "So you need me to find out for sure?"

"That's one thing." He looked around as if someone else might be listening. "But there's something else too."

Frederick's bushy eyebrow shot up.

"How fast can you draw up divorce papers?"

Chapter 17

"Man, what is your problem, coming up in here and asking for a divorce?" Frederick asked, disapproval spreading over his round face faster than an ink stain bleeding onto a white shirt. "You're going to leave your wife for that chick?"

"No, no, and hell no!" Kurt snapped. "I love Val. I don't want to lose her." He picked up the chair he'd knocked over and sat down. "I just want things to go back to the way they were when we met."

Frederick furrowed his eyebrows. "Then you both probably need to seek counseling."

"We can do this ourselves," Kurt balked.

Frederick scoffed, leaned back in his chair and threw his feet onto the desk, clicking the toes of his shoes together. "If you could handle this yourself, things wouldn't be where they are. There's no magic formula to fix this." He interlaced his fingers behind his head. "There's too much pain, bitterness and lies for the two of you to handle alone. If you want your marriage to work, you've got to get help."

Kurt tried to rub the weariness out of his eyes. "You're probably right. But I can't do that, not now."

"If your marriage meant anything to you, you would."

"See, that's the thing." He deliberated a moment on how much to divulge. "There's some stuff you don't know about."

"Well make me know."

Kurt shook his head. "I can't get you involved in some of this, but if I can just get Val to divorce me for the time being, then I'll remarry her *after* I rid myself of a few problems."

"I know you're not talking about harming that other woman, are you?"

"No," Kurt answered, giving Frederick a long look. "But it is a thought."

Frederick advanced from behind his desk. "Kick rocks!" he shouted, shoving the plate of food into Kurt's chest, then hauling him to the door by his collar.

₪ ₪ ₪

Barred from his own home for another twenty-eight hours and unwilling to face off again with his stepfather at "the castle," as Foster called his new home, Kurt drove to Buffalo Wild Wings to loiter for a few hours. He dropped the plate Frederick's wife sent him into the garbage can just outside the restaurant's front door.

The hostess seated him at a booth and handed him a menu. The Chicago White Sox were playing the Detroit Tigers on a nearby television suspended from the ceiling. Feeling the lump of his cell phone in his pants pocket as he worked his brawny frame into the booth, he pulled it out and laid it on the table. As soon as he took it off of silent mode, the Ray Charles "I Need Money" ringtone played. He ignored it. That ringtone was for everyone who was chasing him down to get whatever money Timmons Realty Pros owed them.

Temptation got the best of him, and he couldn't resist looking for a missed call from Val. A part of him was afraid of what she might have to say. A bigger part was deeply concerned that no call meant she was shutting him out of her life for good. He checked the numbers. Nothing from Val.

Twenty-three missed calls, seven voicemails and two texts from Whitley signaled that she hadn't been arrested. She couldn't do all that from a holding tank. Knowing Whitley, she had seduced her way out of trouble.

Kurt yearned to block her calls altogether. *She'd just bring her dumb ass back to my house if I did that.* Until Frederick could confirm whether she'd filed the order of protection, Kurt couldn't take the chance of being anywhere near that woman.

Two baseball games and six beers later, the alcohol had him mellow. He wasn't close to being drunk; not even tipsy. Cocaine had souped up his psyche on much wilder rides than this.

Still in need of a hideout to sort out his problems, he headed to his real estate office ten blocks away.

Chapter 18

"I don't know if this is the right time to bring this up, but since we're knee deep in family chaos anyway, I might as well," Uncle Bubba said as he and Dwayne played pool in Val's basement while she napped upstairs. He made the eight ball jump a quarter-inch off of the pool table and zip into the corner pocket.

Dwayne racked the colorful balls. "Am I going to have to play twenty questions to get you to tell me whatever it is you want to say?"

Uncle Bubba poked him in the side with the butt end of his cue. "Get out the way, boy." His pool stick exploded into the solid white ball. "How do you think Val would react to seein' yo' mama at the church's friends and family dinner?"

"Like a flamethrower in a room full of gasoline," Dwayne answered, tapping the rubber tip of the cue stick on his shoe. "Having mom and us reconnect and be a real family is something you've prayed on for years. But I don't know if this is the right time for Val."

The older man circled the table to take his next shot. "The dinner's not until November, but I was hopin' Val might warm up to the idea if I told her far enough ahead of time." A striped ball nudged a red ball into the pocket on his next shot. "Your turn."

Dwayne bent his towering frame over the table. "Remember when mama first got out of prison a month ago?" He drew his stick back and did a couple of fluid practice strokes.

"You talkin' 'bout the day I saw her when me and Al was on our way to pick up that new power stripper."

"Not power *stripper*. He bought a power *strip* for his TV and DVD player."

"I know the word." He pointed his pool cue at Dwayne. "I just like yankin' yo' chain. Now take yo' shot."

Chuckling at his uncle, Dwayne knocked the green ball in a pocket. "Anyway, remember what Val said when you told her you saw mama at that cheap motel in Harvey?"

Uncle Bubba puckered his lips and mimicked his niece's saucy tone. "She was either over there buyin' drugs, sellin' her body or both."

"And when you told her that mama was pushing a cart full of cleaning supplies and towels because she worked as a maid there, did she lighten up on her?"

"Naw, she didn't," Uncle Bubba whispered, wishing that Val, like her brother, would try to find something redeemable in the mother they barely knew. "Family is everything, son. Even when they mess up." Sadness almost wrestled the words back down his throat.

"Val doesn't hate her," Dwayne said as he walked over and clapped his uncle on the back. "She'll come around. It's just that she doesn't know what to do with the pain mama caused us." He laid his stick across the table. "I can't focus on pool. Give me a rain check."

"All right, but you still owe me two dollars for the last game."

Digging his wallet out of his back pocket, Dwayne thumbed through the bills inside. "Can you break one of these twenties?"

Uncle Bubba shook his head. "I can break open my wallet and drop it in."

"Ha!" Dwayne huffed, then hung the pool cues in the rack on the wall.

"We prob'ly should start dinner," Uncle Bubba said, noticing that the sunlight was now spilling in through the windows on the west side of the rec-room.

"Want me to fire up the grill?" Dwayne went to the far end of the finished basement and rifled through the upright freezer. "I see steak, chicken legs and turkey burgers."

"Some of that yard bird will do," Uncle Bubba suggested.

"Chicken it is."

Uncle Bubba climbed the stairs and opened the door to the kitchen. "You got from now 'til November to tell Val that Francesca's comin' to that church dinner."

"Not happening, old man," Dwayne said as he stepped into the kitchen then shopped in Val's cabinets for spices he would need. "You invited mom, so you have to tell Val."

Putting his hands in his armpits and flapping his arms like wings, Uncle Bubba teased, "Come on over here and let me pluck some of them feathers off yo' chest, ya big chicken."

Dwayne pulled down a rectangular Pyrex dish from the cabinet, looked at his uncle, grinned and said, "Cluck. Cluck."

Chapter 19

The cars of Kurt's two best real estate agents were parked outside of his office when he pulled up. But Ellis and Sade weren't there on a Sunday because they were workaholics. It was more like they were there staking the place out, hoping to confront him about the commissions he owed them.

"Shannon was supposed to take care of them," Kurt mumbled. Cutting the wheel sharply, he veered into an alley and came out on the next street over to avoid detection.

He called his half-sister, Shannon, a successful CPA who managed the books for Timmons Realty Pros. She had warned him regularly about dumping too much money into too many distressed properties at one time. But desperation disguised itself as shrewd business sense and compelled Kurt to keep buying and rehabbing failing malls and shopping plazas, expecting huge profits from the sale of them. Now the properties he held were like slot machines at a casino, hungrily accepting every dollar he fed them and rarely giving a payout.

As soon as he heard Shannon's hello, he jumped right in with, "Didn't I tell you—"

"I'm not available. But please leave a message and I'll get right back to you," her cheerful voicemail greeting said, followed by a beep.

Kurt blew out a lungful of fury. "I need to talk to you now." He ended the call and drove until he found himself outside a boarded-up movie theater in a sprawling defunct mall he owned and couldn't pay to get rid of. Parking in the furthest corner of the abandoned lot, he cracked his windows and set up a makeshift office in his truck, retrieving a leather briefcase from underneath the passenger seat and fanning out its load of unpaid bills on the empty seat beside him.

His phone rang. When Shannon's number appeared on the screen, he answered with a harsh, "Didn't you pay Sade and Ellis?"

"Feel free to say, 'Hello, Shannon. How're you doing, Shannon?'" she said in her usual calm, unaffected manner.

Kurt let out a pent-up breath and weakly recited, "How are you, Shannon?"

"What fire do you want me to put out now?"

"You're supposed to be taking care of my money problems with the business, but I'm sitting here staring at shut-off notices, back rent on the office, overdue contractor invoices, mechanics' liens and maxed out credit cards."

"What do you expect me to do?"

The cooler her voice became, the hotter Kurt got. "I told you to pay everybody I owe a little bit at a time, just enough to pacify them until I got back on track."

"You are two million dollars in the hole," Shannon emphasized. "And you seem to forget that the little money you do have, I can't get access to since the IRS froze the business accounts."

"I'll get back to you," he told his sister and disconnected the call without giving her time to say goodbye. The Internal Revenue Service had gone as far as to call his house. Before then, Kurt had been successful in keeping Val in the dark concerning his mountain of out-of-control debt because all his other creditors only had his cell and office phone numbers.

The initial money Kurt received from his stepfather's lottery winnings would have at least put a dent in his debt. But between paying off Whitley, slapping down twenty grand to keep the owner of that three-flat from taking him to court, and buying cocaine to run from his own reality, nothing was left.

He took long, deep breaths, dreading the trip back to his parents' home. If he could just get his hands on the one-point-five million Foster promised, he'd set everything in order.

Then he'd work on getting things straightened out with his wife.

זו זו זו

When Kurt got back to Burr Ridge, the front door flew open just as he stuck the key in the lock. Foster stood in the doorway.

As grown as he was, Kurt felt like a teenager sneaking in after breaking curfew.

"What possessed you to be all out in public bringing shame on our family's name? Arguing and fighting at the church," Foster said, gritting his tobacco-stained teeth. "And with a woman!"

Kurt didn't wait for his stepfather to move aside. He plowed past Foster, but the cigar-wielding man was right behind him, their footsteps echoing off the marble floor and sounding like wild horses galloping through the house.

Foster dug his fingers into Kurt's bicep and turned him around. "Don't you walk away from me when I'm talking to you, boy!"

"Take your hands off me," Kurt growled. Their arms locked as one scuffled to hold on and the other fought to get loose.

Melva's soft voice penetrated through the fury. "Son?"

Hers was the face of a woman who was tired of having to step in as the shock absorber whenever her son and husband fought.

Both men released their hold on each other. Kurt tucked in his shirttail, all the while glaring at his stepfather, who was stuffing his calloused, bare feet back into the house shoes that slipped off during the fray.

"I've been praying for you all day, son." She beckoned toward the kitchen. "Let's all sit down and try to be civilized with each other."

Kurt ran his hand across his face and let his head slump. "Mama, can't we do this another time? I just want to go get in the bed, close my eyes and forget about everything that's happened this weekend. Can you let me do that?"

"No," Foster shot back. "You're gonna sit here and give us some answers right now."

"Answers to what?" Kurt yelled.

Foster threw his hands up and looked at his wife. "You hear that, Melva? He was all out in the street fighting, and now he wants to act like nothing happened."

"I bet you didn't tell her that you were out there pulling your switchblade on people, did you?" Kurt countered.

"Your father said he had to keep you from jumping on that woman you got pregnant. And he says the police chased you out of the parking lot."

That made Kurt angry enough to break a telephone pole in half with his bare hands. "I'm too tired to discuss my personal business with the two of you tonight. Especially when folks get it twisted."

As he turned and stormed upstairs to the guest room, Foster shouted, "You took that mess public. It won't ever be personal business again."

Chapter 20

A few hours later, Val awoke to Uncle Bubba's laughter. She turned on the bedside lamp and looked at her watch.

She paused for a moment—no pain, no spotting. Sliding into a silk robe, she tipped her way downstairs. From the foot of the stairs, she watched her uncle guffawing at something on the television as he thumped his cane on the hardwood floor to the beat of the Sugar Hill Gang's "Apache." Tearing his eyes away to look up at Val, he made a move to get up. She motioned for him to stay seated. She walked to the doorway of the living room to see what had him so amused.

Will Smith and his sit-com cousin Carlton were dancing at a strip club. Uncle Bubba hooted until tears came out of his eyes as they swiveled their hips and shook their butts. She smiled, despite the gloom in her heart.

"I was worried you was never comin' outta that room again," he said.

Val blew him a kiss and trudged her weary body back toward the stairs.

"Where you goin'?" he asked.

She stopped and turned toward him. "I'm going to lie back down. I just need to turn my brain off and tune everything out until my doctor's appointment in the morning. I'm getting an ultrasound." She touched her stomach, fear invading her as thoughts of her cramps and bleeding resurfaced.

"Back in my day, you didn't see the baby until it came out," he said with a broad grin. "Guess that's a good thing, 'cause if my mama had seen how ugly I was befo'hand, she never woulda let me out of there." He bent over laughing.

Val came back down the stairs, walked over to Uncle Bubba and kissed his bald head. "You're one of the most handsome men I know," she said.

"Besides me, right?"

Dwayne's voice startled Val. She marched over and smacked him on the shoulder. "Don't walk up on me like that."

Uncle Bubba joked, "You almost got shot, sneakin' outta the kitchen like that."

Dwayne held his hands up defensively. "Yeah, I forgot you were packing."

"Val's goin' to her doctor. Wanna come?" Uncle Bubba asked Dwayne.

"When? Now?" Dwayne frowned, patting first one jean pocket then the other until his keys jingled. "Want me to drive?"

Val tugged at her robe. "Hellooo. Would I be wearing this if I were leaving the house now?"

Dwayne gave her a sheepish smile. "I'm rushing and panicking like you're in labor, right?"

Uncle Bubba used his cane and the arm of the couch to lift himself up. "Boy, I hate to see what you're gonna act like when that day really comes."

"He'll pass out," Val chuckled. "And it'll take me, you and Kurt—"

The mention of her husband's name ignited the ache in her heart. His recklessness had permeated their lives, their home and now their church. She looked up at Dwayne and could barely see him through the pools of tears in her eyes.

He rubbed the small of her back. "What time is your appointment?"

"Nine-fifteen tomorrow."

Wiping a tear from her cheek, he said, "That's perfect. I never teach a Monday morning class before noon. Have to give those party-happy college freshmen plenty of time to wake up after the weekend." He smiled and wiggled his eyebrows at her, causing a small lift of the corners of her lips.

A tear dropped onto her bare foot.

"Why don't you head upstairs and try to settle in for the night?" he asked

"Okay."

Uncle Bubba walked over and scolded Dwayne as she walked away. "Boy, why you have to go and bring up Kurt? You made the girl cry."

"I didn't mention him, Unc," he protested.

"Yeah ya did."

Val did an about-face on the stairs and shook her finger at them. "You two sound like a couple of eight-year-olds. Stop all that fussing."

Uncle Bubba gave Dwayne a slight shove and mumbled something she didn't quite catch. She gripped the banister and pulled her tired self up the stairs, hoping to fall into the kind of dreamless sleep that would not bring memories that were better left buried.

Chapter 21

Jungles of Papua, Indonesia
July 2011

"It wasn't my idea!" Zeze protested as Nuri practically dragged him out of the narrow opening of their thatched hut. The ceremonial headdress he wore was knocked to the ground when he failed to duck. He blew dust and leaves off of the brightly-colored bird of paradise feathers and placed the topper that symbolized his position on the elders' council back on his head.

"Zeze, Nuri," Kepala said. "Please take your places—in silence—so that we may start this assembly."

The women sitting to the east of the fire that lit the evening sky gave way to Nuri as she stepped over, around and through their huddle to sit herself right in the middle of the group. Immediately she voiced her outrage to them in irate whispers. Hungry ears wanted to hear her words because, as with every other time that the elders' council had gathered the entire tribe to discuss a crucial matter, Nuri had already wheedled the information out of her life-mate Zeze.

Matius moved over to make room so that Zeze could take his place on the opposite side of the fire, among the elders' council and the rest of the men.

"I would hate to have to lie down in Zeze's hut tonight," Aboweh jeered.

Smirks and grins spread across the many warrior faces decorated with streaks of red clay.

Matius silently prayed, "Lord, give me the right words to say so that we can all leave here on one accord."

Clapping in a slow cadence, he began singing a song that told of the trials and victories of the Berani people through the years. Other voices and hands joined in. The men sat shoulder-to-shoulder, rocking side-to-side in unison. The women—all except Nuri—mirrored them on the other side of the fire.

When the singing morphed into a soft chant near the end of the anthem, Matius stood. Before he could open his mouth, Nuri shouted out, "I don't agree with what you're asking of us."

"Your voice has been heard," Matius replied with a polite nod in her direction. "Now please allow the others to learn why we've gathered."

"You may speak." Her dictator-like tone caused more than a few of the men to furrow their brows at her brashness.

"Stay in a woman's place!" Aboweh commanded, saying aloud what most of the men were thinking.

Zeze was a mess by now. A feather in his headpiece drooped, as if it were embarrassed to stand atop the man's head.

Words were tossed back and forth across the fire. This was not a good preamble to tonight's topic.

Matius shouted over the exchange. "Berani men! Berani women!" The hostile chatter cut off all at once, probably because no one had ever heard him raise his voice in the eleven years that he'd been there.

Satisfied that he had everyone's full attention, he addressed the crowd in a softer voice. "Am I my brother's keeper? I heard those words before—where I don't know. But the Berani tribe is bringing much honor to those words as we organize this alliance of tribes that will enable us to protect ourselves from the attacks of the Setan."

The elders sat up a little straighter, their rheumy eyes beaming with pride at the fact that theirs had been the one tribe wise enough, resourceful enough, influential enough to bring that to pass.

Matius walked to the women's side and stretched out his hand. Madra and Toma got up and joined him in the center of the gathering. There were a few sideways glances from both sides of the fire.

"I know it's not customary for women to address a gathering," he stated. "But I have spoken with Kepala and the council, and they agree that it's fitting that Madra and Toma speak. Now, as they stand before you, don't merely look at their beautiful faces."

Toma sashayed in a little circle, swinging her frail hips to get a laugh and break the tension.

"And don't be distracted by their gorgeous bodies," Matius added, smiling down at her. He then scanned the face of each person present. "But hear them tonight. Hear their hearts." He stepped back so that the two women were now the center of attention.

"Are we our sister's keeper?" Madra asked. Some of the women leaned forward.

Like two minds with one purpose, Toma's words flowed seamlessly behind Madra's. "Right now, there is a village within a three-day walk where all of the men have been killed."

Grumbles of discomfort echoed.

"Matius and Madra came upon it yesterday while returning from a meeting with the Yorda tribe. Those women and their young ones are alone. Many are afraid. Some are without hope. And all are vulnerable to repeated attacks by the Setan."

Madra placed a hand over her heart. "That could be me." Her eyes bore into the faces of the women before her as she said, "That could be you."

"Or your mothers. Your daughters. Your sisters or life-mates," Toma added, turning to face the men.

Matius winced at the thought that with just one twist of fate, her words could be true.

"What we're doing to bring the tribes into an alliance is wonderful," Toma said. "But it's not enough. Those sisters and their young ones need—"

"They are no sisters of mine," Nuri snapped. "Leave them be."

Toma whirled her head toward Nuri. Her body was a little slower, but it followed the move. "May the gods forbid this ever happening, but would you want that answer if Zeze and all of our men were killed? Would you not hope that someone would come and try to comfort you through your sorrow and give you hope that life will one day be worth living again?"

Bossy Nuri was uncharacteristically silent for a moment.

"May I speak for a moment?" Matius asked. Madra and Toma nodded. He stepped near the flames. "First let me say that I know these women's fear. Madra and I stumbled upon two of them who were gathering coconut palms. When they saw us, their eyes reminded me of a monkey I once saw whose arm was caught in the jaws of a crocodile at the bank of the river. The poor little animal was looking death in the face and could do nothing about it. I know these women's terror. It is what I felt when I was first pulled out of that pit and saw all of those dead bodies on the ground." He picked up a stick and tossed it into the fire.

"Having Madra there is the only reason we were able to break through that wall of fear. Had the wife of the Yorda chief not requested Madra's presence, it would have been just us men passing through the bush. There's no way we could have convinced those women that we were not the Setan." Gazing into the fire gave him a moment to gather his strength. Thinking of those women always brought a lump to his throat.

"They let us talk to them for a little while. We learned that more than anything, they were tired of being afraid. Those two begged us to bring them and several other women and children to our village. They told us there were others who couldn't bear to leave, but who vowed to try their best to defend what's left of the village against another attack of the Setan." He paused, giving his words time to sink in.

"We can't be aware of such suffering, yet do nothing about it. But at the same time, I can't act on it without consulting each of you because helping them will impact every life here."

"I'm not concerned about the ones who want to stay and fight. Let them," Nuri snarled. "But as for the others, why would I invite a strange woman to live in my hut with me and my life-mate?"

The "don't go getting any ideas" glare that she gave Zeze wiped away the smile that had crept across his face. "After being with you, what man in his right mind would want another woman in his hut?" he muttered just loudly enough for the men to hear.

Again the sexes tossed cross words at each other. Kepala stood and raised his hands, causing the voices to become silent. "The women would not live in your huts. We would build one large dwelling to hold them and their children."

Another woman spoke up. "Their children will eat up our children's food." She shook her head. "No, this is not a good move at all."

Matius knew these people. The bickering and dissension were coming from a select few who were against the idea. Many of the others were reasonable people with good hearts. But they would be afraid to publicly stand against those who were so vocal and domineering. If a vote was called right now on whether or not to bring the attacked women to the Berani village, those meeker villagers in favor of it would be goaded and harassed into voting against it.

Kepala moved toward the flame and spoke again. "The council has decided to send a group of men to train those women who want to learn to defend themselves." He cast a glance at Aboweh. "It would please the council if you would choose the men and lead them in the training."

Ever competitive, Aboweh's first reaction was to cast a childish "he chose me, not you" look at Matius. But when he caught the elders watching with disapproval, the warrior put a closed fist over his heart and said, "It would be my honor to fulfill the council's wish."

That's one part taken care of. In Matius' heart, he again prayed. "It's the moment of truth. Show me how to help the people honor their convictions and follow their hearts."

In the time it took to blink, an entire scene unfolded in his mind. The council formed a tight circle. In the middle were two tall baskets. One-by-one, the villagers were called into the circle and given one berry. Away from the prying eyes of any of their kinsmen, they dropped their berry in the brown "no" basket or the green "yes" basket.

Matius whispered a silent "thank you," then explained to the people how the vote would be carried out, much to the chagrin of Nuri and her minions.

Thirty minutes and ninety-seven berries later, the Berani people had come to an agreement to help those attacked women who asked to be integrated into their community.

Kepala pulled Matius aside. "The gods are pleased."

"We can't say the same for Nuri," Matius answered.

"Nothing ever pleases that woman," the chief countered. "Mark my words, by the time we have the hut built and the women come, she will have found something else more deserving of her anger."

Chapter 22

Matteson, Illinois
8:30 a.m. Monday, July 18, 2011

Val emerged from her room fully dressed, with her natural, spiral curls freshly washed and her face complemented by a light dusting of makeup, though her skin really didn't require enhancement. She greeted her brother and uncle, who were waiting for her in the kitchen.

"I got shotgun," Uncle Bubba cried as they went out of the front door.

Val cringed. "You can't take that thing with you!"

"Naw, girl," he said, chuckling. "I didn't mean I'm *bringin'* the shotgun. I meant I'm *ridin'* shotgun." He lifted his eyebrows in a comedic fashion. "What kinda man you think I am?"

Laughing, the men headed to Dwayne's car as Val locked the house. But their fun was cut short when Val doubled over in pain. "Val!" they shouted, rushing to her. As if it were a synchronized dance, Uncle Bubba grabbed her left arm, and Dwayne anchored himself at her right side.

"You in pain, baby?" Uncle Bubba asked, his voice peppered with fear as his hand tightened around her bicep.

Searing pain in her abdomen brought her closer to the ground. Her head felt like a red-hot furnace. Sweat leaked from her pores and danced down her skin.

Dwayne's arms closed around her midsection. "Get the door, Uncle Bubba," he commanded. "I'm carrying her to the car."

Val felt her feet leaving the ground as Dwayne lifted her into his arms. She was vaguely aware of her head tilting forward against his neck, then flopping backward. She wanted to snap to attention when she heard Uncle Bubba exclaim, "Her eyes are rollin' back in her head. She's passin' out." But she couldn't fight the compulsion to close her eyes and fade away.

ℕ ℕ ℕ

"We need some help over here," Uncle Bubba barked as Dwayne carried her through the sliding glass doors leading to the emergency room. Val's body flip-flopped between feeling like it was on fire and feeling like she was making snow angels in the nude. Bringing her knees up to her abdomen, she wedged herself further into the crook of Dwayne's arms and used his broad chest as a pillow.

Unconsciousness threatened to swallow Val again. Her left eye didn't even try to fight. It just slowly closed, urging the rest of her to follow. Through a crack in her barely open right eye, she took in a distorted glimpse of the room. A guard folded his newspaper and stood up from the desk he was seated behind near the door. A woman pointed to a weather map on a muted TV. A custodian with a mop bucket positioned a "wet floor" sign on a slick spot.

"My sister's pregnant and she passed out at home. In the car, she told us she's bleeding and having pain," Dwayne said with urgency.

Val pressed her ear to his body to feel the rumble of words resonating through his chest. She tracked the guard when he dashed past them. When she lost sight of him, a bawling toddler drew her attention. "No," said the exasperated woman holding his wiggling body. "I don't care if you cry. I'm not letting you crawl around on this floor."

The security guard reappeared, rolling a wheelchair in their direction. As Dwayne headed toward him, each step he took made Val's head feel like a stick of dynamite was detonating between her ears.

The uniform-clad man locked the brakes on the chair. Dwayne placed her in as gently as possible. Before he could straighten back up, Val head-butted him when her body bucked forward with the urge for her last meal to make an untimely return. The dry-heaves brought a soreness she hadn't felt since that time in high school when she had bet Dwayne she could do two hundred sit-ups without stopping. She saw the security guard scrambling to grab a plastic garbage can and set it at her feet.

Uncle Bubba's voice faded in and out. "... somebody over here ... make me come back there ... girl is sick ..."

A wave of stabbing abdominal pains knocked the air out of her.

Uncle Bubba's cane swatted the security guard's feet. "Don't just stand there! Go get a doctor."

Agonizing cramps made Val's face contort. Her arms locked around her stomach and she dug sharp fingernails into her side as her head came to rest in her lap.

"Everybody move!" an authoritative female voice commanded. "Now!" She clapped twice, and Val saw the security guard's feet step aside to make room. The woman lowered to her haunches and lifted Val's head an inch off of her knees, then looked up and asked Dwayne, "What's going on?"

His voice shaky, he answered, "My sister's pregnant and she's—"

"Bleedin' and crampin'," Uncle Bubba finished.

A nurse burst into the waiting room through a set of heavy wooden doors marked AUTHORIZED PERSONNEL ONLY. The doctor shouted some orders at her, then gave instructions to the two anxious men hovering near the wheelchair. "I'm going to need you two to go to the registration desk over there and give them as much information as you can. I've got to get her in a room right now so I can examine her."

Another pain ravaged Val's abdomen, folding her in two again like a stick of gum. "Please," she pleaded, taking hold of the doctor's hand. "Please save my baby."

"What's your name, Miss?" the doctor asked, placing her cool hand on Val's forehead then pulling it away as though the boiler-like heat from her patient's skin had singed her.

Val sat up slowly, wiping tears off of her face with her index finger. "Valencia Timmons."

"But we all call her Val," Uncle Bubba said.

The gentle, self-assured woman kneeling in front of her cupped Val's trembling chin in her hand. "Well Val, I'm Dr. King, and I'm gonna take good care of you."

The nurse unlocked the wheelchair brakes and whisked Val toward the locked double doors that led to the emergency room.

"Wait!" Uncle Bubba shouted. The rubber wheels squealed on the waxed floor as the nurse stopped just short of the heavy wooden doors. He and Dwayne crowded around Val. "We'll come back there as soon as we take care of this paperwork," her uncle promised.

Dwayne snapped his fingers as if remembering something. "Val, do you have your insurance card on you?"

She handed him her purse. "Look in my wallet."

He reached in and came up with a beat-up bag of Skittles before finding the wallet. He placed the purse back in Val's lap.

"Hold on to that while we get her examined," Dr. King said.

Taking the bag and tucking it under his arm, Dwayne bent down and kissed Val's cheek. "I love you, li'l sis. Everything's gonna be fine. Okay?"

She nodded, tears clouding her vision.

Uncle Bubba gave a soft squeeze to the tip of her nose. The tentative smile they shared spoke of their sadness and apprehension.

"We really have to be going now," Dr. King nudged.

Dwayne and Uncle Bubba reluctantly moved aside and allowed Val to be taken through the doors. Before the doors shut behind her, Val heard them arguing over who was going to hold onto her purse.

"Uh-uh, you keep up with it. I ain't walkin' around with no

pocketbook on my shoulder, boy," Uncle Bubba complained.

"But it matches your shirt," Dwayne shot back.

Chapter 23

10:15 a.m.

"Val," Dr. King said, "I'm going to examine you, but first I need a blood draw."

Within minutes, a nurse who was a pretty good vampire was putting a Band-Aid on the crook of Val's elbow and handing vials of Val's blood to the other nurse in the room.

"Lonnie, as soon as you get that to the lab, I need you to have radiology bring their portable ultrasound machine down here stat," Dr. King said.

"I'm on it, boss," the petite nurse said as she left the room. Dr. King turned to Val and nodded toward the other nurse. "This is Kierra. We'll help you onto the bed."

When Val stood, a woozy feeling almost knocked her back down, but the doctor's and nurse's firm grip around her waist supported her as she took the few steps toward the bed. As soon as she was on her back, Kierra went to work, taking Val's pulse, blood pressure and temperature. After jotting down the numbers, Kierra hurried out of the room.

"How long have you had bleeding and pain?" Dr. King asked.

"They started yesterday," Val responded. "But it's just been a little spotting here and there. And the pain has never been this bad."

"I'm gonna need you to get out of your clothes and put this on." The doctor opened up a drawer and took out a green cotton hospital gown. "Let it open in front. Do you need Kierra to help you when she comes back?" When Val shook her head, Dr. King said, "Radiology will be here shortly. I'll be back in as soon as the tech finishes your ultrasound."

Though it didn't take long for the radiologist to get there, the ultrasound itself went on forever. The tech's face, registering concern every few seconds, made it even more torturous for Val. She was evasive when Val asked, "What is it?"

Snapping the latex gloves off her hands, the technician reached for the door and said, "Sit tight, Mrs. Timmons. I'll send the doctor back in."

₪ ₪ ₪

Val was getting more distraught by the moment. It helped that Dwayne and Uncle Bubba were now in the room, but it felt like a whole decade passed before a quiet knock on the door was followed by the doctor's voice. "Val?"

"Uh-huh," she responded.

Dwayne pulled the door open and Dr. King came in. She slid a short stool from under a desk fixed to the wall, sat down and rolled herself closer to Val. After removing a pair of glasses from her pocket, she rustled through some papers in the file she held. "The good news is that you aren't miscarrying."

Relieved sighs from Val, Uncle Bubba and Dwayne filled the room.

"We saw a good fetal heartbeat. And your blood work shows that your hormone levels are in the normal range for sustaining a pregnancy. So I'm not sure why you're bleeding and having abdominal pains. But about twenty to thirty percent of expectant mothers spot during their entire pregnancy, then give birth to perfectly healthy babies."

"That's what the doctor on call told me last night," Val said.

"Maybe that's what's going on with Val," Uncle Bubba said hopefully.

Dr. King hooked her feet around the base of her stool. "That's possible. But usually there's no cramping with it. That's what has me most concerned. As far as you know Val, did your mother or grandmother have these problems in their pregnancies?"

"My grandmother's dead."

"Her grandmother was my sister," Uncle Bubba offered. "She had miscarriages for ten years before she finally had Francesca, her only child. That's Val's mother."

Dr. King's eyebrows drew in. "Oh, then what about your mother, Val? Did she have problems like this?"

Val felt the blood rush to her face, crushed at the notion that her mother had probably never wanted her as much as she wanted this baby.

Dwayne cleared his throat. "Our mom's been in and out of prison since we were small, so we don't know much about her."

Spasms tore into Val's abdomen with a pain too unbearable to describe. Eyes closed, she writhed in agony.

Dr. King leaped off of the stool. "Val, Val." She gently tapped her patient on the cheek. "Look at me, Val. Tell me where it hurts."

Gasping in distress, Val pointed to the left side of her navel.

The doctor placed her fingers there and applied pressure. There was no discomfort—until she removed her hand. The resulting explosion of pain caused Val to let out a loud shriek and grip the sheet so tightly that she almost ripped it. Dr. King repeated the movement, and the jab of pain it caused almost made Val jump off of the table.

"N-n-n-no," Val groaned, grabbing Dr. King's hand. "It doesn't hurt when you push in," she said, her voice coming in ragged bursts. "But when you let go, it feels like somebody's stabbing me from the inside."

Dr. King went to the door and stuck her head into the hallway. "Kierra, get radiology back down here stat to do another ultrasound, a vaginal one this time."

Rolling her stool back against the wall, she said, "Excuse me for a moment. I have to do a bit of research. I've got a hunch about what might be going on in Val's body." She went out the door again, still giving orders. "Kierra, tell the ultrasound tech to focus on the area around her left fallopian tube."

₪ ₪ ₪

"So what's the verdict, doc?" Dwayne asked forty minutes later. He, Uncle Bubba and Dr. King were all standing beside Val's bed again after having left the room while she underwent a second ultrasound.

Dr. King looked at her iPad. "It's pretty serious." She slid in between Dwayne and Uncle Bubba so she could talk to Val. "The ultrasound images they scanned to me shows that you have a baby developing in your tube. He can't survive, and if we leave him there, that tube will rupture. You could die."

"Nooooo. Pleeease, no." Val pawed at the iPad in the doctor's hand. "Look again. There's got to be some kind of mistake. You said my baby was okay."

Dwayne sat on the bed, pulling Val to his chest.

"If it's in her tube, can't you go in and move the little critter, like nudge it until it gets in the right spot?" Uncle Bubba asked, frowning.

The remorseful woman shook her head. "I'm so sorry. The medical field hasn't figured out a way to move a tubal pregnancy into the womb and still have the embryo survive. But we need to do emergency surgery because your niece's life and the healthy baby's life are at stake."

"What healthy baby? You said it wasn't going to survive," Dwayne said,, gently stroking his sister's hair as she soaked his shirt with her tears.

Dr. King put her hand on Val's shoulder and held it there firmly, speaking in an even, serene tone. "Val, listen to me." When Val's watery eyes finally latched onto hers, the doctor slowly inhaled and exhaled. "Breathe with me."

Like volunteers at a hypnotist's show, Val, Uncle Bubba and Dwayne simultaneously took deep breaths and let them out as one.

"That's better." Dr. King rubbed a soothing hand on Val's arm. "I'm not being clear." She took her glasses off. "What I was getting at is that the second ultrasound showed that there are two babies inside of you, one of which is healthy and exactly where it's supposed to be."

Val's mouth fell open. The tears that flowed down her cheek this time were accompanied by an ecstatic smile. Dwayne's face replicated her jubilation.

"Lord, have mercy," Uncle Bubba said, pulling a handkerchief from his pocket and mopping his forehead. "You were gonna have twins, just like yo' mama had." He lifted his eyes to the ceiling.

"Not quite," the doctor corrected. "See, Val has an extremely rare and dangerous condition called heterotopic pregnancy. That's when one embryo implants in the womb and another implants outside of it, like in a fallopian tube."

"Maybe we should call Kurt?" Val said in a pensive voice.

"We ain't callin' that scoundrel," Uncle Bubba growled, tapping his cane on the floor. "I'm still mad at him."

Patting the old man's shoulder, Dwayne confessed, "I'm mad at him too, Uncle Bubba, but this isn't about us." Looking at Val, he asked, "You sure about this, li'l sis? I mean—"

"No, I'm not sure," she answered. "But call him anyway."

Chapter 24

1:45 p.m.

"That crazy woman didn't get a restraining order against you." Frederick had sent Kurt a text instructing him to meet him in the park where he took an hour-long run every day. The well-conditioned attorney put a foot on the bench next to the space where Kurt was seated. He leaned into a long hamstring stretch and groaned.

"I checked with a friend at the Matteson Police Department, and they don't know anything about an order of protection with your name on it." Spreading his feet apart and holding his arms out to his side, Frederick rotated his torso left, then right. "I had a contact at the courthouse in Markham look into it too. Nada."

"Can you check back in a week or so?" Kurt asked, unfolding a wrinkled piece of paper he had in his hand and holding it out to Frederick.

"Oh Lord, what's this?" the attorney asked.

"Read it."

Frederick gave it back. "I don't want to read it."

Huffing in frustration, Kurt laid his shades on the bench, sat the paper on his thigh and used his hand to iron the creases out of it before reading it aloud to Frederick. "I, Whitley Moore, accept the sum of one hundred fifty thousand dollars cash as full and final payment of all monies I am owed from Kurt Timmons for the support of our child. My signature acknowledges that I have received the cash and agreed to terminate our friendship immediately."

Frederick shook his head. "What law school dropout threw that thing together?"

"I did," Kurt said. "Just trying to protect myself."

Frederick nodded and stroked his goatee. "Riiiight. And how's that working out for you?" He took the towel from around his neck and snapped it like a whip at Kurt's arm.

"Ow!" Kurt cursed and rubbed the sore spot.

When Frederick stopped guffawing, he said, "I thought you were crazy when you asked me to draw up papers for you to divorce Val and remarry her. But this ..." He pointed to the paper in Kurt's hand. "This is so crazy that I can't even give it any more of my time."

He turned and walked away, leaving Kurt fuming on the bench.

ℾ ℾ ℾ

Kurt's cell phone was sounding off in the cup holder when he opened the door to his truck. He slipped into the driver's seat and picked it up. The number on the display was one he didn't recognize. *Please, please, be a buyer for one of my properties.* The phone's battery was down to two percent.

"Kurt Timmons here," he said, searching in the center console for the charger.

"It's about time you picked up."

He slammed the truck door closed. "Dammit, Whitley. I told you to leave me alone!" Still unable to find his charger, he smashed the top of the center console down.

"Oh, poor baby," she drawled. "I just thought you might want to know that your precious wife is here at the hospital."

"How long did it take you to come up with that lie?" Kurt said, offended that she would think he'd be stupid enough to believe her.

"I'm not lying," she protested. "My friend in the emergency department remembered me mentioning I was kicking it with a guy named Timmons."

The woman had his business all out in the street.

"So when she saw someone had come into the E.R. with that last name, she called to ask if I knew her. I've got no reason to lie."

"No reason?" he snapped, starting the engine and almost stripping the gears as he backed up, shifted into drive and floored the gas. "Try this one: you missed your chance to get an order of protection against me yesterday, so now you're trying to lure me to your job so you can cause a commotion and get me arrested."

"I just know that your wife is up here having your baby." She paused, then taunted, "Wait, I forgot. She's not even showing yet. So I guess she's probably not *having* your baby; she's *losing* your baby!"

Chapter 25

Forty minutes later, Kurt sat parked across the street from his real estate office. As badly as he wanted to stay invisible to the people inside, he couldn't work from his mobile command center indefinitely. He stretched his neck left and right trying to see around the Timmons Realty Pros lettering on the plate glass window. There was movement inside and two silhouettes, but the glare of the afternoon sun reflecting off the glass made it hard to determine who it was.

A city bus passed, letting off a few passengers before Kurt grabbed his briefcase and got out of the truck. When he crossed the street and stepped up onto the curb, he could see Ellis and Sade inside comparing notes on green sheets of paper. Kurt remembered the day he decreed to his staff, "When this green paper hits your inbox, it means that some green money has hit your bank account."

Well, that hadn't happened in a while.

A bell tinkled when he opened the door and walked in. Ellis and Sade both looked his way.

"Got our money today, boss man?" Ellis asked. His tan face wore an expression that signaled that he already knew the answer.

A few people had warned Kurt not to hire Ellis Reyes. One person who knew that Ellis had been to juvenile detention for shoplifting had said, "That boy will steal the paint off your car." But Ellis had turned out to be the best salesman Kurt had ever run across.

"I wish I did have something for you, my man," Kurt said, feeling the hot sticky July air on his back and the cool, dry office air on his face. He stepped over the threshold and closed the door. "If you and Sade can give me just a little more time, I'll—"

"You owe me six large," Ellis snarled, smacking his palm with the green paper he held. "How much longer do you expect me to wait?"

Sade came alongside him and waved her sheet at Kurt. "Me and my husband have three mouths at home to feed. We need two salaries—two *consistent* salaries—to make ends meet. I can't do this anymore. I'm starting with Coldwell Banker next week."

Kurt grimaced.

"I'm leaving too," Ellis added, working two keys off of his key ring and tossing them onto a desk.

"You can't go." Kurt put his briefcase on the reception desk and flicked the locks open. "You're my two best salespeople." A ringing phone on the desk went unanswered as he took out his checkbook. "Let me write you a check for a portion of what I owe."

Sade stepped up and slammed the briefcase closed. "Too little, too late."

Kurt hurriedly wrote a check anyway. Sade took it, scanned the print, then tore it to shreds. "Only cash or a cashier's check at this point," she said. "I'm not racking up any more bank fees for depositing another one of your rubber checks."

Nobody paid the ringing phone any attention as Kurt rambled through his wallet and pulled out a credit card. "I'll go to the cash station and take an advance off of this."

Can't use this one, he thought as he pulled out one card after the other.

Ellis headed to the door. Sade wriggled two keys off her key ring and dropped them on top of Kurt's briefcase.

The never-ending ringing of the phone made it hard for Kurt to concentrate as he flipped through his wallet. "Sade, can you *please* answer that?"

"Nope—don't work here anymore." She retrieved a designer tote from the top right drawer and caught up with Ellis at the door. "And check your inbox."

"Yeah," Ellis said. "You got a dozen calls today from some old dude named Bubba."

Kurt didn't wait to see them leave. It was just one more reminder of his failure as a businessman. Instead, he trudged into his office, snatched the messages out of the inbox on his desk and collapsed into the chair. "If that old man thinks I'm calling him back so he can bust my chops again, he's got another think coming."

The glowing red voicemail light on Kurt's phone begged for his attention. Putting it on speaker, he dialed the voicemail code and deleted message after message without even listening to them. But a voice prompt announcing an urgent message made his finger hover above the keypad. He let it play. "Kurt, this is Uncle Bubba. We been callin' yo' cell phone and yo' office all mornin'. They're takin' Val to surgery right now over at Franciscan St. James Hospital in Olympia Fields."

Kurt's heart slammed in his chest. His wife being at the same place where his crazy ex worked would not be a good thing.

Chapter 26

Val's eyes popped open in the recovery room after surgery. Her hand shot to her stomach, as though her fingertips were stethoscopes that could detect a fetal heartbeat inside her.

"Oh, I see someone's awake," crooned a recovery nurse with smooth charcoal skin. Her nametag said Natalie. She was swapping out an empty saline bag on Val's I.V. pole. "Dr. King should be here in a minute."

Val grabbed her sleeve. "Is my baby all right? Am I still pregnant?"

The nurse gave Val's hand a reassuring pat, but her next words were anything but. "I'm sorry, I can't answer that for you. Dr. King will be here shortly."

Val's heart sank. She forced herself not to tear up as she asked, "Natalie, can you at least tell me where my family is?"

Natalie smiled, which lit up her entire face. "That I can do, sweetheart. Dr. King's in the waiting room talking to your uncle and brother now."

Val was both angry and hurt that her husband hadn't shown up. She groaned while trying to prop herself up in the bed.

"Here, let me help you." Natalie rushed to push a button on the side of the bed, inclining the head of the bed just a touch.

The curtain swung open and Dr. King stepped in, pulling it closed behind her. "So how're you doing, mommy?"

Mommy. So much elation filled Val upon hearing that one word. She thought she might need wrist and ankle restraints to keep her from floating up to the ceiling.

Dr. King's eyes danced with delight. "Everything went well. And it's a good thing you got here when you did."

Val hadn't even realized she was crying until the doctor reached for a tissue on the bedside table and blotted her tears away. "Had you gotten here a day later—maybe even just hours later—that tubal pregnancy would have ruptured and we could have lost you and the baby in your womb." With a smooth bank shot, she fired the balled-up piece of tissue into a mesh trash can.

"You've got skills," Val joked, feeling the tentacles of relief for the first time in days.

"Who do you think taught Jordan how to play back in the day?" asked Dr. King, grinning as she pulled out a few more tissues and stuffed them into Val's hand.

"When can I see my family?"

"I'll send them right in." She gave Val a gentle squeeze on the shoulder. "You'll be transferred to a room shortly. I'll stop by to check on you in the morning. Until then, the nurses on your floor will take good care of you. If all goes well overnight, I might be able to release you tomorrow."

Chapter 27

3:45 p.m.

Kurt pressed his palms on the information desk and gritted his teeth at Whitley. "I'm not in the mood"—he leaned deeper over the desk so the nosey security guard couldn't overhear him—"for your silly ass games right now."

Whitley sneered at him then typed something into the computer. Taking an adhesive tag and a Sharpie marker off of the desk, she said, "They're taking her to 401-East," and wrote the room number in scribbly letters on the visitor pass.

He snatched it, peeled the back off and slapped the visitor pass on his navy and white striped dress shirt.

"You'd better keep an eye on her," Whitley taunted, her eyes promising a retribution he would regret. "You never know when I might get the notion to mosey on up to her room and smother her while she's doped up on those painkillers. Then it would be just me and you. The way things should be."

She laughed out loud as Kurt spun on his heels and hurried away.

ℿ ℿ ℿ

"None of the nurses will tell me what's going on with my wife. And now you two are keeping some code of silence," Kurt said, pointing an accusing finger toward Dwayne and Uncle Bubba. He resented the judgmental looks swinging his way.

Uncle Bubba waved his cane in Kurt's direction. "If you got here when we called you the first time and not the twentieth time, then you'd know what's happenin'." He rested the cane across his knee and glared at Kurt. "Ask yo' wife when she gets here."

Kurt groaned, scrubbed his hands down his face and growled, "How many times do I have to tell you that my phone went dead and I didn't get your messages until an hour ago?" If he could get rid of them, he could be alone with Val when she was brought back from surgery. "Can't y'all go to the chapel and pray?"

"I ain't never stopped prayin'," Uncle Bubba rebutted. "Can you say the same?"

God's not too pleased with me at the moment, thought Kurt. *He hasn't been for a long time.*

Kurt plopped down in a chair by the window and tried to ignore Dwayne and Uncle Bubba as they held hushed conversations that were sure to be about him. He envied the bond they shared. His father had died when he was just a few months old. A year later, Foster Timmons was in his life. Most women were only enamored with Foster's outer appearance, the wavy ebony hair and ivory skin of a man who was of mixed heritage. But what swept Melva off of her feet was his ambition and his dreams of owning a chain of grocery stores.

The Saturday morning after Melva and Foster's nuptials, a three-and-a-half-feet tall golden-skinned girl holding a brown paper shopping bag rang their doorbell. That's how Melva found out about the ex-wife Foster had never mentioned and the custody arrangement that let him keep his six-year-old daughter on weekends. How he had managed to keep it a secret was a mystery.

Foster openly favored his daughter Shannon over Kurt. Every

Saturday morning when Melva would leave for her beauty shop appointment, Foster would give Shannon some type of special gift— crayons, new white gloves for church, barrettes for her hair. At those times, Kurt felt like the family pet that people ignore when a new baby comes home.

In Dwayne and Uncle Bubba, Kurt had found the male acceptance and camaraderie he'd thirsted for all his life. Well, until now.

They had shut him out and closed ranks around Val because he'd hurt her. But what about what she had done to him? That didn't seem to matter.

Now it was him against them. And they seemed to have the upper hand.

Chapter 28

Dwayne, Uncle Bubba and Kurt created a human traffic jam when they heard the wheels of a gurney approaching the room. All three of them had barreled toward the door, getting wedged in the opening as they each jockeyed for position.

Dwayne, who was closest to Val when she was wheeled to the door, leaned over the railing of the bed and kissed her forehead. "The doctor told us it was a close call."

Uncle Bubba was squeezed in beside him. "I prayed mighty hard for you." He blew her a kiss.

Kurt hated the feeling that he had to compete with those two for his wife's attention. From the opposite side of the gurney, he put his finger under her chin and tilted her head in his direction. "As soon as you get out of here, baby, I'm going to get you home and take good care of you."

"You will do no such thing." Uncle Bubba's frigid tone was lethal.

These two needed a reminder that he was the alpha male as far as Val was concerned. "She's my wife and don't you forget it," Kurt responded, his words spiked with cyanide.

"I'm not the one who forgot," Uncle Bubba shot back.

"Gentlemen," the clean-shaven young orderly interrupted. "You can work things out after I get her in bed." When none of them moved, he looked at Val and said, "Your highness, will you order your loyal subjects to move?"

Val grinned and closed her eyes. "Don't make me laugh," she told him, holding her hand over her stitches and trying to stifle a giggle.

The men gave terse chuckles and allowed the orderly to pass, but he still had to shoo them away several more times before he could get Val fully situated in the bed. As soon as he finished, the men played musical chairs, dashing toward the two seats on either side of Val's bed. Uncle Bubba took the one by the curtain and Kurt beat Dwayne to the one against the wall. Dwayne made himself comfortable leaning against another wall.

A nurse came in the room just as the orderly left. "Mrs. Timmons?" she asked, plucking a pair of glasses from the mass of curly gray hair loosely piled on top of her head. Only her hair color accused her of being a senior citizen. The vibrant bronze skin on her oval face and her nimble movements as she walked toward the foot of the bed contradicted that charge. "I'm Greta, and I'll be your nurse until we change shifts in about three hours." She looked at the three men positioned around the room. "And who are they, your not-so-secret admirers?"

Dwayne stepped up with a grin and an outstretched hand. "I'm her brother, Dwayne."

Kurt stood and reached his arm across Val, unwilling to relinquish his spot, and said, "I'm Kurt, her husband."

Uncle Bubba got up from his seat. "And I'm her uncle, but you can call me Bubba," he said with added bass in his voice that caused Dwayne and Val to share an amused glance.

When Uncle Bubba looked at them and winked, Dwayne's lips twitched as he strained to seal in his laughter.

The three of them were a tight circle, leaving Kurt on the outside looking in. He wanted to shout to Val, "What, I don't exist in your world anymore?" But that would make him sound pitiful and whiny. He leaned on the arm of the chair and covered his face with his hand, hoping to not let the fact that he was being made to feel invisible cause him to do something counterproductive like storming out of the room.

"Well, nice to meet you all," Greta said, walking to the curtain that separated the room into two halves. "And since you don't have a roommate for the time being, Mrs. Timmons, let's get some sunshine over here on your side of the room."

Kurt slumped in his chair, his patience wearing thin. He wanted to be alone with his wife.

Greta reached out for the curtain, but Uncle Bubba stepped in. "Allow me, uh, Greta, did you say?" In a move that wasn't completely spry but was far from rickety, he sprung to her side and slid the curtain back.

Greta put a hand on her ample breast. "My, what a gentleman you are."

Uncle Bubba took a bow, beaming. "At yo' service, my dear."

She pointed toward the window, where two colorful balloon arrangements were dancing around, billowing from the flow of air coming out of the vent along the windowsill. Uncle Bubba stuck his chest out. "Me and Dwayne got those balloons for my niece," he gushed.

Not to be outdone, Kurt popped out of his chair and picked up a gigantic panda and a vase full of festive red roses that were on a wooden table below the television. "I brought these for you. I hope you like them," he said to Val, laying the stuffed animal at her feet and waving the bouquet under her nose to sniff.

"They're beautiful," she said with a weak smile.

He was thankful that she didn't kick the big bear out of the bed or knock the vase out of his hands.

Uncle Bubba went to the window, gathered the balloon strings in his hands and walked to the bed, a trail of balloons bobbing behind him. He twisted the strings around his hands to bring the balloons to eye level so Val could read what each one said.

When she rewarded Dwayne and Uncle Bubba with a warmer, more genuine smile for their gifts, resentment and jealousy raced through Kurt. He placed the vase on the bedside table, certain that he would crush the glass with his bare hands if he didn't.

"You're one lucky young lady," Greta said as she set out to take Val's vitals. "And those roses are gorgeous. I love roses. Any kind of plants, actually. My friends all wonder why I don't retire and work in my garden full time." She took Val's blood pressure and typed the results into the laptop she'd brought into the room on a rolling metal stand.

"You like flowers, huh?" Uncle Bubba said, rubbing his chin. "That's good to know."

Under the watchful eyes of Uncle Bubba, Dwayne and Kurt, Greta finished assessing her patient. Before she left, she fished around the edges of the bed until she found the remote tucked between the railings. She handed it to Val and said, "If you need me, just hit this button, the one with the little stick person on it."

"Greta," Uncle Bubba interjected, giving her an appreciative once-over. "If you don't mind me sayin', you got too many curves to look like that stick person."

"You behave," Greta said with a mischievous wink. She left the room with a wave and a little dip in her hip.

Uncle Bubba turned to Val and said, "I'd wax my chest for that woman right there."

"All three hairs?" Dwayne joked. As the old man and his nephew quibbled, Kurt cleared his throat and looked at Uncle Bubba, casting his eyes at the doorway to indicate that he wanted him and Dwayne to leave.

Uncle Bubba frowned at Kurt, but gave his niece a kiss on the forehead and said, "Me and your brother gonna go get somethin' to eat."

"Uh-uh, I'm staying put," Dwayne declared.

Uncle Bubba put his hat on his head and teased the crease with his fingers. "I said we need to go, son."

When Dwayne didn't move, Uncle Bubba clapped a hand on his shoulder. "Come on." Over his shoulder, he told Val, "We'll be back in no time."

Dwayne reluctantly pushed off from the wall. "Whatever you say, Unc." He moved toward the doorway, but gave Kurt a warning look over his shoulder.

Chapter 29

"I ain't sayin' I agree with the way Val got pregnant," Uncle Bubba said to his nephew as they slid their trays up to a gum-popping teen working the cash register in the cafeteria. "But I understand why she felt like she had to do it." He handed her ten dollars and scooped up the coins that clanked to the bottom of the change dispenser.

"I see an empty table," Dwayne said and weaved them through the crowded dining area.

"Yo' Aunt Rebecca—God rest her soul—was exactly like Val," Uncle Bubba said as they sat down in hard plastic chairs. "Me and her tried every trick in the book to have a baby. That was back when they didn't have fertility clinics like they do now, at least not for black folks. For all I know, I could have had reptile dysfunction."

He wanted to smile at the joke he'd made, but sadness captured his smile like a butterfly in a net. "Everything changed when Rebecca faced the fact that she wasn't gonna have children. She started actin' like she had nothin' to live for." His chin dipped to his chest as regret began bubbling through his thoughts. "I stayed mad at her a long time 'cause my pride was hurt. I felt like she wanted kids more than she wanted me."

"Everything worked out when me and Val came to live with you, though, right?" Dwayne remarked, and there was an anxious tinge in his voice that put Uncle Bubba on notice.

He looked into his nephew's face and saw the grown-up version of the little boy who had stolen his heart. "Yeah, it did."

At first, Uncle Bubba had thought that nothing could top his love for his wife. But when he brought those children into his home, the way they depended on him and trusted him with their lives took his heart to a place he had never imagined. He had instantly realized that that very feeling was what his wife had been longing for.

His mouth turned down at the bittersweet memory.

A college-age girl passed by, her arms loaded with books. She sat down at a nearby table and cracked one open.

"That girl there reminds me of yo' mama," Uncle Bubba said, casting his glance toward the bookworm. Dwayne turned around to get a look. "Yo' mama used to keep her head buried in books, just like her."

Francesca, the only child of Uncle Bubba's sister Mae, was the daughter any parent dreamed of. Quiet and respectful. Always thinking of others. "Yo' mama used to say she was gonna be a nurse. And I believe she woulda made it, too." Feeling his appetite sneak out the back door, he placed his hot dog on the plate and nudged the tray away from him. "But she changed so much after she got pregnant with you and Val. Plus she got all mouthy, became rebellious. A regular hellion."

Dwayne wiped crumbs off of his mouth with the back of his hand and took a sip of his Coke. "I know that didn't go over well with Grandma Mae."

"Woo-wee!" Uncle Bubba gave a little snort. "Mae was ready to ring that girl's neck like she was a barnyard chicken." He brought his leg out from under the table and stretched it, ankle popping as he rotated his foot. "But she decided that instead of trying to beat the devil out of Francesca, she would love the hell out of her." He crossed one leg on top of his knee. "I don't know what happened after that, though, 'cause they got into it one day when you and yo' sister was just little bitty things, the biggest showdown they ever had."

Opening the chocolate pudding on his tray and scooping out a spoonful, Dwayne said, "I remember it. I didn't know what it was about, but I thought back then that me and Val were the reason."

Uncle Bubba grimaced, thinking how, even at four years old, a child would take responsibility for what the adults in their lives did. "No, it didn't have nothin' to do with you or yo' sister."

Dwayne got a faraway look in his eyes. "I just remember that the night they had that big argument was the last time I saw my mama."

"Yeah," Uncle Bubba sighed. "Yo' grandmama woke up the next day and found that Francesca had run off. That tore Mae up somethin' awful. The doctor said it was a heart attack that killed Mae a year later. But he was wrong. She died from a broken heart."

"I don't know what would've happened to us if you and Aunt Rebecca hadn't been there to take us in."

Silence.

"Unc?"

"Yeah?"

"I don't know if I tell you enough but …"

He gave Dwayne's hand a reassuring pat. "I know, son. I know."

They both looked away. Hidden secrets began tumbling through Uncle Bubba's head like laundry flipping end over end in a dryer. Finally he said, "I used to think that yo' mama was crazy about whoever got her pregnant, 'cause she protected that boy to the end and never did tell us who he was."

"She knew you and Grandma Mae would've killed him," Dwayne said, sprinkling salt on his fries and dunking one in a small paper cup full of ketchup.

"You're right I guess," Uncle Bubba laughed. He gazed toward a stack of dirty dishes hitching a ride to the kitchen on a conveyor belt. "But I found out not too long ago that I was wrong about her coverin' for the boy that got her pregnant."

Dwayne's fry paused midway to his mouth. "Why do you say that?"

"Because," Uncle Bubba sighed, "the last time I saw Francesca when she was still in prison, she said that when she got out, she was gonna kill the man who raped her when she was a girl."

Chapter 30

Jungles of Papua, Indonesia
July 2011

Matius slid his arms around her midsection and pulled her to him. The way she melted into his embrace never failed to set him on fire. There was something so provocative about the way this strong, self-assured woman had chosen to give herself only to him. He nibbled at her earlobe and she inhaled deeply, her warm, moist breath against his neck causing desire to course through his veins.

"I love you," he whispered as he pulled her closer still. With a trail of soft kisses, he anointed her temple, forehead and the tip of her nose. She tilted her head back to meet his lips, and he could barely restrain himself. He kissed her so long, so deeply, that her knees buckled. "I've got you, baby," he said, his strong arms holding her up. "I won't let you fall."

He pressed his manhood against her. Rising on her tiptoes, she matched his every move. When she was overcome with ecstasy, she threw her head back and released a breathy whisper. "I love you, too—"

Matius bolted upright on his straw sleeping mat, startled awake once again. It was always the same dream; with the same unsatisfying ending. The moment she fixed her lips to say his name, she vanished.

Lying alone in the pitch black of his hut, he inhaled. Her fragrance had been so alluring while he slept. But it was gone now. If only he could conjure up that scent at will, he'd breathe it in until his brain was forced to surrender the identity of the shadowy woman who wore it.

When Toma had called the woman in his dreams the "shadow woman," she didn't know how right that term was. In every dream, her body and face were mere silhouettes. But the fire that passed between him and her was real. The love had once been real.

Matius reclined on his mat with one assurance on his mind: a shadow is never created without there being a concrete object blocking a stream of light.

His shadow woman was real—somewhere.

Chapter 31

Olympia Fields, Illinois

"Are you comfortable, Val? You need anything?" Kurt asked once they were finally alone. "Nobody will tell me what happened." He settled in the chair beside the bed.

Her eyes zeroed in on him, taking in his counterfeit concern. "So now you wanna be Mr. Caring Husband." The air she forced through her nostrils felt hot enough to set her nose hairs on fire. "Where was that man yesterday when your woman tried to take me out in the church parking lot? Or Saturday when she showed up on my front porch?" If her eyes could shoot flames, he would have been cremated by now.

Kurt took her hand and patted it. "I know you're not going to let me get away with any of that, but ... just ... let's not deal with that right now. Okay?" he asked in a placating tone.

"Then when, Kurt? When is the right time to talk about all this? When Whitley gives birth to your child?"

Giving her an unsympathetic look, he snapped back, "You're making this harder than it has to be."

She snatched her hand from his and snarled, "You don't know what hard is."

He turned away and sighed.

Val caught his chin in her fingers and forced him to look at her. "Hard is every time you hear someone's baby whimpering, you can almost feel the sensation of laying his warm, squirming little body against your chest to soothe him. Hard is always wondering 'When will I get my turn?'" The I.V. in her hand dug into her flesh as she balled her fist up to wipe away her tears. "I couldn't understand why God would fill me with such longing to have a child, then deny me the privilege of becoming a mother."

"I already know this stuff," he snapped. "You've said it a hundred times."

"Obviously your brain set up a roadblock and never let my words get to your heart."

Kurt stood and paced at the foot of her bed. "I told you we'd adopt if you weren't able to have children—when the time was right. Even Mama thought adopting was a good idea."

She tracked his every step. "You still don't get it, do you? I didn't want to try that option yet." She rubbed her stomach. "I wanted to feel a child moving inside my body." Some people told her that was selfish, especially given the number of children who needed good homes. "I wanted to look at that child and see *my* face."

He sighed again. "I know, and that's why I'm so sorry you lost the baby."

Val snapped her head toward him. "You self-centered—"

Kurt stopped pacing and turned fully to her.

Disgust rattling through Val made the room spin. "Is that why you came here? To find out if I miscarried so you can run back and play house with your mistress?"

Kurt's hands flew up. "No, no, that's not what I want."

"You're so full of it," Val tossed back. "For your information, I didn't miscarry."

His hands dropped to his sides and he slumped into a chair. "When I finally got Uncle Bubba's message, he said to get over here because you were having emergency surgery for a tubal pregnancy."

"I had a baby in my tube and a baby in my uterus. They removed the tubal pregnancy, and the one in my womb is fine." For some reason, she ached for him to hold her and tell her how glad he was to hear that news.

"You happy now?" he sneered, his eyes flickering with a mean light. "You got what you wanted. And while you've been wrapped up in your own issues, you didn't have a clue about what I've been going through."

Val crossed her arms, tilted her head down and glared up at Kurt. "Like what?" she challenged. "What *exactly* have you been going through, Mr. Timmons?"

Kurt burst out of his seat and marched toward the door. "See, that right there is why our marriage is so shaky now."

"Oh, so *I'm* the reason?" she exclaimed.

He turned and gave her a snide look. "Yeah." He spread his arms like expanding wings. "In the whole world, nothing matters except you and your issues."

Marching back over to the bed, he towered over her. "And Lord knows you've made it clear that there's no room for anyone's mistakes but your own. Oh wait, I forgot—you're perfect. You don't make mistakes."

To Val, it felt like Kurt was doing nothing more than pulling rabbits out of a hat, trying to turn the tables so he wouldn't be the one in the hot seat. "I don't have to listen to this." She picked up the remote and searched for the button to turn on the television.

Kurt collected the device from her hand. "Oh yes, you do." He put it on the side table and blocked it from her reach. "You made yourself out to be the poor helpless victim in all this and me to be the big bad wolf."

"You must be out of your mind!" Her pores were little volcanoes with sweat hot as lava seeping out of them. "I waited years longer than I wanted to start a family because of *you*. Until it was almost too late for me to have one."

"Fifty-year-old women are having babies nowadays," he protested.

"Don't say that crap to me!" she countered. "You got some other chick pregnant, then had the gall to tell me to get rid of my child!"

Dropping his head, he spoke quietly. "I was wrong for that, and I'm sorry. If I could go back and do things all over again, I never would've let that happen."

This time, his words sounded genuine. His expression looked sincere. But pride and pain made it impossible for Val to acknowledge it. "Oh, you would have strapped up so she wouldn't get pregnant, right?" she cracked.

"No, I mean I wouldn't have been with her in the first place."

"And now I guess you're going to tell me that I drove you to be with her."

"I *was* driven to her!"

Val could tell he was trying to keep a muzzle on his volume.

"But not by you."

She thought his eyes looked teary when he focused her way.

"That's part of what I need to talk to you about."

When he hesitated, she snapped, "I'm listening."

"This is going to sound strange, but hear me out before you make a decision." He cleared his throat. "I don't plan on being with Whitley ... but I do need to ask you for a divorce."

Chapter 32

"Somebody raped mom when she was growing up?" Dwayne asked, giving his uncle a double take.

Uncle Bubba leaned forward in his chair until his chest rested on the edge of the table. "When she told me, I was just as surprised as you are now. But it kinda explains a lot of stuff. That's why she changed so much after she got pregnant." He held his nephew's gaze until he heard the sound of Dwayne crushing the empty Coke can in his hand.

"Who was it?!" Dwayne demanded.

"I don't know."

Dwayne dropped the can on the table and wiped his hand on a napkin. He put his elbows on the table, looking as though he were watching answers unfold in his mind one by one. "A lot of things sort of make more sense now. I always thought she left because she hated me and Val. But maybe she didn't."

"I think she hated what you reminded her of," Uncle Bubba offered, saddened that such an early memory of rejection could still be a fresh wound in his nephew's heart decades later.

He tried to lighten the mood. "Boy, when you was little, you used to look after yo' twin sister like you was a Pit Bull instead of a little pipsqueak. You didn't hardly even trust the preacher around Val."

Dwayne's eyebrows relaxed a little and a smile dawned across his face.

Uncle Bubba continued. "I remember the whole congregation crowdin' around the little baptismal pool in the church the day Val got baptized. 'Member that? Y'all was six then."

"When the preacher covered Val's mouth and nose with his hand and bent her back to dunk her in the water, I thought—" Laughter trapped Dwayne's words.

"You thought he was tryin' to kill her," Uncle Bubba said with a wide grin. "You climbed yo' scrawny little butt up those pulpit steps so fast that none of those old deacons could catch you. Water splashed all over everybody when you jumped yo' crazy self into that pool."

Uncle Bubba smashed his palms together to make the sound of a body doing a belly flop into the water, and Dwayne laughed until tears came out of his eyes. "You was flappin' yo' puny arms so much that I couldn't tell if you was swimmin' or tryin' to fly."

"I *couldn't* swim!" Dwayne exclaimed. "But I didn't think of that until *after* I threw myself into the pool."

Their laughter died down, and gloominess blotted Dwayne's face again. "If you really look at it, I've lost every mother I've ever known."

Uncle Bubba shook his head. He had suffered those losses right along with Dwayne. First when Francesca ran away. Then when her mother died a year later. The final blow the family suffered was the death of Uncle Bubba's beloved wife Rebecca.

"On the day Mama started accepting our visits at the prison," Dwayne said, "it felt like I could maybe get one of my mothers back. And now that she's been released and we've started working toward building a relationship ..." His voice cracked a little. "Do you think she meant what she said about killing the man who raped her?"

"Let me put it to you like this," Uncle Bubba said, absently rubbing his finger back and forth across the prongs of his plastic fork. "If I knew who the bastard was, I woulda already put him in the grave."

Chapter 33

"A divorce?" Val scoffed, gritting her teeth so hard that Kurt thought her jawbone was about to break.

He turned an angry face toward his wife. "Stop talking for a minute and listen, okay?!?"

"You want to kick me and our baby to the curb so you and that hooker can set up housekeeping?" She didn't seem to care that her voice might be carrying through the walls.

"Shhh!" he hissed. "You don't have to tell everybody our business. And no, that's not why I'm proposing divorce."

She poked her tongue in her cheek. "I'm confused. I thought a man proposes marriage, not divorce."

"You know what I mean."

"No, I don't," Val flung at him. "I don't even know who you are anymore."

Kurt walked to the window, wishing he could open it and let all the hostility be sucked out of the room. "Will you just let me talk?" He turned from the window, pleading with his eyes.

Val opened her mouth to say more but held it instead.

He took a deep breath. "I'm asking for a divorce because of ... the money."

"What? So you can keep the quarter mil your stepdad gave us? You must think I'm a fool. I've cried too many tears in this marriage to turn around and let you walk off with that money."

Kurt flinched and his eyebrows drew in. "Woman, would you please just listen?" He hesitated, rubbing the back of his neck. "I'm trying to come clean about some things."

"Oh, there's more dirty laundry that I don't know about?" She kicked her feet from under the cover. "Your life is just one big shockumentary."

If he didn't find the right way to explain it, he'd never get her to go along with it. "My stepfather can't stand you."

Val gave a phony gasp and pretended to swoon.

He squeezed the bridge of his nose and counted to ten in his mind, realizing he only had one chance to get this right. "I never really stood up to him about how he treats you, and I'm sorry about that. I know it's late in the game and that apology probably doesn't mean anything to you, but I had to say it just the same. That money he gave me—"

"*Us*, Kurt. He gave *us* money."

Kurt exhaled deeply. "When he gave *us* the money, he promised me he'd give me a million-and-a-half more next year."

Val's eyes bucked. "Why didn't I know about this? You never said anything about any extra cash."

"That's because ... he said I could only have it if ... I divorced you."

She drummed her fingertips on the bed. "And you saaaid ..." She was hotter than a branding iron. He didn't open his mouth.

"Come on," she urged. "Fill in the blank. You said ..."

"I told him no."

Val gave a sigh of relief.

"Well, at first I said no." Her startled look made his recent encounter with the police come to mind. He might need to call them now to keep Val from killing him right there in the hospital room. Kurt blew out what could be his last breath and said, "Then I went back and accepted his offer."

Her eyes rolled over every inch of him, from head to toe, as if she were looking at a mass murderer. "And you wonder why I wanted to leave your sneaky, spineless—"

"But you've got to let me tell you why I did it."

"As if I don't already know," she snapped.

Now his voice escalated almost loud enough to be heard outside the room. "You *don't* know. Shut up a minute, will you?!"

In an over-the-top show of submission, she bowed her head. "Yes, my king. Your humble servant shall shut her mouth so that thou mayest bless me with thy words—which are filled with enough manure to clog a thousand toilets."

Anger was a ventilator forcing his chest to heave up and down. He flexed his fingers, fighting for self-control.

"I know things between us got bad. And I know I haven't been the husband you needed me to be. But you have to believe that I never, ever stopped loving you." Sensing that he needed to bring out the big guns, he said, "Oh hell, I may as well come on out and tell you. When I got the two hundred—"

Val's narrowed eyes administered the antidote for that little slip of the tongue.

"When *we* got that two hundred fifty thousand, it was just a drop in the bucket compared to what I needed to get my business back in the black again. And now all that money is gone—every dime of it. My business is in a lot more trouble than I told you. And I just ... I got desperate ... so I told my stepfather I wanted the rest of the money."

He wished he could hook Val up to some kind of machine that would read her brain waves and tell him if he was making any headway in getting her on his side. Her stoic face and mummified body gave no clues.

Quick to make an addendum, he said, "I was hoping you'd agree to the divorce. Once I show him the divorce decree, *we* get the million-and-a-half." He looked out of the window just as an airliner passed overhead and wished he was in the economy seats. "Then we can go somewhere far away and start a whole new life together. I mean, what can he do? Sue me if I get back with my wife after I take his money?"

As hard as it was, Kurt sat down and said no more. He used to preach, manipulate, badger and finagle his way into getting Val to fall in line with his ideas. But more often than not, pressuring her into doing something didn't turn out the way he planned. In time, he had learned to make his point then give her time to mull it over. Sometimes she wised up and came around to his way of seeing things. Hopefully, it would work this time.

To Kurt's delight, Val beckoned him closer with her index finger and puckered her lips. Ah, she did get it. She saw the logic in what he'd said. He leaned in, closing his eyes and parting his lips just a touch to give her a sensual kiss. She'd earned this one.

Live electric wires must have touched his skin. He jerked back, rubbing his cheeks where Val had delivered a forehand smack to one and a backhand to the other.

"By the time I get home tomorrow, you had better found some other place to live—permanently," she growled.

Rottweilers were less menacing than the woman lying in that bed glaring at him. But Kurt was not about to be pushed around. "Either you give me a divorce so we can get the money and start to rebuild our life together, or I'll divorce you and get sole custody of that child you're carrying. Remember, I can make it happen because I'll have more money than you. You choose."

Given his drug addiction, no judge in his right mind would grant him custody. But Val didn't know that. He strutted out of the room with an air of confidence. One way or the other, he was going to get what he wanted.

Chapter 34

"You know somethin' that really bothers me?" Uncle Bubba asked after Dwayne finished responding to an email from the person who took over his class at the college for the day.

Dwayne clipped the phone back onto his belt. "No, Unc. What?"

"That invisible noose Foster's got around Kurt's neck. That ol' goat has his hooks in that boy somehow."

Dwayne turned his nose up. "Don't mention that man to me."

"Which one, Kurt or Foster?"

"Neither one of them." Dwayne piled all their trash onto one tray. "Foster treats Val like she has a contagious disease. I've had a hard time with that from day one because I want to jump in and protect her, but she always says to let them work it out. I almost lost my mind when Foster was going off on her yesterday and Kurt didn't say anything. If that's her definition of working it out ..."

"I don't know what made Kurt act that way." The Kurt Uncle Bubba used to know loved Val as much as he did. He would never have allowed anybody to hurt her. Uncle Bubba drank the last few sips of Mountain Dew then added the can to Dwayne's garbage heap. "But Foster didn't surprise me. He's always been an ass."

A five-dollar bill glided off of the tray of a woman in a snazzy navy blue suit as she passed their table. In her effort to catch the money, her tray slipped out of her hand. Every voice in the cafeteria hushed simultaneously at the sound of the tray of food crashing to the floor. Her pale skin turned crimson.

Dwayne got up and helped her wipe up the food that had landed on her shoes and the floor. When he came back, Uncle Bubba asked, "What was I sayin'?"

"That Foster's behavior doesn't surprise you," he said as he sat back down.

"I used to know him way back when me, yo' auntie, yo' grandmama and yo mama all lived in a two-flat on 66th and Vernon."

"I don't remember him."

"That's 'cause y'all was just little babies when his family moved across town." He covertly pointed and whispered, "Here comes butterfingers."

The woman who had dropped the tray came up to the table. She flashed a smile at Uncle Bubba and extended a hand to Dwayne, bending at the waist and exposing an ample amount of cleavage. "Thank you so much for your help." She switched away from the table before Dwayne could answer.

"She gave you that little peep show hopin' you'd chase after her," Uncle Bubba teased.

"Believe me; one woman is enough for me." Dwayne rubbed the back of his head. "Tiffany understands enough to give me space to deal with family issues like this. But she'd go upside my head if she thought I was out here flirting."

Uncle Bubba frowned as he said, "Back to Foster. You know how every street has that one crazy neighbor that everybody avoids?"

Dwayne nodded.

"Foster was that man on our block." Uncle Bubba let out a long, slow whistle. "He was mean as the day is long. Somebody walked on his grass, he would come bustin' out the front door like a junkyard dog. Somebody parked in front of his house—wasn't even no driveway for them to block—but he would come out yellin' that they had to move their car." His index finger made a circling motion near his head. "Biggest fool I ever did see."

"Once a fool, always a fool I guess." Dwayne stepped away to empty their trash, then went back to the table and turned the chair backward, straddling it as he said, "Foster is mean to Val, but Melva is crazy about her. She's more like a second mother to Val than a mother-in-law. Li'l sis tells her everything."

"Maybe, but I bet she didn't tell Melva that she was determined to have a baby—with or without her son's blessin'." He scanned the cafeteria, noticing a group of people in scrubs moving toward the exit. "Speakin' of babies, we need to get back to the room and check on Val. How long we been gone?"

Dwayne checked his cell phone. "Almost forty minutes."

Uncle Bubba stood. "Let's get on back to see 'bout her."

Chapter 35

Val pinned her eyes to the doorway when she heard voices. Greta entered, followed by a set of curvy hips that backed into the room while the person attached to them talked to someone down the hall.

"Blaire," Greta said as she pulled the other woman into the room and shut the door. "This is Val Timmons. Dr. King just performed surgery on her a couple hours ago, and we'll be monitoring her pregnancy overnight."

The woman stopped short when she looked at the patient in the bed. A mahogany undertone illuminated her sepia skin. "Val? Is that you?" she asked, eyes roaming over Val's features.

Val hoped the heart monitor didn't register her surprise. Uncle Bubba and Dwayne were back in the room. She certainly didn't want them to see how spooked she was right now. Her response was a curt, "Blaire."

"And you're pregnant? Congratulations," Blaire beamed as she reached out to take Val's hand. The woman didn't seem to catch on to the fact that Val was uncomfortable being around her. Val wiped her sweaty palm on her gown before shaking the nurse's hand.

"You two know each other?" Uncle Bubba asked from where he stood near the window.

"Yeah, we met at the fertility clinic where I used to work," Blaire volunteered.

Val wished she could blink the words *shut up* to Blaire in Morse Code. "That was a really long time ago," she answered, hoping Blaire would catch her drift and stop talking.

She didn't.

"How far along are you?"

"Three months," Val said, wishing she had magical powers to make Blaire disappear.

"That's about how long you've been working here, isn't it Blaire?" Greta asked.

"Yeah. I left when the fertility clinic got that new supervisor," she stated to Val. "He was about to make me catch a case. Told me he couldn't work with people who didn't flow with his vision."

Greta erased her name from the whiteboard that listed the nursing staff. "If I know you, you had something to say about that." She handed Blaire a green magic marker.

"You know I did." Blaire wrote her name in bold blocked letters on the dry-erase board. "And he wrote me up for insubordination."

Greta lowered her head and looked at Blaire from under hooded eyes. "Sounds like you brought that one on yourself." She moved closer to Val's bed.

"He just wanted the people under him to drop their brains in the lost-and-found and treat him like he was the only one who knew anything." She snapped the top onto the marker. "But I'm not the one. I just think he was threatened by me. Thank God I was able to find this job right after he fired me." She slid a glance at Val. "When I saw you back in April—"

Val feigned a coughing fit.

Greta patted her on the back, then put her hands on her hips and said to Blaire, "I'm sure our patient doesn't want to hear your life story. And besides, I'm trying to get out of here, so pay attention while I tell you what's going on."

Val glanced at Uncle Bubba and Dwayne. Uncle Bubba was eyeing

Greta while whispering to Dwayne. Whatever was shared made the men do a fist bump.

When Greta finished updating Blaire on Val's status, she told Val, "I'll see you tomorrow, okay?" and turned for the door.

Uncle Bubba cleared his throat dramatically. "You ain't gonna say bye to nobody else?"

She looked over her shoulder and winked. "Only if you promise I'll see you again tomorrow."

Uncle Bubba elbowed Dwayne's side like he was the school nerd who just won a date with the prom queen. He was still grinning when Greta left the room.

Blaire remained behind, punching buttons on Val's I.V. machine. "Who are these handsome men, Val?"

Still on cloud nine from his encounter with Greta, Uncle Bubba stepped up and kissed the back of Blaire's hand. "I'm her Uncle Bubba and that's her brother Dwayne."

"You're just a regular charmer today," Dwayne teased.

Uncle Bubba ignored him and asked Val, "By the way, where's that husband of yours?"

Blaire gave a quizzical look. "Wait, I thought your husband died."

Val cut her eyes at Blaire.

"Naw, that rascal's alive. By the way he's been actin', though, he's just askin' for the good Lord to strike him dead."

"But I handled your paperwork at the fertility clinic, and it said you were a widow," Blaire announced a little too loudly.

Val looked at Dwayne and Uncle Bubba, who had both taken too much interest in the conversation for her liking and were now giving her suspicious looks. Squeezing her eyes shut and opening her mouth wide, she forced out a yawn that her body hadn't asked for. She put a pained look on her face and touched her incision site with her fingertips.

"Blaire, can you look at my bandage before you go? The tape is pulling my skin."

"I'm gonna have to ask you gentlemen to wait outside for a minute while I check the dressing on her wound," Blaire announced. She walked behind them and closed the door, then pulled a pair of rubber gloves from a box on the wall and slipped them on. She came to the bedside and reached for Val's gown. A biting grip around her wrist stopped her cold.

"I would thank you to keep *my* business out of *your* mouth," Val said, her fury amplified ten times more than her volume.

Blaire drew back her hand. Her eyebrows rose to her hairline. "Why? You got something to hide?"

Val waved her index finger in the air as she spoke. "I don't have to tell you anything other than this: whatever you *think* you know about me, keep it to yourself."

Blaire crossed her arms. "Correct me if I'm wrong. When I first saw you at the fertility clinic a few months ago, your paperwork said you were widowed and wanted to have your frozen embryos implanted inside you."

"You just go around spying on everybody's medical history?"

"I was putting some information in your file when I saw that," the nurse retaliated, neck swerving. "And your paperwork didn't mention anything about you having a new husband."

Val was ready to shut Blaire down, but she needed to find out how much the woman knew. "What does me having a new husband have to do with you?"

Blaire's nostrils flared. "You gave us consent forms showing that you and your *late* husband had both agreed that if one of you died, the other one would have full control over the embryos you had frozen."

"And that's the truth. So why do you have your nose all up—"

"Because you lied about being a widow. You falsified consent forms with respect to your marital status. That's illegal! Your uncle said you're married. If you lied about that, then what else did you lie about?"

Val wasn't proud of what she had done, but this was her business to tell—when the time was right. "Who are you, the fertility police?" she said, her tone simmering with indignation. "What gives you the right to question me about my personal business?"

"Me being a single woman trying to find a good man gives me that right," Blaire snapped. "It's women like you—"

Val's hand went up. "Whoa, what do you mean women like me?"

"Pretty girls," she shot back. "You think you're better than the rest of us, but all of you are just manipulative and conniving." She stripped the rubber gloves from her hands. "I'll bet your husband is a good man. That's what your type of woman always seems to get, and then you mess up their heads and their hearts with your shifty ways. When you cut him loose, he'll be just another good brother that can no longer trust his heart to a good sister like me." She fired the gloves into the trash as if they had done her wrong.

"You don't know the first thing about my husband." Val folded her arms across her stomach but quickly moved them because it made her incision hurt. "And don't turn your issues with men into my issues."

Blaire shifted her weight to one side, her unforgiving eyes shining into Val's like lasers. "I might not know everything, but I know enough to figure out that this right here"—she gestured to Val's abdomen—"is as lowdown and sneaky as it comes." Propping her hands on her hips, she asked, "What's gonna happen when your new husband finds out that your pregnancy is from a fertility clinic? A clinic that implanted your *dead husband's* frozen embryos inside you?"

"Get your supervisor in here," Val snarled, gripping the edge of the sheets. "I don't know how you treat all your other patients, but—"

"When this baby comes out looking just like your dead husband, your current husband will certainly figure it out." Blair smirked, again casting an accusing finger at Val's abdomen.

Those words pierced Val's armor, but instead of showing it, she blew a raspberry with her lips and said, "You don't know what you're talking about."

"Yeah, well—"

There was a rap on the door, followed by Uncle Bubba peeking in. "Okay to come in?"

Glaring at Blaire, Val answered, "Sure. The nurse was just leaving."

"That's right," Blaire added, giving Val a challenging look before heading out of the room. "Just leaving."

Like two hound dogs that had caught a whiff of a fox and now wouldn't stop sniffing around until they found it, Dwayne and Uncle Bubba kept their focus on Val. "Val … uh … is there somethin' you need to tell us?" her uncle asked.

She pulled the covers over her head and tried to reposition her hips on the hard mattress. Fear of having done the wrong thing laid a load of guilt on her so heavy that her shoulders shook from the weight of it all.

Gently lowering the covers, Dwayne sat on the bed and allowed her to lean into his chest. Whenever she was distressed when they were kids, he would wrap his arms around her shoulders like a protective cocoon. But she knew his strong arms couldn't shield her now because what threatened her wasn't an outside force. It was inner guilt that smothered her.

"Before we left the room, did I hear that nurse say she saw you at the fertility clinic in April? That was just three months ago," Dwayne said. There was no condemnation or judgment in his voice, just confusion and concern. "You told us you got pregnant using fertility drugs you ordered off the Internet."

"And you didn't say nothin' 'bout goin' to no clinic." Uncle Bubba hooked his thumbs in his suspenders. She wondered if he realized that he always did that when he was trying to dig up an answer to something that puzzled him.

"Why is that important?" She kicked the covers off of her feet and tried to sit up to swing her legs over the side of the bed, but her sore incision area halted that idea. Allowing her back to sink into the pile of pillows behind her, she said, "The only thing that matters is that I'm pregnant for the first time ever and I've made it to the end of my third month."

"You ran that girl outta here 'cause you didn't want her talkin' 'bout somethin' in front of us. That says it's important. Mighty important." Uncle Bubba gave her a pointed look. "So we're askin' you again. Why didn't you tell us you went to the fertility clinic?"

"I don't want to talk about it," she mumbled and poured herself a cup of water from a pitcher on her bedside tray. Taking several long sips, she stopped when the ice cold liquid gave her brain freeze.

"Val ..." Uncle Bubba edged.

"Please … I really don't want to talk about it."

Relief washed over her when Uncle Bubba got up and said, "All right, then." He came near and brought his fingers to her face to give her nose a soft goodbye tweak.

"Me and Dwayne gonna leave now 'cause I know you need yo' rest." He rubbed his hand down his face. "And I ain't gonna lie; I'm tired too."

"That makes three of us," Dwayne admitted, giving her a kiss on the forehead. "We'll be back first thing in the morning, li'l sis."

She rubbed her eyes and acted like her eyelids were almost too heavy to keep open. "No, I don't want you missing another day of work. Besides, Dr. King said she's letting me go home tomorrow. I'll call you when she discharges me."

"You got a deal," Uncle Bubba said as they went to the door.

Within seconds, their footsteps were reverberating down the hall. But a moment later she heard the step-step-tap of Uncle Bubba's footsteps and cane. When his three-legged rhythm stopped, Val opened her eyes and glanced toward the door.

Uncle Bubba stepped inside her room but didn't approach. "I know you're all grown up and you're tellin' me and yo' brother it ain't our business, but it sounded like that Blaire person was sayin' that that baby you got inside you ain't Kurt's."

Val opened her mouth to protest, but a wave of his hand silenced it.

"Now I've lived a long time, and I can tell you that lyin' ain't never good. Don't matter if you lie *on* someone, *for* someone or *to* someone. You need to straighten this mess out before it blows up in yo' face."

She didn't respond, just looked at him like he was an apparition. His words echoed as he left the room.

Chapter 36

Jungles of Papua, Indonesia
August 2011

The last few weeks had Matius on edge. He was not sure if it was because of the upcoming talks with the next group of tribes or this meddlesome notion that he was close to a breakthrough concerning his memories. Madra sensed it too. Sensed something was coming— something big and powerful enough to pull him away from her forever. Each fed off of the other's strange fear that the end was near. Never with words did she voice her fears, but with her body, she laid out her soul to him each time he held her like he was holding her now.

They had stolen away to his living space. He stared down at her, lying on the pallet in the oversized hut that the villagers had helped him build as a gift of comfort and gratitude for the many years of aid he had given them. Marveling at Madra's exquisiteness, he wondered if this enormous change they both sensed would destroy the woman he now loved.

When she drifted off to sleep, Matius rose and inched quietly to the other side of the hut. It was becoming increasingly harder for him to find slumber because he couldn't quell the murmurings of his mind. Shadows became dreams, dreams became visions, visions began to take root, and the voices in them became that much louder. A seductive, fruity, flowery scent that was familiar yet unlike any in the jungle toyed with him each time he did manage to fall asleep. The shadow woman. Amnesia hadn't erased the feel of her touch on his skin, the tinkling sound of her laugh. It was too real to only be his imagination.

He kneeled to pray. The Berani people believed in many gods, but Matius had an internal knowing that he had always believed in just one— One who was the sole and omnipotent ruler of heaven and earth. Looking to this God for guidance is something Matius had done all his life. Of this he was absolutely certain. Amnesia tried to cloak all memories that supported this fact, but specific words that had been imprinted in his spirit found a way to sneak past his barricaded recollections. These words he recited every sunrise and sunset because they spoke to the essence of who he once was.

"The Lord is my shepherd; I shall not want ..."

"Our Father, who art in heaven, hallowed be thy name ..."

"For God so loved the world, that He gave His only begotten Son ..."

The prayer in his heart right now was different from what he usually offered up. "Dear God, Heavenly Father," he murmured. "I've come to You asking for forgiveness of sins. I've prayed for my memory to return. I've prayed for wisdom to help Kepala save the Berani tribe from the Setan. I've prayed for so many things."

He clenched his hands tighter and glanced once again at Madra, still curled innocently on the mat. Matius closed his eyes and continued. "Today God, I finally realize that I've prayed selfishly. I only wanted what would ease my burden. I've prayed for answers that could destroy the woman I love. So God, please hear my prayer and know it comes from a man whose heart is riddled with shame. I ask you now to forgive me for this unworthy act of selfishness. Sweet Merciful Father, if You only answer this one prayer, I will forever be grateful. Precious Lord, whatever You have coming for me, whatever fate You have deemed my shoulders to bear, I beg You now that it not hurt Madra. She has never forsaken me. I love her so much. If You've chosen for me a path that leads me away from Madra, please don't let that destroy her."

He dropped his forehead to his folded hands and mumbled in deep meditation as quiet tears rivered down his cheeks.

Chapter 37

"I'm suing her ass to kingdom come," Kurt yelled, watching the computer screen that Frederick had swiveled around so that both of them could see.

The video clip of last night's news began with the anchor doing a voiceover as Whitley was rolled out of a hospital in a wheelchair. "Real estate tycoon Zhang Cái today revealed what he calls the two best acquisitions of his entire life: his new wife, the former Whitley Moore, and their new son Zhang Chéng."

Husband and wife smiled down at a baby wrapped like a papoose. Whitley loosened the blanket, and the cameraman panned between a close-up of the infant's face and a head-shot of the proud dad leaning over him. They were the spitting image of each other. Straight, jet black hair. Smooth skin with a butterscotch hue. Ebony eyes hooded by an extra fold of skin on the upper eyelid.

"Look at them," Kurt jeered. "She knew when she took my money that I wasn't that baby's father." Anger and embarrassment were like two wild animals tearing at his flesh.

"Regardless of how hurt you might—"

"I'm not hurt!" Kurt interrupted. "I'm pissed that I let her make a fool out of me." Hefting his heavy briefcase onto Frederick's desk and opening it so hard that he almost snapped the hinges in two, Kurt fished a piece of paper out of an inner pocket and scribbled some digits. "Here," he said as he threw it across the desk at Frederick.

Spinning the piece of paper so that the handwriting was facing his direction, Frederick said, "And this is?"

"Whitley's cell phone number." Kurt pushed the desk phone closer to Frederick. "I need you to call her." He picked the receiver up and handed it to his attorney.

Frederick sat back in his seat.

Waving the receiver in the air by its cord, Kurt began to rant, "That hooker's gonna give me my money back. Here I was trying to be a good guy and do the right thing by giving her money for the baby."

Frederick gave a stare that seemed to say, "Are you serious?"

Kurt was too much on edge to yield to reason. "I needed that money for my business, and she swindled it out of me." He let the receiver drop to the floor as he stood and placed his palms on two neat stacks of paper on the desk, leaning close enough to count the whiskers in Frederick's goatee. "People go to jail for swindling money. So do what you do, counselor!"

Frederick inched forward, his scowling face filling in the millimeter or two of empty space between him and Kurt. "Sit your silly ass down!" The crisp smell of his spearmint gum didn't cover the biting sharpness in his words.

Kurt plopped back into his seat, a few papers sliding off one of the stacks as his hands dragged across it. He eyed the man on the other side of the desk, silently letting him know he only sat down because he was in need of his help, not because he was afraid of him. "After I saw her on the news last night, I left voicemails, I texted, but she won't respond."

"And you think she'll answer when she sees Law Offices of George

& Associates on the caller i.d.?"

"You're right," Kurt said. He pointed at Frederick's pocket. "Use your cell."

Three beeps from the landline receiver prompted them to look down toward the floor as a robotic voice called out, "If you'd like to make a call, please hang up and try again." Frederick grabbed the cord on his desk and reeled the receiver in like it was a trout at the end of a fishing pole. Slamming the receiver onto the phone, he asked, "What good is going to come out of me calling this woman?"

"Just get her on the phone. She blackmailed me into giving her money. And I'm gonna blackmail her to get it back."

"I can tell you now that you're going nowhere fast with that, but if making this call is what it takes to get you out of my face, let's do it." His squinting eyes spoke his displeasure at having to reorganize the papers that had fallen when Kurt got in his face. Setting them to the side, he found the slip of paper containing Whitley's phone number, dialed it into his cell and put it on speaker.

"Hello?" The scratchy female voice was one that Kurt didn't recognize.

Frederick looked at Kurt, who frowned and waved him on. Clearing his throat, the attorney said, "Um, may I speak to Mrs. Zhang?"

"One moment please." They heard footsteps then, "It's for you, Mrs. Zhang."

Kurt sat up upon hearing Whitley's faint voice in the background. "Who is it, Annette?"

"I don't know, ma'am. I'll find out." Her finger accidentally mashed a few buttons as she put the phone back up to her mouth. "Who's calling, please?"

"I work for *Essence* magazine, and I was hoping Mrs. Zhang and her husband would let me schedule an interview for our next issue. We're doing a story on most-eligible-bachelors who have settled down."

Kurt dropped his head and shook it, then looked up to see Frederick giving a "that's the first thing that came to my mind" shrug of his shoulders. When the lady relayed the message and Whitley said from the background, "Bring me the phone," Kurt cracked a smile. He heard footsteps, then Whitley said hello in her most sweet and welcoming voice.

Kurt could tell she was gloating in the notoriety that her fifteen minutes of fame was giving her. Her head had to be as big as a hot air balloon. He was all too happy to be the stickpin that popped it open. "Have you told your new husband about me?" he asked.

There was a deep gasp, then, "What do you want, Kurt?" Whitley's tone was quiet but bitter.

"Only what's rightfully mine," he said.

"I know you're not trying to take my baby from me."

He could picture the ashen look that accompanied her panic-stricken voice. "Please, you can keep that little joker. I want my money." He waited in silence, expecting her to hang up. Instead, he heard something akin to a door being slammed, then Whitley's voice came back on the line.

"You don't call here threatening me." Her voice was so loud that she could have been right there in the room with him.

"I want my money back—every last dime—by tomorrow evening, or I'll let that fool who married you know everything."

"Everything like what?"

"Like you were with me and him at the same time!"

Arrogance replaced the fright he had heard in Whitley's voice before. "You know how I do it," she said with a heaping dose of conceit and haughtiness. "The first time I got him in the bed, he swore he would leave his fiancée for me."

"You tried to pull that same crap with me," Kurt retaliated in a gruff tone. "I was too slick for you, but his stupid ass fell for it." His self-esteem got on an elevator and hit the button for the top floor.

"Well I gave Zhang Cái a little lovin' now and then, here and there," she added, "just to remind him of what was waiting for him. And while he was trying to get untangled from that *thing* that he called a fiancée, I hooked up with men like you."

Kurt's outrage burned like a bonfire. "Men? As in more than one?"

"You got it, partner," Whitley sighed. "All of you had a little money. But you were the only one," she added with tartness, "who also had a little *thing*."

From the way she stressed that last word, he guessed that she was squeezing her thumb and index finger together like she had once before when she saw a man with a 'teeny weenie peenie' in a porn flick. Kurt's pride, ego, outrage and resentment stepped up to the microphone like a barbershop quartet. "I had more than enough to handle you!"

"No, you *got* handled. By the time Zhang Cái proposed to me, I'd racked up close to a half mil from my stable."

If somebody was going to lie to him, Kurt at least wished they'd give a convincing lie and not insult his intelligence. "If you have so much money, why were you working at that minimum-wage information booth job?"

"That wasn't a job," she said with a laugh. "I was finishing up some community service at the hospital to keep from getting locked up for some stupid stuff I did."

Frederick shrugged and shook his head at Kurt.

"I've never had to work. Men line up to take care of me. I knew one day I'd hit the jackpot, and BAM, Zhang Cái showed up."

Kurt's fist clobbered the desk. "Give me back my damn money!"

"The only thing I can give you is a hard way to go," she cracked.

"That'll change when I give your husband a copy of our agreement."

There was dead air on the phone, then she piped up, "And what's that supposed to do?" Kurt could just see her snapping her neck.

"He'll know that you were with me and that you're such a lowlife whore that you took a payoff to stay out of my life." Finally something worked in his favor. He glowered at his attorney as if to say, "My common sense is more helpful than your useless law degree."

"You can't prove anything with that piddly piece of paper," Whitley taunted.

"Oh, it'll back me up all right. I've got bank statements that show when I took the money out and the signed agreement showing that I gave the money to you that same day."

Whitley's cackling laughter boomed through the speaker, sending a chill through him. "Did you ever wonder why my writing was so messy?"

He filled his cheeks with air and blew out his irritation. "Because nobody could write with those claws you call nails. So stop changing the subject."

"You idiot," she shot back. "It was because I did everything with my right hand whenever I was around you."

"So!"

"I'm left-handed! None of that junk you're relying on has my real signature."

Frederick grabbed the phone and ended the call.

"The bank statements and that agreement prove my story!" Kurt said to spur his attorney into action.

"Maybe," Frederick said, drumming his fingers on the desk. "But the money you'd have to pay me to fight this case—"

"Pay you?!"

"Oh yes, my brother. I wouldn't handle this mess for free. And right now, you can't afford me." He dropped the cell back into his shirt pocket. "Go home and try to put the rest of your life back together."

Chapter 38

Harvey, Illinois

"Francesca, you in there? It's me, Uncle Bubba." Looking up into the hot sun, he took his hat off and ran his hand along the band where perspiration from his forehead made a little ring of sweat. The flimsy screen door rattled when he banged on it again. Hearing "Here I come" from inside the motel room, he looked back at the car.

A blast of Lysol-scented air escaped when she opened the inner wooden door. The smile she wore was so bright that the sun paled in comparison. She unhooked the latch on the screen door and stepped outside, wrapping her arms around Uncle Bubba and letting her head rest on his shoulder. "I'm so glad to see you," she said, her voice full of joy.

"I'm glad to see you too, baby. And lookie here." He unwrapped her arms from his midsection, took a step back and pointed to the parking lot. "I brought ya somethin'."

Dwayne hurried from the car and began walking up to them.

Francesca gasped, placed a hand on her bosom and nearly choked on her words by the time he reached her. "Dwayne!" She threw herself into his arms, standing on her tippy toes in rubber flip-flops. With his eyes closed and his mouth pulled into what Uncle Bubba would call a "show every tooth in yo' head" smile, Dwayne gave his mom a consoling pat as they rocked from side to side.

She eased from his embrace, her face wet with tears. She wiped her chin on her shoulder and opened the screen door wide. "Y'all come on in and make yourselves at home."

Uncle Bubba had been in outhouses bigger than the room Francesca called home. But he could see that she took pride in her cubby hole. Although most of the furnishings were old and the room had seen better days, it was clean. Cleaner, he suspected, than any of the other rooms in the cheap motel where she lived and worked.

"Make yourselves comfortable while I get us something cold to drink."

They settled into two mismatched chairs on either side of a square wooden table in front of the window. She walked three paces to the "kitchen," which consisted of a microwave on a dresser, a roll of paper towels and unopened packages of Styrofoam cups, plastic cutlery and paper plates. A large Styrofoam ice chest set atop a mini-refrigerator. "The fridge broke, and they won't be able to replace it for another couple of weeks," she explained.

"Well yo' air conditioner is in tip-top shape, I can tell you that," Uncle Bubba said. The heavy monstrosity mounted in the lower portion of the window blew arctic air that nearly gave his legs freezer burn.

Francesca threw her head back and laughed. "Turn the temperature up and it'll stop blowing. It's that big dial on the right." She sloshed her hand around in the ice chest and brought out a can of Mountain Dew with ice chips still clinging to it.

"Just what the doctor ordered," Uncle Bubba said as she wrapped it in a paper towel and handed it to him.

"What would you like, Dwayne?" Francesca asked. "A Coke or some bottled water?"

"I'm not choosy."

"Okay, you're getting the first thing I lay my hand on," she joked as she went ice-fishing again. "My fingertips are getting frostbite." When she drew her hand out, she had hooked a bottled water and a small bottle of Tropicana.

Uncle Bubba pointed his cane toward the orange juice. "You tried to hold back the good stuff, huh?"

She laughed the way she used to laugh—before her life had turned into a tragedy. But when she turned back toward them, her smile faltered and she pursed her lips.

Wrapping the two bottles in paper towels, she took them to the table then perched on the bed. She looked at Dwayne, a remorseful veil covering her face and telling of her regrets. "Feels like we've got so much catching up to do."

Uncle Bubba resisted the urge to reach over, touch her and speak comforting words to her. She had already cried her apologies to him the first few times he visited her after she got out of prison. Right now it was between her and Dwayne.

Just by scooting a couple inches forward in his chair, Dwayne's knee was touching his mother's. "Don't beat yourself up over the past. We're together. Now. Here."

She looked first at Uncle Bubba, then back to Dwayne and hiccupped words in between sobs. "It's okay ... to say you hate me ... for leaving you. I don't ... deserve your love," she cried.

It had taken a long time for Uncle Bubba to convince her that Dwayne had forgiven her and wanted her to be a part of his life. Her tears told him that she still couldn't forgive herself for running away from her babies.

Dwayne rose from his chair and filled the space beside her. Pulling her close to him, he kissed her forehead. "It feels like I've waited all my life for this. And I have to ask your forgiveness too."

She squinted up at him, then looked at Uncle Bubba with her brow furrowed in confusion.

"Here I was driving Uncle Bubba to the prison four times a year to see you, but I never went in again to see you after that first time." He rubbed the side of his face. "I guess it was kind of selfish, but I couldn't take it. When that first visit was over and I had to watch the guard take you through that big iron door and lock you back up, I couldn't handle that."

Uncle Bubba's legs had just thawed out when the air conditioner kicked back on. Instead of adjusting the temperature again, he sat still, not wanting to disturb the open and honest exchange between mother and son.

"You don't owe me an apology, baby," she said, splaying a hand on the floral bedspread. "But I want to apologize to you for not saying thanks for offering me a room in your home when I got out." She took Dwayne's massive hand in her more delicate one. "I couldn't live with you, though. It was important to me to do it for myself once I got out. You understand that, don't you?"

"Yeah, but we were worried," he protested. "We didn't know what would become of you."

"I know, and I'm sorry." She pulled at the thick braid flowing down the middle of her back. "My cellmate in prison had lupus. Sometimes she was in so much pain that all I could do was sit and hold her while she cried. Every visiting day, she told her mother about me taking care of her. Shortly before I got released, she told me that her family owned a few motels—she actually called them roach motels." Francesca found another smile to share with her son, and he smiled back. "Her mother offered to set me up with a job and a place to stay because of what I'd done for her daughter." She smoothed a hand over the worn bedspread. "It's not the Taj Mahal, but it's home and it's mine. And I earn an honest living."

She let her words hang in the air before offering a timid, "How's Val?"

The men looked at each other. "A lot has happened since I came to see you last month," Uncle Bubba answered. He filled her in on everything from Whitley's visit to Val's hospital stay.

Francesca's pain spread across her face. "I wish she would let me be there for her."

"In time, baby. In time," Uncle Bubba promised. He hoped his words sounded more convincing to her than they felt to him.

Chapter 39

Labor Day

Val was virtually alone in her office building, except for two die-hard office managers who'd forsaken holiday cookouts to come in and catch up on paperwork.

She had chosen to become a psychiatrist because she wanted to help make people feel whole. Plus she wanted a field that would give her the resources to be comfortable staying home raising her child for the first five years of its life. She wanted to hear the first words. Wanted to see the first steps. Wanted to immerse herself in the motherhood experience and be the best mother and wife she could. Her husband deserved that. Their child deserved it. She deserved that happiness.

Eleven years ago, she had poured herself into building up her practice, hoping that the busyness would help her ignore the hole that was in her heart after Hunter's death. Now she was once again making it a point to stay engrossed in work—this time to keep her mind off of the problems in her current marriage. But that wasn't working today. Her mind kept going back in time, wondering how life would have turned out if she had not lost Hunter.

נ נ נ

It was July of 2000. Summer wasn't summer until Val and Hunter spent a day or two at the annual Taste of Chicago. Hundreds of thousands of people walked the expanse of Grant Park during the ten-day festival. Val and Hunter always went to The Taste on an empty stomach. Upwards of sixty food vendors sold everything from lobster tails, to stuffed artichokes, chocolate-covered frozen bananas on a stick, and cups of tiny beads of ice cream called Dippin' Dots.

When the pair first arrived, they gravitated to the foods they had fallen in love with the year before. Hunter got a slice of Chicago-style pizza. They both bent over laughing when he took a big bite and began fanning his mouth as the hot cheese sat on his tongue like burning coal. Next, they went on the hunt for the sweet, juicy, buttery corn on the cob. It was better than any Val had eaten in her whole life. The throng pressed in on the happy couple, and every passerby had a handful or mouthful of a treat from one of the food trucks.

"Patti LaBelle's going to hit the stage soon," Hunter said, tossing his stripped corncob into a trash receptacle. "Want to head over there?" he asked Val as she flicked a kernel of corn from his chin. Patti LaBelle was at the Petrillo Band Shell, one of six outdoor venues for the myriad of entertainers that performed at The Taste.

"Sounds like a plan." She smiled at the handsome man she had married, unbothered by the appreciative looks that women passing by gave him.

They worked their way into the crowd of people. Hunter's cell rang just as they were in the midst of the throng. He put the phone up to one ear and stuck his index finger in the other ear to block out the noise and excited chatter. Val followed close behind as he sidestepped his way out of the noisy, flowing crowd and onto a grassy area.

She ambled a few feet away and leaned back against a tree, people-watching until she saw Hunter's expression change from nonchalant to deep concern as he latched the phone back onto the holder on his belt. He walked in her direction in slow, heavy steps.

"I'm almost afraid to ask," she said when he was in front of her. "But what was that about?"

Taking her in his arms, he held her so close that she could feel the pulse at the base of his neck. He rested his chin on the top of her head as he said, "That was Cole calling."

Val had been awakened out of a sound sleep too many times to count in the last three months as Cole called Hunter at all hours, asking questions or making suggestions about surgery to remove a life-threatening facial tumor from a little boy in Indonesia. Being the newest physician on Hunter's surgical team, the upcoming mission was Dr. Kellstrom Cole's first such trip.

"He's probably been packed for this trip since the day you assigned him to it six months ago," Val said.

It unnerved her how her normally good-humored husband didn't think her quip was funny. She pulled away and examined his face. Was that sorrow, sadness or frustration etched across it? More like an even mixture of all three.

"I mentioned to you that Cole switched secretaries a few months ago, didn't I?" he asked, his voice solemn enough to make Val worry.

"Yes, and?"

"Cole just found out that there was a miscommunication between the new secretary and the one who took a leave of absence. Neither one of them sent in his passport application."

Val stared blankly at her husband, knowing what this meant but hoping to God that she was wrong. "So he can't go?" she asked, unable to keep her voice from shaking. The couple had been so relieved months ago that the surgical mission would be fully staffed without Hunter.

He gave her hands a gentle squeeze. "I'm going to find someone else to go so I don't have to take Cole's place. I can't go back on my word to you."

After their third failed in-vitro fertilization attempt, Hunter had persuaded her that it might be good for both of them to schedule days off from their demanding careers—Val, to see if reducing stress would heighten her chance for conception, and Hunter, to give her an extra dose of his already generous love, pampering and moral support. And it seemed to work. Just before they left the house to go to The Taste, the fertility clinic had called and told them that the eggs Val's body produced this time around had begun to mature into healthy zygotes after they'd been fertilized with Hunter's sperm. That had never happened in their past attempts. She was so hopeful they'd have a child by springtime.

Hunter pulled his phone out. "Dr. Swanson's the only one in the group who might be able to help. And he owes me a favor. Maybe he can take Cole's place." He switched the phone on.

"That won't work," Val said, easing the phone from his hand. "Didn't you tell me at dinner that he just got in from a surgical mission in the Amazon? I can't see him being able to jump back on a twenty-hour plane ride, then perform a surgery that you said would take about twelve hours."

"Stranger things have happened. At least let me find out."

She pinned her eyes on her husband's muscular form as she slipped his phone into her purse. Laying her hand on his broad chest, she said, "I knew when I married you how much sacrifice it took for you to be a part of this foundation. And I admired that." Knowing this was the right thing to do didn't make it an easy thing to do. But she loved the man standing before her more than life itself. "We should call the doctor and have him freeze our fertilized eggs," she said.

Hunter opened his mouth to speak, but Val pressed her finger to his lips. "Baby, if you don't make this trip, that little boy won't live much longer. I can't bring my child to life at the expense of another child."

Placing a hand on the nape of her curly hair, he drew her closer. She allowed him to pull her in, resting her head just under the curve of his neck as he whispered, "Our child is in a petri dish at the fertility clinic right now, waiting to be implanted in your womb two days from now. How can I choose another child over my own?" The catch in his voice spoke of how conflicted he was.

She laid a hand on either side of his face. "This is why I'm so glad you'll be the father of my children. How many men would choose their family over their career? You are one of a kind Hunter Jamal Pierce." She got on her tiptoes, wrapped her arms around his neck and gave him a full-on kiss.

"I love you too much to keep you from helping that little boy. You have to go on the surgical trip. Okay?" She rubbed noses with him. "It'll only be two months. Our child will be with us for a lifetime."

"I could never find another woman like you," he said, holding her tight enough to almost cut her breath off. "As soon as I'm back, we'll re-schedule the implantation. Everything will be fine. You'll see."

נ נ נ

What Val wouldn't give to be able to edit the script of her life. If she had that power, she would have found the chapter where Hunter died in the jungles of Indonesia. *Delete.* She would have only left three scenes in the script—the day they fell in love, the day they married and the day they solidified their love with the birth of their first child. Yes, that was the way her life was supposed to turn out.

Instead, she'd been left with no husband, no child and no love. Then Kurt dropped into her life eight years later, showed all the outward signs of a loving, loyal, devoted husband, but in the end had none of the character, valor and kindness that Hunter Pierce had. How had she missed the signs back then?

Soon after they married, she found herself becoming less of who she was in order to make Kurt feel better about who he was. Putting his needs before her own became the template for their marriage, even to the point where she had put off the only thing she most desired. Now the time was fast approaching when she wouldn't be able to enjoy the fruit of her womb at all. Yet he considered her selfish for wanting that one thing.

Kurt not wanting her to have a child had even recently begun to seem to be about not wanting to share Val with anyone else—not even his own offspring. More and more, he expressed his resentment at how close she was to Uncle Bubba and Dwayne; even went so far as to hint that they were "coming over too often." That same complaint had worked to separate her from a few girlfriends she'd been close to all this time, but her family wasn't having it. Thank God.

The phone on her desk rang, and she crinkled her brow when she saw Kurt's number on the display. Slowly she placed the receiver to her ear.

"I'm glad I caught you," he said.

"What do you want, Kurt?" she asked dryly.

"I just want to talk to you, baby."

She shifted her eyes and sucked her teeth. "We don't have anything to talk about. I haven't seen you in over six weeks, and I want to keep it that way."

"Look, I just called—would you please consider signing the divorce papers and after I get the money from Foster, I'll fix this mess I made. Then we'll renew our vows in the biggest celebration you've ever seen."

Swiveling in her chair, she eyed their wedding photo on the bookshelf behind her. This Kurt on the phone was nowhere near the man she thought she'd married. "You can't guarantee that your stepfather will honor his word and hand the money over," she warned, not really caring one way or the other.

"I know," he said, resignation filling his voice. "But I have to at least try. My business depends on it."

"And if by some miracle he does, what makes you so sure that I'll come back to you?"

The silence on the line brought home the realization that he wanted what he wanted so badly that he'd brainwashed himself into believing that her not coming back after a divorce wasn't a possibility.

"Bye, Kurt," she said, shaking her head.

Chapter 40

The two-day trek to the Kahlo village left Matius both rejuvenated and leery at the same time. Aboweh's presence didn't help the situation. Matius sensed that the hostility the cocky brat displayed was being fueled not by resentment but by stark fear. Aboweh had never taken part in negotiations before, but his heated words with Matius and Kepala two moons earlier had led to his forced attendance today. Chief Kepala would be watching Aboweh's every move. If Aboweh failed to convince this last and strongest tribe to join the united effort against the tribal executioners, his pride would be doubly wounded. First, because he would have failed in front of Kepala. Second, because Madra would hear of his shortcoming.

Matius was certain that before it was over, the pig-headed warrior would learn a hard lesson he wouldn't soon forget: never demand what you cannot deliver.

As they cleared the tree line and saw the approaching small group from the Kahlo tribe, they knew the main village was not far off.

"Kepala," Chief Ushi greeted in their first tongue. "Welcome to the Kahlo tribe."

"Ushi," Kepala replied. "Let us join as brothers and find strength in peace together." The two leaders embraced, then Kepala directed Ushi's attention to Matius. "This is Matius, a great warrior, an honorable and courageous man, and the healer of the Berani tribe."

Ushi stared oddly at the giant. "If he is all you say he is, I see why he is called 'gift from the gods.'" He blinked several times, as if trying to fit an invisible puzzle piece into place.

Kepala then turned to Aboweh. "This is Aboweh, also from the Berani tribe."

Aboweh frowned his displeasure at being introduced with so little fanfare.

"Come," Ushi said, beckoning them forward. "We are about to have our meal gathering in the large hut near the trees. Join us, and then we can speak words of union." He motioned for Matius and Aboweh to go first. Kepala walked alongside Ushi, following behind the two younger men.

The Kahlo village was vibrant with frantic activity. Daily meal gatherings were a source of great pride and preparation. Even more so with visitors from another tribe. All families contributed food, and the meals were cooked together and enjoyed by everyone. It was a way for them to gather and bond as a people of the elements.

When Matius strolled past the first small hut, many stared at him in dumbfounded awe. His sheer height stopped people in their tracks. Young women excitedly moved into his path to reach out and stroke him. He kept his eyes straight ahead.

Ushi chuckled and said to Kepala, "It seems many anxious females in my tribe are setting their net for your healer. He will start tongues wagging long before we speak words of union."

Kepala laughed. "Then my daughter Madra may need to come and have words with them."

Ushi laughed and slapped Kepala on the shoulder.

ꑭ ꑭ ꑭ

Many hours later, Matius, Kepala, Aboweh, Ushi and several Kahlo elders were in the chief's hut discussing the union of the tribes. Aboweh's presentation was abysmal. After listening patiently for several minutes, Ushi subtly but effectively dismissed Aboweh's speech by turning all his attention to Matius and asking for his ideas. Ushi's action was all the proof Kepala needed to confirm his suspicions about Aboweh. He was not ready to lead. He was not chief material.

After Matius was given the opportunity to speak, the negotiations moved in a positive direction and concluded successfully.

Frilly females entered the hut several times during the talks, feigning that they were seeing to the men's needs with offerings of clean water, extra bowls of fresh fruit or more dried meat. The men shared knowing glances. Those females wanted Matius' attention. None of them succeeded.

Another woman walked in, causing the Kahlo men to rise to their feet and the worrisome women to bow before her. Matius, Kepala and Aboweh followed suit and stood in her presence. She shooed the women out of the hut with a wry smile.

Ushi turned to his guests. "This is my soul and heart, my life-mate Elsa." The woman blushed and bowed respectfully. He said to her with a smile, "Thank you for saving our new brothers from the women."

Elsa nodded and turned to leave, but stopped cold and pivoted directly in front of Matius. Instantly her eyes watered and she screamed with joy, embracing him. Matius stiffened, looking to Ushi and Kepala, scared to even breathe. It was strictly forbidden for a common person to touch a member of a noble tribal house. This woman's shocking act could provoke a tribal war and destroy the union he had just negotiated.

Elsa was crying, mumbling and shaking her head, lost in a world none of the men could enter. Carefully, her chief came behind her and pulled her away from Matius.

His first words to his wife were heated and swift. Then as she sniffled and explained in gasping whispers, Ushi's eyes sought out Matius'. No one moved. Slowly Ushi turned Elsa again to Matius, and she ran back into his arms, laughing and crying with gratitude that left the entire room shocked.

After a few moments, she returned to her husband, who now had water brimming from his eyes. He nodded and whispered to Elsa. She hastily left the hut.

Ushi offered for the men to join him again. Cautiously—very cautiously—they did.

"Gift from the gods," Ushi breathed, bringing his bloodshot eyes up to Matius. "There are words I must share with you." He looked at Kepala then back at Matius. "For many seasons I believed that the devil warriors were only focused on my people." He inhaled a ragged breath, as though momentarily lost in horrid images of the past. "The Kahlo believed the Setan preyed on us as punishment from the gods because I had not sired sons. My mate and I tried for many seasons to have babies. None of them lived long enough to draw their first breath once leaving her body."

Ushi stared squarely at Matius. "Then our son, Rashi, was born. He was our blessing. For seven seasons, our people moved around and knew peace. Then Rashi became ill—very ill. I feared the gods would call him home before his time and the raids would begin again." The small chief shivered with haunted memories. "But one day a tribal guide for outsiders brought a gift from the gods to save and heal my son."

Matius could feel every drop of blood leech out of his face.

"Matius," Ushi croaked. "You were that gift."

Barriers in Matius' mind started to give way to his past. He swallowed hard. "I've been here before?" he asked. The chief nodded, and Matius asked, "When?"

"Eleven seasons ago you appeared with others to cut into my child and save his life."

Elsa rushed into the hut. She glanced at her husband before walking back to the entrance of the hut and pulling a teenager into the room. "This is our son, Rashi, who you saved eleven seasons ago."

Matius stared at the boy—really looked at him. There was something about the lanky eighteen-year-old. Matius' eyes snagged on a scar that began along the young man's hairline and ended around his chin and neck. Easing up to Rashi, he reached out and traced a trembling hand over the keloid skin. Touching the hard tissue caused memories to burst forth in Matius' mind. Two distraught parents putting the life of their deathly-ill child in his hands. Hours in an Indonesian operating room delicately cutting away bit by bit of a tough, fibrous growth that had invaded a child's skin and become thoroughly enmeshed in his network of vessels, choking off the blood supply to his face. Parents begging Matius and his team to come back to their village so that they could honor them for saving the child. Traversing through the jungle weeks later.

"Dear God," Matius heaved. "I remember it all, even my name." He sagged bonelessly back to the dirt-covered floor and gasped, "I am ... Dr. Hunter Pierce."

Chapter 41

5:00 p.m. Saturday, November 5, 2011

When Val came into the fellowship hall for the friends and family dinner, people hugged her, then patted her distended stomach as though she and the baby inside of her needed separate greetings. After stopping to mingle at a few tables, she wound her way toward two girlfriends who waved her over. She was jovial—until Francesca entered stage right with Dwayne. Then Val's buoyant disposition sunk faster than a cement block dropping to the bottom of a lake.

Uncle Bubba didn't miss that fact as he stood across the room. Ever since his niece was four years old, she had camouflaged the pain of abandonment with anger toward her absent mother. It stood to reason that her first face-to-face meeting with Francesca might be awkward and strained. He walked to Val.

"'Scuse us," he said to the young women she was talking to. They took a glance at each other, then hurriedly stepped away. He looked deep into Val's eyes, asking without words if she would allow him to walk her over to greet her mother. She closed her eyes and laid a hand on her stomach. When she looked at him again and gave a small nod, he took her clammy hand in his own. "Girl, the last time I felt a grip this tight was when I was a young soldier goin' up against the man who claimed to be the arm wrestlin' champion at the army base."

Touching the small of her back, he led her to the table where Dwayne and Francesca were holding seats for them. Uncle Bubba tapped Francesca on the shoulder. Francesca arose and gave Uncle Bubba a hug. She smiled at her daughter and held her arms out for a hug. He thought Val was going to leave her hanging, but after a second or two, Val inched forward into her embrace. Francesca kissed the side of Val's head and fought back tears.

"Why don't we all sit down?" Dwayne suggested. He stood and pulled the chairs out for his mother and sister.

Francesca ventured a glance at Val. "How've you been?"

"All right."

"And the pregnancy, has it been a difficult one?"

"No," Val answered, fiddling with the bow on the front of her dress.

"You look really good."

Getting no response from her daughter, Francesca leaned back and looked at Uncle Bubba. Things weren't going as smoothly as he'd hoped, but Val hadn't lashed out at Francesca either. That was something to be grateful for. Still, this relationship was going to need a little help.

Uncle Bubba pointed and said to Francesca, "See that table over there with the orange-lookin' tablecloth?" She scooted her chair sideways and shifted her focus in that direction. "I think that's the one with the macaroni and cheese I really like," he said.

"You want me to get you some?" she asked.

"I want you to do more than that." He pulled a large rectangular plastic container out of a canvas bag hanging from the back of Dwayne's chair. "That's Sister Tate behind the table. Remind her that she promised to make a whole batch for me and I'm holdin' her to it."

Dwayne took the bowl out of his uncle's hand. "If she fills this big thing up, there won't be any mac and cheese for anybody else here, Unc."

"Yeah, it will," he shot back, snatching the bowl from Dwayne and handing it to Francesca. "Brother Boatwright's daughter sent two big bowls by him. They're on the table too."

"Nobody ever eats her cooking," Dwayne pointed out.

"That's exactly why yo' mama's got to get me some of the good stuff befo' it's all gone." Uncle Bubba shooed Francesca in the direction of the mac-and-cheese shrine.

As she crossed the room, two toddlers chased after each other, their little legs moving them around at turtle speed. One bumped into the back of Francesca's shin and grabbed the hem of her dress to keep from falling onto his bottom. The other must have thought their romp had turned into a game of tag where this unknown woman was the safe place, so he grabbed Francesca's other leg and held on.

Uncle Bubba watched as Francesca turned and knelt down in front of the little frolickers. Each of them leaned into her for a hug, as though she were some celebrity and they were fans who had been waiting all day to see her. When she straightened and walked away, they followed her for a moment until a man that Uncle Bubba presumed to be their father came up and escorted them back to a table. With her groupies gone, Francesca went back to her macaroni mission.

Val took it all in, then gave a pained look to Uncle Bubba. "Was she ever that way with us?" She looked like her four-year-old self, her eyes carrying the same rejection as back then.

"She wanted to be, but now I know that she was in so much pain that she couldn't do it half the time." He pushed his chair back and stood, walking around to the other side of the table and bending down to whisper in Val's ear. "We need to talk about somethin'."

Dwayne left his chair and squatted on the other side of his sister's chair. "You should try to get to know her now," he whispered. "If she's unconcerned about you, then shut her out." He placed a hand on her knee. "But if she's changed from what you remember, if she's sorry and wants to make it up to—"

"What? Are you gonna preach forgiveness? That it's my Christian duty?" Val voiced her words through the side of her mouth.

"Val, baby," Uncle Bubba said, steeling a glance at nosey Sister Sullivan, who was seated at their table. She couldn't have been more obvious in her eavesdropping if she held a glass up to her ear. He positioned himself so that Sister Sullivan would get a snapshot of his backside if she insisted on turning her face toward them. She was always checking out that part of his anatomy anyway. Might as well give her a close-up.

"Yo' brother ain't sayin' that yo' mama can take back the past. What's done is done. But if she wants to try for a better future, you should give her a chance."

"Why, so *she* can feel better?" Val challenged.

"No," he said, catching her chin with his thumb and index finger. "So *you* can feel better."

Uncle Bubba felt a fluttering movement when his arm brushed against Val's belly. The baby was poking her from the inside. Uncle Bubba placed his hand on the spot, uncle and nephew communicating through the layer of skin. "Don't you think that this little baby deserves every bit of love that the world has to give him?" he asked Val quietly. "Francesca has changed. The woman you saw with those two little boys is who she is now. It wouldn't be right to keep that kind of love from baby Caleb."

She rubbed her stomach. "Caleb has all the love he needs from the rest of his family. I'll never let him fall in love with her just so she can run off and desert him like she did us."

Dwayne leaned near her ear as he stood. "Unc is right, li'l sis. I was hurt just as much as you were, but I've been spending time with her. I know she's not perfect, but she wants to be there for us now."

As afraid as she was of being hurt again, something in Val's expression told Uncle Bubba that she longed to have her mother as much as she longed to have this child. But he was wise enough to know not to push this on her. He walked back around to his side of the table. "You want some more punch, Val?" he asked, looking into her empty paper cup.

She wobbled backward and forward, trying to rise. When she put out her hand to Dwayne, he clasped it and drew her out of the seat.

"I'd better pass," she said as she gathered up the long skirt she had on to avoid tripping over it. "I live in the bathroom as it is." As if to carry her point, she waddled toward the ladies' room outside of the fellowship hall.

"You think she'll come around?" Dwayne asked Uncle Bubba. "It's been four months since she separated from Kurt, and I don't ever hear her talk about getting back with him. I don't want the baby to be without his father and without his other grandmother, too."

Now, Uncle Bubba approved of the child being without the influence of a knucklehead like Kurt Timmons. But Francesca deserved a whole different type of consideration. He rubbed his chin thoughtfully. "We just gotta give Val time."

His eyes caught Francesca returning. He whispered to Dwayne, "I hope that bowl she's totin' is full."

Chapter 42

Francesca squirreled over to Uncle Bubba and Dwayne, juggling four forks and four paper cups atop the closed container she held. They all headed out into the hallway, giggling like kids who were cutting class.

Grabbing one of the paper cups, Uncle Bubba exclaimed, "What you say! Sister Tate threw in a right-now-helpin'." He took a fork and dug into the cupful of mac-and-cheese, closing his eyes as he relished the savory goodness.

Extending the bowl to Dwayne, Francesca said, "Will you take this to the car? I'll hold on to the other cups so Uncle Bubba doesn't eat them up before you get back," she teased.

While Dwayne dashed out to the car, she stayed right by the door, holding it open so he wouldn't get locked out and have to walk to the front of the church.

Once they were all together again, they munched on their mac and cheese. Francesca pointed to the fellowship hall with her eyes. "I know you two were talking to Val about me in there. I read people pretty well, and I could just tell by her body language that my baby girl hates me." She placed a hand on Uncle Bubba's shoulder. "I can live with that. But

I can't live with either of you straining your relationship with her on my behalf. It'll happen if it's meant to be." She did a group hug with her son and her uncle. "But thank you for giving it a try."

Soft music flowed out of the fellowship hall. Dwayne gave his and Francesca's empty cups to Uncle Bubba and took his mother's hands to lead her in an impromptu mother-son waltz.

Uncle Bubba studied her face. A certain warmth emanated from her. His tortured niece had almost had her life destroyed, but somehow she was fighting her way back from the darkness. If only he had known back then what had sent her to that place, he could have … he would have … he wasn't quite sure. But he did know one thing—she would not have had to face it alone, whatever it was.

He smiled at her as Dwayne twirled her around the hallway. In spite of everything, Francesca had cultivated a positive attitude, even some hope and joy, from the ruins of her life. Uncle Bubba set the macaroni cups on a nearby table as he whispered, "Thank you, God, for keepin' her and for bringin' her back to us—not broken like when she left, but whole and complete. Thank you."

When the song was finished, Dwayne waltzed his mother back toward Uncle Bubba.

"All this dancing has made me hot," she said, fanning her hand in front of her face. Dwayne propped open the outside door to help her cool off.

Uncle Bubba squinted at the slightly bowed legs coming down the stairs on the other end of the hall. As more of the person's body was revealed, he asked Dwayne, "Ain't that Melva?"

"Yeah, I think it is," he confirmed after looking down the hall.

"That there is Val's mother-in-law," he said to Francesca as the bubbly woman headed toward them. "Think you ready to meet her?"

Francesca looked more ready to take flight.

"Don't worry, she's good people," Dwayne added. "You'll like her."

Uncle Bubba stepped close to Francesca. "And she'll like you too." He beckoned for Melva to come over. "Girl, you ain't in the country no mo'," he teased as he looked down and saw Melva's pretty feet sinking into the plush carpet. "Where yo' shoes at?" He bent down to give her a hug, careful not to step on her bare toes.

She hugged him, then stepped back, lifted her foot and wiggled her pedicured toes. "My dogs wanted to get off of their leash," she joked. "Foster's outside getting my flats out of the car."

Dwayne stepped up and kissed her on the cheek. "How are you doing, Mrs. Timmons?"

"I'm fine, baby. How are you?" She looked around. "And where's Val?"

"She went to the bathroom."

"Again," Uncle Bubba added with a chuckle.

Melva laughed. "I remember those days with a baby sitting on your bladder."

Dwayne nudged Francesca forward. "Mrs. Timmons, this is my mother Francesca Harper."

Francesca stretched out her hand. Melva looked at it and said with a wink, "Get out of here. We're family, co-grandmas. No handshakes here, just hugs." She reached out and embraced Francesca.

To Uncle Bubba, his niece looked pensive at first, but then her shoulders relaxed and she patted Melva's back.

"Aren't you dying with excitement over baby Caleb?" Melva asked Francesca as the two stepped out of their embrace. "He can't get here soon enough."

With eyes sparkling like five-carat diamonds at the mention of her grandson, Francesca gently squeezed Melva's hand. "You're right about that."

"We already have a nursery set up in our house. You and I will be first-time grandmas together."

They whispered excitedly to one another until Francesca tilted her head and sniffed the air. She must have smelt the same acrid cigar smoke that was curling into Uncle Bubba's nose. He turned to see Foster at the door behind them. The slimy wet tip of the cigar he pulled out from between his teeth nearly turned Uncle Bubba's cast iron stomach.

Melva ordered, "Foster, put that thing out. Some people are allergic to smoke. You're not supposed to be smoking on the church grounds anyway."

"But this isn't church; it's a meeting hall," he protested.

"A hall *inside* a church," she shot back.

He grumbled and put the stogie away.

"Foster," Uncle Bubba said, tipping his head and letting his voice relay his disapproval. In reality, the smoking didn't bother him as much as the man's presence did.

"Bubba," Foster replied. A pair of ballerina slippers dangled from his fingers. "Here, Melva. Take these shoes."

Uncle Bubba hissed at what felt like someone twisting the skin on his arm with a pair of pliers. He looked down. Francesca was holding onto him with all of her might, her nails sinking into his skin through his sleeve. Fear radiated from her.

"Girl, what's done come over you?" he whispered as he turned around and looked into eyes that were wide with fear. He pried her nails out of his arm. "Melva, Dwayne, y'all 'scuse us a minute." Shielding Francesca's meltdown from the others, he turned and escorted her to the water fountain a few feet away. Her hands were shaking so hard that he had to squeeze them between his own to calm them. "What is it, baby?"

Her mouth opened, but the chattering of her teeth was the only sound that came out. Her eyes resembled laser beams locked onto the back of Foster's head. Uncle Bubba snapped his finger in front of her eyes, and she blinked and turned her eyes to her uncle. "Who's that man?" she asked in a voice just above a whisper.

Uncle Bubba looked back where they'd come from. "Who, Foster? That's Melva's husband, Val's father-in-law. He used to live down the street from us—"

Francesca transformed right before his eyes. Her shoulders hunched up. Her chin quivered with involuntary spasms. "T—T—take me home," she stammered. "Take me home *now*, Uncle Bubba. I wanna go home." Her voice was even shakier than her body was.

From the corners of his eyes, Uncle Bubba caught Dwayne approaching. Somehow the young man had sensed something was off.

"What's wrong, Mama?" he whispered.

She didn't respond.

"Go find yo' sister," Uncle Bubba instructed. "Tell her somethin's wrong with yo' mama and we gotta take her home right now."

Dwayne got his keys from his pocket and gave them to his uncle. "Get mama to the car. I'll be out in a minute."

Francesca leaned so heavily on Uncle Bubba that he thought she might need his cane more than he did for the short walk to the front door. With his arm wrapped tightly around her shoulder, he could feel every tremor that ran through her.

Once outside, he sat in the back seat of the car with her, keeping her close as her body shuddered. She stared into nothingness. Moving his hand up and down in her line of vision made her blink and pull her face back from his hand. Her shallow breathing turned into the stymied breathing of one trying not to cry. He pulled her head to his chest and felt hot tears drench his shirt.

Opening up the back door, Dwayne bent down and said in a quiet voice to Uncle Bubba, "Val said her stomach is upset and she's leaving too. I'll call her when I think she has made it home." He looked at his mother and asked his uncle, "What happened in there?"

Uncle Bubba shook his head at the questioning look Dwayne threw his way. He had no answers. Dwayne closed the door and hopped into the driver's seat.

Other than Francesca's muffled sobs, the ride to her place was silent.

Chapter 43

Francesca leaned over the sink in her room, throwing handfuls of water on her face. Uncle Bubba and Dwayne stood by the window. She had yet to open up about what happened at the church. Uncle Bubba leaned his head toward his nephew. "Did you call to see if Val made it home all right?"

"She texted and said she did. Her stomach's still upset though."

Francesca pulled a towel off the rack and buried her face in it. When she went in the bathroom and closed the door, Dwayne whispered to Uncle Bubba, "Val asked how mom is doing."

Uncle Bubba was glad that Val was trying to open her heart to her mother. He looked expectantly toward the bathroom door. Francesca came out, placing her hand against the wall for support. Dwayne ran over and helped her to the bed.

"I don't want to lie down," she said as she lowered herself to sit on the edge of the bed. Dwayne went to stand by the door. Uncle Bubba settled at the table by the window.

Seeing her red, puffy eyes made Uncle Bubba frown. His niece had seen enough hardship to last a lifetime. That something was bringing her pain now hurt him to no end.

Throwing her head back and exhaling deeply, she murmured something, but all he caught was the tail end, "... was him."

Dwayne squinted and leaned in.

"That man at the church," she said, tears dribbling down her cheek and spilling into her lap. "That was *him*." Her nose turned up as though a vile odor had just violated it.

Realization curled a knot in Uncle Bubba's gut.

"He looks a little different, a lot older," she added, "but I can't ever forget the smell of that stinky cigar and the sound of his voice." Her lip curled up, and contempt laced her words. "That's the man who raped me."

Francesca nearly jumped off the bed when Dwayne's fist jutted out and struck the door at the same time that the old man pounded the table next to him and shouted, "Foster Timmons?"

"I never knew his name," she said. "But I remember his funky cigar-breath all in my face, that hoarse voice and that straight, slicked-back hair. He ... raped ... me."

"He's a dead man!" Dwayne bellowed, opening the door. Francesca ran over and locked her arms around her son's bicep, leaning back and using her body weight to try to keep him from leaving. Adrenaline rushed through Uncle Bubba's veins, and he leaped out of his seat, grabbing Dwayne's other arm and helping to pull him back in the room.

The herculean effort wore Uncle Bubba down faster than he would like. He plunked himself down on the bed beside Francesca. "Whew!" he said as he wiped the sweat off of his brow.

Dwayne rubbed his fist. "Mama, I can't let him get away with doing that to you."

"I understand, baby." She pulled him down beside her so they were eye-to-eye. "But you and Uncle Bubba can't go over there hurting that man."

"After what he did to you?" Dwayne exclaimed. "We sure as hell can."

She flicked her gaze between the two men. "If you go after that man, you could end up in jail, in the hospital or in the morgue."

"The hell you say!" Uncle Bubba interjected. Knowing that his niece had been raped was one thing. Knowing who did it took this to a whole other level.

"I never told a soul about it all this time because he told me everyone would say it was my fault. And I shouldn't have said anything now." She looked squarely into Uncle Bubba's eyes and then into Dwayne's. "Neither one of you is thinking of the consequences." Tapping her index finger on her temple, she said, "God gave you a brain. Use it."

Uncle Bubba growled, "He gave me a gun too—that's what I plan to use."

Her tears came in earnest. "You don't get it. If you hurt him, I'll lose you. Because if he doesn't kill you, then the courts will put you away for trying to kill him. Either way, I'll lose you. He's not worth it." She rocked back and forth, wringing her hands. "I've lost so much already."

Uncle Bubba rubbed his temple hard enough to almost scour the skin off of it. "I never liked that man. Ever."

Dwayne's voice was quiet but deadly. "No man hurts my mama like that and gets away with it. Trust me; I know a better way to put a hurting on him."

"You read my mind," Uncle Bubba said. The bed was low to the ground and his adrenalin had leveled off, so he had to ask Dwayne to help him up. "Come on, boy. We gonna pay Foster a visit."

Chapter 44

Jungles of Papua, Indonesia
November 2011

Shaking as rapid images and events flashed across his mind's eye, Matius nearly hyperventilated. Elsa retrieved a tattered backpack from inside a hand-woven basket in a corner of the hut and offered it to him. "I kept this. I told my son that it once belonged to the great healer who had saved his life at the price of his own."

Matius took the backpack and unzipped it. Inside was a collection of plastic bags containing his personal possessions. He remembered now. He'd stored them all away in zippered plastic for safe keeping. The rainy season in this part of Indonesia could destroy anything that wasn't waterproof. He found his passport, an uncharged satellite phone, a stethoscope, disposable gloves, an assortment of medicinal items and painkillers and finally, his wallet.

Now he really trembled. Carefully he pulled out the wallet. Taking a deep breath, he cracked it open. And there it was—his entire life. He found a hospital i.d., his driver's license, several credit cards and three photos.

"Oh my God." He shivered as he fell to his knees. "Valencia." Finally, the shadow woman had come into the light. He traced the delicate features of her face with his fingers. His wife, his beautiful wife Val. Matius looked directly at Elsa and lifted the backpack. "How did you get this?"

She turned to Ushi, and he said, "After you left, the elders' council insisted that we head upriver because the rogue killers were moving in our direction. On our journey, we came across the men who were with you." His eyes dipped. "They were all dead. We searched for you among them and never found you."

"We sorrowed for your loss," Elsa gulped. "You came and helped my son to live, and—" Her words were cut off by the effort it took to hold back a sob.

"Elsa found your pouch," Ushi said. "We prayed for your soul because we believed the Setan had killed you too and left your body for animals to enjoy as a tasty meal."

Matius rocked back and forth then shot to his feet. "Kepala!" he gasped. "Do you know what this means?"

His chief looked at him with devastated eyes. "Yes, Matius. It means you must go to your home—you must leave."

The impact of that heartbroken statement crumbled Matius to his knees. The first thought that hit his mind—*Madra.*

ᴫ ᴫ ᴫ

A look of absolute agony streaked across Madra's face two days later as Matius rocked her through the retelling of what he had learned from Ushi and Elsa.

"Matius, don't leave. Not yet," she cried, letting her head fall against his chest. "Stay a while longer."

He gently pulled her away and wiped the tears from her eyes. "I love you, Madra. Please believe that. And I'm dying inside knowing that what I have to do will change your life forever. But now that I know who I am and who I left behind, I would never be able to give you all the love you deserve. Please try to understand that my staying and only giving you part of my heart would bring more hurt to you than my leaving."

Madra dried his tears while her own eyes glassed over with fresh ones. "A woman knows things in here," she said as she put her hand over her heart. "I knew I might lose you one day." Her lips trembled and she burrowed into his arms. When she crumpled to the floor, Matius knelt by her side. She wrapped her arms around his neck and kissed him wildly. "Remember me, Matius," she implored, taking the kiss even deeper. "I will never love another."

"Oh God, Madra." He crushed her in his arms. "I will carry you in my heart until the day I die."

ﬠ ﬠ ﬠ

Ushi and Rashi, being fierce trackers and guides, had offered to come see Matius safely to the mainland. But they wouldn't be able to do that until after the dry season returned in seven moons because the deluges of the rainy season would start any day now. Seven moons was sufficient time to implement the plan for warriors from neighboring tribes to join together in ridding the jungles of the plague of the Setan.

But was seven moons long enough where it concerned him and Madra? His heart had never given Val up during the eleven years that she had been a mere shadow to him. How much harder would it be to give Madra up, the woman who had been his reality for those same eleven years?

Chapter 45

"Bubba, Dwayne," Melva said, giving them a flustered look. "I didn't know you were coming by." She buttoned up her coat.

"Yes, ma'am, and we 'pologize for that," Uncle Bubba offered, trying to peer around her and into the house.

"I would invite you in, but I'm on my way out." She pulled her purse off of the foyer table and slipped a pair of Isotoner gloves on her hands. "Sister Cooper waited until eight o'clock tonight to call and tell me she needs help finishing up the praise dancer outfits she's supposed to have ready for tomorrow morning. I'm going to be up half the night with her sewing those things. Can you come back another time?"

"Well actually, we needed to talk to your husband," Dwayne said. "Is he here?"

Melva looked curious but walked them a few paces to a closed door. She opened it. Uncle Bubba looked around her. Foster was stretched out in a recliner, snoring with his mouth wide open.

"He's sleeping," she said. "Maybe you can come back tomor—"

"Foster!" Uncle Bubba shouted over her shoulder.

Sleeping beauty stirred, stretching his arms then scratching his chest before opening his eyes and looking their way.

"We gotta talk to you," Uncle Bubba said.

Coming into his fully grumpy self, Foster stood and walked over. "You got three minutes."

"We only need two," Dwayne shot back as he and Uncle Bubba entered the room.

Melva tilted her cheek to Foster for a kiss. "I'll probably be gone until way up in the middle of the night," she said.

"Just come on home whenever you get done. And don't be calling and waking me up unless it's an emergency," he added as she backed out of the room and closed the door.

Foster crossed in front of Uncle Bubba and Uncle Bubba deliberately mashed the man's foot with the tip of his cane.

"Excuse you!" Foster snarled. The two old-timers stared each other down like they were facing off for a duel. He stepped around Uncle Bubba to get to the recliner. "Now what do y'all want, coming to my house at this hour of the night?"

Dwayne stepped up to Foster, clamping his hand onto Foster's shoulder and shoving him down into the La-Z-Boy so violently that the footrest popped out. Foster tried to use the back of his legs to push the footrest back in so he could get up. "Sit!" Dwayne commanded. "And shut your damn mouth."

Foster breathed fire. "I don't know what y'all think you're doing, but you better get the hell outta my house before I throw you out," he threatened, still trying to rise up in the chair.

"You don't want to do that," came Dwayne's deadly growl. Foster gave Dwayne a menacing glare but stayed put and shut up. Dwayne got two chairs from a card table in the corner and positioned them side by side in front of the recliner. He put his foot on the recliner's footrest, shoved down hard, and Foster was bolted into an upright position, his head rebounding twice off the back cushion. The younger man grabbed the chair behind him and pulled it closer to the recliner. He was knee-to-knee with Foster when he sat down.

Ignoring the chair Dwayne had dragged over for him, Uncle Bubba stood closer to the door than to Foster. If there wasn't enough space between him and Foster when Foster started acting crazy—and Foster *would* start acting crazy—Uncle Bubba knew he wouldn't be able to keep from beating the man to within an inch of his life. He examined Foster Timmons' face. He never particularly cared for the man, mainly because he was a fool. If emotions were housed in buildings, it would take a skyscraper to contain this whole new level of disdain he felt for Foster now.

"You meet anybody today from yo' past?" Uncle Bubba eventually asked. He looked down at his nails. One second too much of eye contact with Foster, and Dwayne would have to pull his uncle off of the man.

"How you gonna come in my house talking all this crazy—"

Knowing his nephew was at the end of his fuse too, Uncle Bubba looked up just as Dwayne got so close to Foster's face that their foreheads nearly touched. Foster wheezed his anger through clenched teeth. Uncle Bubba smelled his polluted breath from where he stood. He wasn't sure what was keeping his nephew from retching at the stench.

Foster reached for something in his back pocket, and Uncle Bubba scuttled across the room and grabbed his hand. Foster tried to snatch away. Uncle Bubba bent his fingers back until the man let out a muffled shriek.

"Don't try to get bold 'cause you think I'm old," Uncle Bubba warned. When he turned Foster's hand loose, Foster slowly opened and closed his fist as if testing to see if his fingers still worked.

"Don't worry; I didn't break 'em," Uncle Bubba warned. "That was just practice." He pushed on Foster's forehead with two fingers and sat down.

Foster's bloodshot eyes bore holes through the men. "Say what you got to say and get the hell outta my house."

"When we get finished with what we have to say, *we* will own this house," Dwayne said with a satisfied grin.

Foster cursed under his breath.

Uncle Bubba pulled out a small notepad and a pencil from the pocket of his overalls, then touched Dwayne's shoulder with them. Dwayne looked his way, took the items and gave them to Foster.

"What am I supposed to do with this?" Foster protested.

"Write exactly what I tell you to write," Uncle Bubba instructed, sounding like a school teacher talking to a slow learner. "F-r-a-n-c—".

Dwayne slammed his hand on the arm of the recliner. "Write it down!"

The pencil in Foster's hand made a scribble on the paper when he jumped at the sound of Dwayne's voice.

Uncle Bubba noticed the vein throbbing in Dwayne's temple. His own pressure was rising as well. It felt like a kickboxer was using the inside of his cranium as a punching bag. Seeing Foster nervously wet the tip of the pencil on his tongue, Uncle Bubba began spelling again. "F-r-a-n-c-e-s-c-a. H-a-r-p-e-r."

"Okay, I wrote it down. Now will you leave?"

"Oh, no. I don't think we will just yet," Uncle Bubba answered as he settled back into his chair. "Least not 'til you write a check with that name on the payee line."

A ripping sound filled the room as Foster snatched the sheet off the pad, tore it to shreds and threw it up in the air.

"You outta your damn mind if you think you gonna make me give somebody my money!"

"This ain't just any ol' somebody," Uncle Bubba corrected, getting up and coming to stand over Foster. "It's Francesca Harper. The girl you raped when you lived on our block. That"—he punched Foster in the chest—"Was"—another punch—"My"—final blow—"Niece!" His hands were around Foster's neck so fast that he couldn't even remember getting out of the chair.

He vaguely heard Dwayne calling his name, felt him digging his fingers into his upper arm as he tried to pry his uncle's hands loose from Foster's windpipe.

Although Foster was scratching the back of Uncle Bubba's hand hard enough to draw blood, Uncle Bubba couldn't feel any pain. His hands only felt Foster's Adam's apple bobbing up and down against his palm.

Chapter 46

Foster struggled like a madman. When Uncle Bubba finally gained enough control to release him, Foster crumpled to the floor like road kill.

"Get up," Uncle Bubba shouted. "You ain't had nearly enough!" His fist delivered an angry blow.

"Unc! No!" Dwayne's arms constricted around the old man's chest and dragged him away from his prey.

"If this boy wasn't here, I'da killed yo' ass by now," Uncle Bubba growled, trembling with every effort to keep his rage under control.

Foster rolled onto his stomach and dug his cell phone out of his back pocket. "Y'all better haul ass because I'm calling the police right now." He crawled back over to the recliner and held onto it the way a drowning man hangs onto the side of a liferaft. Pulling himself up into the chair, he heaved a series of breaths and yelled, "The police *will* come knocking at your door because I'm pressing charges." The phone made three beeps as Foster dialed 911.

"Let 'em come!" Uncle Bubba challenged.

"So we can tell them what you did to my mother!" Dwayne added with a sly grin.

Foster looked like his liferaft sprung a leak.

"Go on and hit the send button," Dwayne dared.

Foster pressed another button and let the phone fall into his lap. "Whatever that girl told you is a lie. I never raped nobody."

"Tell that to the judge," Dwayne huffed.

"I don't have to tell anything to anybody because I didn't do anything!"

"She wouldn't lie about this!" Uncle Bubba was seething with anger.

"You raised a dopehead and a convict. What judge is gonna believe her over me?"

"What the hell is going on in here?!" a voice yelled over the commotion.

All heads snapped to the door.

Kurt stood there with his half-sister Shannon peeking around his shoulder. Foster's bottom lip drooped like a flag on a windless day. "Wh— what y'all doing here?"

"Mom called and asked me to come back home because she didn't get a good vibe about y'all being here."

Shannon glanced at Kurt, then at her father. "And I was meeting Kurt here to bring some tax papers I needed him to sign before I leave for my cruise tomorrow."

Kurt moved into the room, his gaze sweeping over the three men before him. "But never mind all that. Before I got the front door open, I could hear y'all in here hollering about rape and judges and convicts." He glared at the three men. "Somebody had better tell me something, and I mean like right now." His fist slammed into his palm with the last two words.

Dwayne made a sweeping gesture, yielding the floor to Foster. "Go ahead, *Dad*! Tell your *other* son how you raped *my* mother when she was just fifteen years old!"

Kurt's eyebrow shot up.

Shannon's jaw went slack.

"That's a lie!" Foster got up and rushed toward Kurt. "Don't believe these jackasses, son. They just want my money. And anyway, if that *did* happen—and I'm not saying it did—but if it did happen, it's too late to do anything about it now." He pointed a taunting finger at Dwayne and Uncle Bubba. "The statute of limitations already expired."

"Most people who ain't raped somebody don't fall back on that kind of thinkin'," Uncle Bubba challenged.

"I ... uh ... picked it up when I was ... uh ... watching TV the other night," Foster said, beady eyes shifting between the four people in the room.

A piercing sound like a city's emergency warning siren permeated the room. Every man clamped his hands over his ears and followed the noise back to ... Shannon. She was shaking her head so hard that her glasses fell off. "If that woman said he raped her, he did." She inched back, trembling. "I know because—he raped me, too! He raped me! He raped me!"

Kurt clasped her head in his hands, calling her name over and over to get her to stop screaming.

She pulled away and wrapped her arms tightly around her stomach, as though trying to push all the vile memories out of her. Eyes glassy with tears, she told Kurt and everyone in the room, "I used to come to spend the weekends ..."

Kurt barely nodded.

She gulped and said, "He would take me ... take me in the bedroom and ... do things to me. I always hated when your mama had to go to the beauty shop. She'd leave me alone with him, and he hurt me. Every time she left, he ..." Only some of the words that followed could surf through the tidal wave of fresh tears. "... touched ... said it was because he loved me."

In one smooth motion, Kurt hefted Shannon clean off of her feet and set her fully in the hallway. He launched himself back into the room, slamming the door on Shannon and advancing toward Foster in a heated wave. "That's why you tried to tear me and my wife apart, so you could protect your dirty secret? You vile snake."

Foster sat like a stalled car in the path of a speeding train. He didn't move one inch.

Kurt glared at Foster. "And if you raped Val's mother—" He stopped, the realization seeming to slam into him like a WWE wrestler. "You knew the woman I married was my *sister*!"

"Quit whining," Foster snarled. "She ain't your blood sister or even your half-sister, because I'm not your real father."

With Kurt in the lead, the three men swarmed to Foster's chair like a pack of hyenas. Foster went for his pocketknife. "I'll slice you like three pounds of bad bologna!"

Kurt caught him with a punch to the jaw and a second one to the nose before Foster could get the weapon completely in his hand. Uncle Bubba had to summon every ounce of strength he had to help Dwayne drag Kurt off of Foster. They each had one of Kurt's arms, pulling in opposite directions.

With blood painting his beard and the front of his shirt red, Foster popped up out of the chair and tried to get a lick or two in on Kurt while he was restrained. Uncle Bubba released his hold on Kurt. Foster had been begging for this ass whipping. Who was he to stand in the way of what the man wanted?

Jerking his other arm out of Dwayne's clutches, Kurt shoved his stepfather so hard it seemed that he was trying to push the man's lungs out of his chest. Foster sat where he fell, shaking his head, trying to get his bearings.

"Get up, you no-good son-of-a—"

"Who're you calling names?" Foster shouted at Kurt from the floor. "You're no better than that heifer that said I raped her. Do your in-laws know that you're a drug addict, just like she is? And did you tell them you're divorcing Val so you can get more money from me and shack up with that other girl?"

Foster rolled away just as Kurt pounced down on the spot where he had been. Dwayne jumped on Kurt's back and wrestled him face down to the ground, yelling, "That's the last time you ever hurt my sister!"

The younger men rolled across the floor, first Dwayne on top of Kurt, then Kurt on top of Dwayne. Foster yanked a lamp off of the nearby bookshelf and crashed it over the two bodies grappling on the floor.

Uncle Bubba jabbed Foster in the rib cage with his cane. He followed with a crack upside the man's head.

ロ ロ ロ

When the police responded to Shannon's 911 call, they questioned the four men in the back of separate squad cars. Soon afterward, the procession of cruisers chauffeured their passengers to the Burr Ridge Police Department.

Chapter 47

Baby Caleb chose to make his entry into the world two months early. When Val first felt those contractions, she had left messages on every number she had for Dwayne, Uncle Bubba and Melva. She even got desperate enough to call Kurt and Foster. There had to be somebody to take her to the hospital—and to tell her why everyone had suddenly gone AWOL. She picked up the phone and called the one person she never thought she'd reach out to.

"Mother?" The word felt strange on her lips. But it was more respectful than calling her by her first name and less intimate than calling her 'mom.'

"Val?" There was a warmth in Francesca's voice that Val hadn't expected.

"Do you happen to know where my uncle and brother are?"

There was a pause on the other end. "No, I haven't talked to them since last night. Is something wrong?" The warm tone was replaced by unease.

Another contraction hit. "I called both of them, and it keeps going to voicemail. Melva, too. I can't reach anyone."

"Hold on, let me try." Francesca clicked over, and there was a short span of time before she came back and said, "It went straight to voicemail for me too. Sweetheart, what's wrong?"

"I ... I think I'm in labor."

"But I thought you were only seven months along."

Shocked by the fact that her mother had been keeping tabs, Val said, "I am. It's much too early."

There was a pause before Francesca said, "I'm on my way."

"I can't ask you to do that."

"You're not asking. I'm coming because you need someone for the moment. I won't read any more into it than that." Then there was a short intake of breath. "If you don't want me there, I understand. I'll call you an ambulance."

Val thought things over a minute before her heart made the decision for her. "I need you. Will you please come?"

"Say no more. I'll be there in twenty minutes. Ten if the police don't stop me."

₪ ₪ ₪

From the time they arrived at the hospital, Francesca was right by Val's side. It would have been hard for her to leave anyway. Val's grip on the woman's hand was just that tight.

"I'm scared," Val whispered from the bed.

"Everything's going to be fine." Francesca slipped her crushed hand out of Val's grasp, shaking it back to life while she allowed Val to take hold of her other hand.

"Seven months," Val said. "Suppose something's not fully developed. You know, suppose he hasn't finished cooking."

Francesca brushed Val's curls away from her eyes. "Then they'll let him finish cooking in an incubator," she quipped, stroking Val's shoulder.

"What if ..." Val turned away. Yesterday she wouldn't have cared what her mother thought of her. Today she was afraid of seeing disapproval in her eyes. But the burning question had to be asked. "What if things are happening this way because of some lies I've told, some things I've done?"

"The greatest lesson I learned when I was locked up was that God is a forgiving God. So I don't care what it is you think you did to deserve this, God still loves you and He wants to forgive you. Never forget that."

Val searched her eyes. "How can you know for sure?"

"Because I'm right here with my baby girl and I'm about to meet my grandchild, all because of God's grace and mercy," Francesca said, dabbing the edge of her blouse on Val's teary eyes. "I'm more proud of you than you'll ever know. And whether you let me be a part of your life or not, nothing will ever take away that pride."

Hours passed.

Contractions intensified.

Conversation dwindled.

Much later, the nurse came in and unlocked the bed to wheel Val into the delivery room. Francesca released Val's hand, nearly sending her daughter into a panic.

"Mother!" she shrieked.

"I'm here, sweetheart. I just needed to move out of the way so they could get to the I.V. pole. I'm not going anywhere."

₪ ₪ ₪

When baby Caleb screamed his way into the world, his heavily lashed eyes, curly hair and nose with the little rounded tip resembled Val. His long limbs and strong-looking hands resembled both Hunter and Kurt.

She still had not told Kurt that Caleb was not his child. She almost told him the day that he threatened to take Caleb from her if she didn't divorce and remarry him. But she caught herself, not because she was concerned about Kurt at that moment, but because it occurred to her that it would break her mother-in-law's heart to find out. She wasn't ready to deal with that.

Caleb cried to the top of his lungs as the nurse laid him on the scale and weighed him. Nothing in Val's life had ever felt as good as this. But her glee was tempered by the fear of not knowing the whereabouts of her family for almost a whole day.

She brought it up to Francesca again when they were alone in the room.

The response was, "I'm sure they're fine," but her apprehensive expression and tone contradicted that statement. "Let me try to reach them again," she said as she grabbed her purse and hurriedly slipped out into the hallway. When she came back in, she said, "I finally talked to Dwayne. He wouldn't tell me where they've been, but he says they're okay. They'll be here shortly, and they'll tell us everything then."

ℕ ℕ ℕ

"Wake up, Mommy."

Groggy, Val tried to swat away a voice that sounded like a mosquito humming in her ear.

"Let me see your wristband, mommy, so I can make sure I've got the right little bundle of joy here." Val felt someone lift her hand and twist it a little to the side. "Yep, Valencia Timmons."

Val brought her hand up to her forehead to cover her eyes from the bright light that clicked on directly over her head. She smiled when she saw the swaddled infant in the bassinette the nurse had wheeled in the room.

"I'm Raven," the young R.N. said. She looked at Francesca, who was sitting in a chair next to the bed. "Are you a relative?" she asked as she took Caleb out of the bassinette.

Francesca parted her lips, but swallowed her words and looked at Val with moist eyes.

Val held her gaze, giving a smile as she said, "Yes, this is my mother Francesca."

"Pleased to meet you, Miss Francesca," Raven said. "Want a peek before I give the baby to his mom for his feeding?" As if he comprehended what was being said, Caleb began making sucking noises.

If love ever ran an ad campaign, Francesca's face could be the billboard. She shed tears as the nurse brought Caleb near enough for her to kiss the tip of his nose.

Raven turned towards the bed and gently shifted the baby from her arms to Val's arms. Val smiled and kissed the silky dark hair covering the crown of his head. The nurse gave Val a few tips about keeping the baby from swallowing too much air while feeding. Caleb wasted no time latching onto Val's breast. "Oh, he's a fast learner," Raven joked as she left the room.

�◆ ᴍ ᴍ ᴍ

Val's newborn was less than two hours old when Uncle Bubba and Dwayne walked into the room. Caleb had finished his feeding and Val was in the process of burping him. The sight of them first made her angry, then caused her to fall apart. Caleb squirmed and let out a cry of his own.

"You ain't gonna kill us, are you?" Uncle Bubba asked, taking his hat off but not crossing the threshold. He looked adoringly at the bundle she held, then his gaze locked onto Francesca, and his smile made a true appearance.

"Get in here," Val said through her tears.

"Dead men walkin'," Uncle Bubba said as he stepped inside. He stopped at Francesca's chair first. "Seein' you here is a dream come true," he said as he gave her a kiss.

Both men followed her gaze when she glanced at Val. "You have her to thank for that. But I think you have more important stuff to sort out right now."

Dwayne came over and kissed Francesca, then leaned in to kiss his nephew and his sister. "Can you forgive me?"

Val handed him the bawling baby. "I don't know. Ask him," she said, wiping her tears and managing a smile of relief.

Dwayne held Caleb close to his heart, rocking him up and down. "Shh, little man. Don't cry. Uncle Dwayne's got you." He walked in a circle, nuzzling Caleb and whispering to him until he grew quiet.

Uncle Bubba made a spot for himself on the edge of Val's bed. Squeezing her shoulders, he mumbled into her hair how much he loved her. When Dwayne brought Caleb over to him, Uncle Bubba laid the baby over his shoulder and prayed aloud over the next generation of his bloodline. By the time he said amen, baby Caleb was softly snoring.

Val glared at the two men while Uncle Bubba laid Caleb in her arms. "Is somebody going to tell me where everybody's been?"

"It ain't a pretty story," Uncle Bubba confessed, radiating shame.

"Well somebody had better be dead because that's the only excuse that'll get you two off the hook."

With a sheepish look, Dwayne hammered out the words, "We were in jail."

Francesca gasped. She had been so still and quiet that Val had almost forgotten she was there.

Her brother had never been arrested before. And the only time her uncle had been behind bars was when he was arrested along with Martin Luther King, Jr. during a 1963 civil rights march in Birmingham, Alabama. She studied her uncle a moment, expecting him to burst out laughing or at least to chastise Dwayne for telling such a see-through lie. He did neither.

"Me, Dwayne, Kurt and Foster," Uncle Bubba said, putting a finger in the air with each name. "We got … we were … uh …"

"We were arrested," Dwayne said, tugging at his ear. "The police had our phones, so that's why you couldn't reach us. We just got out a couple hours ago."

She scrunched her nose up, as though that would make the jumble of words he just said make any more sense.

"And I think Kurt's phone was probably on the floor at his folks' house," Uncle Bubba added. "It slipped out of his pocket during the fight."

Francesca's head snapped to them.

Val gripped the railing of her bed. "The fight?!"

The men nodded like errant schoolboys who'd been caught throwing spitballs. "Yeah," Dwayne finally conceded. "The police let the two of us go." He maneuvered around the bed. "I think they were letting Kurt out too."

"Not Foster, though," Uncle Bubba added. "I called my friend Al to pick me and yo' brother up and take us back to Melva's house so we could get the car. Then we went back to our house so we could scour away that jailhouse funk before we came here."

Giving a "rewind" sign with her hand, she said, "Back up. What started the fight?"

Uncle Bubba looked deeply into Francesca's eyes. "You gonna be okay with me tellin' this?" Only when she gave a nod of consent did he start talking.

ꀸ ꀸ ꀸ

The hair on the back of Val's neck shot out like porcupine quills as they told her the full story, starting with Francesca identifying Foster as her rapist, then Shannon's confession that he had raped her too, and ending with the fight at the Timmons compound.

Two things clicked into place as Val took it all in. First, Foster had hated her all this time because of something *he* did. Second—and most earth-shattering—her mother had run away because of him, not because she hated her children. Val looked at the woman who had dropped whatever she had going on and stayed with her all night and day, nurturing and calming her through a long labor and delivery.

"Mother, I'm … I'm sorry," Val began. "I thought—"

"Sweetheart, I wanted to love you." Francesca's gaze shifted to take in Dwayne. "I wanted to love you both." She inhaled sharply. "But there was so much pain." She didn't try to wipe away her tears.

"I thought the drugs would help. Or the men … one after the other. Anything to make me forget the pain." Looking at her daughter and grandson, she said, "This is too happy of an occasion for me to go into details. But I will say that I'm sorry for not loving you. For a long time, I couldn't love myself. I was a good girl growing up, did everything I was expected to do. So I couldn't figure out why that bad thing happened to me. And because of it, I couldn't be the mother that you needed. I'm so, so sorry."

Val extended her hand and Francesca rushed forward, taking it into her hands before leaning in to kiss her daughter's forehead.

"Are you okay with holding the baby for a while … Mom?" Val asked.

Francesca's smile was as wide as the Mississippi River. "Most definitely." She took her sleeping grandson, pulling the blanket back to plant a kiss on his chubby cheek and adjust the little knit cap on his head.

Uncle Bubba and Dwayne looked on, both of them too choked up to say a word.

Chapter 48

Burr Ridge, Illinois

Kurt slid into the leather seat of his mother's car in the parking lot of the police station. "I'm sorry for all of this," he said, pulling the door shut. "You gonna be okay?"

"You tell me," she answered, pursing her lips in staunch disapproval. "My first grandchild was just born, and I've been stuck here waiting for my son to be released from jail."

Kurt opened his mouth in shock. "He's premature, isn't he? Is he all right?"

"I don't know yet. Val called me a few times while I was at Sister Cooper's house, but my phone was in my purse in another room, so I didn't hear it. And I missed several calls from Shannon."

A UPS truck pulled into the lot, double parked behind them, and the driver jumped out to take an armful of boxes into the station.

"By the time we got finished sewing and ironing," Melva continued, "I didn't get home until six o'clock this morning. Foster wasn't in bed when I got upstairs. I just assumed he fell asleep again in the family room. I laid down to get a catnap before church, but I accidentally overslept. When I got up, it was noon. Foster wasn't home, so I checked to see if he left a message. I found out about the arrests and the baby at the same time."

That accounted for her appearance. Barring a life or death situation, Kurt knew his mother would never have been caught dead in public wearing those starched slacks, a sweatshirt, her fur coat and sneakers.

"I didn't know where to go first," she said. "But I decided I'd rather get y'all out of jail and let it fall on you to tell Val what happened, than to show up at the hospital all by myself and have to explain everybody's absence."

The UPS driver came back to the truck and hurled out of the parking lot. Melva started her car and put it in reverse. "I'm headed to the hospital to be with Val. You're welcome to come along." She gave him a once-over and a sniff, adding, "Or not." She inched the car backward out of the parking space and shifted into drive.

Kurt knew that Uncle Bubba and Dwayne had already been released. He was certain that they were with Val right now. Though he felt a little concerned about Val and his son, he couldn't see himself being around those two men without another fight breaking out. Anyway, the last time he was in Val's hospital room with them, he had gotten the short end of the stick. He wasn't ready for a repeat performance. "I'll check on her and the baby later," he told his mother.

"Suit yourself," she said, pulling up to the stop sign at the parking lot exit.

"You don't have to wait for *him*?" Kurt asked, wondering where Foster was.

She turned onto 77th Street, wrenching the steering wheel so hard that it should have popped off of the steering column. "The police won't say how much longer it'll be before they finish questioning him."

It was a brisk November day, but she let her window all the way down when Kurt asked, "What did he tell you?" Cold air rustled through her grayish-black hair. He guessed it was talking about Foster, and not the frigid temperature, that made the blood rush to her cheeks.

Her mouth turned down. "They only let me see him for a few minutes, but he said that a fight broke out after I left him, Bubba and Dwayne in the house. Something about those two trying to con him out of his money by making up a lie about him raping Francesca. He begged me not to believe what anybody else told me. Said Bubba and Dwayne had even connived to get Shannon to say he raped her too so that Francesca's lie would seem more believable." Shaking her head, she added, "Even the Chicago Police Department is in on it, let him tell it."

"What do they have to do with this?" he asked as she stopped at the intersection of 77th Street and County Line Road.

"One of the Burr Ridge Police officers who saw Foster being brought into the station last night said he looked just like a Chicago Police Department sketch artist's drawing from a description a little girl gave. She claimed that a man at the library tried to molest her a couple months ago."

Kurt almost got whiplash snapping his head around. Getting away with sexual abuse decades ago must have made Foster think he was invincible. Who knew how many more girls he had done this to? Kurt was beginning to wonder if anything short of castration could make a pedophile change his ways.

Melva lingered longer than necessary before proceeding through the intersection. "Chicago Police showed the sketch to people who worked in the library. One or two remembered seeing him before, but he hadn't been around for a long time, and nobody knew his name. The library's security cameras had been on the blink for a while, so the cops didn't have anything to back up the little girl's claim. But they circulated the sketch to other police departments on the off chance that the man would show up in one of the libraries in their districts." A red light caught them at the next intersection. "Turns out, the sketch matched the description of a man wanted in several areas for the very same thing."

Melva seemed to deflate as she whispered, "Shannon told me everything about last night." She reached a trembling right hand toward her son. He took hold of it and kissed the back of it. When he released it, she wiped away tears that tumbled from her eyes one after another.

"What kind of woman am I? How could I have been so blind?" The light turned green, but her tears were coming so fast now that Kurt didn't think she should drive.

"Pull over there," he said, pointing to the Burr Ridge Village Center Mall.

She clicked on her signal light and changed lanes to turn onto Burr Ridge Parkway. They trailed behind a slow car, and when it stopped to let the passengers out, she threw her car into park and traded sides with her son.

While Kurt adjusted the driver's seat and mirrors, she sat in the passenger seat and wiped the tears that bathed her cheeks. "The signs were all there … Shannon's uneasiness around her father all her life … the way he seemed obsessed with her."

"And the way he hated me as much as he loved her," Kurt interjected.

"That too," she confessed. "He would get so angry when I questioned him about it that I eventually just kept my mouth shut. I'm sorry for that. I failed you and I failed her."

Those years had left Kurt feeling that his mother had chosen her husband and stepdaughter over her son. When he looked her way, her eyes begged his forgiveness while her lips formed the words, "I'm sorry." She was too choked up to vocalize them.

Laying her head against the headrest, she placed a hand on her forehead. "I got your daddy out of jail so many times when you were a boy that it ain't even funny. He was always getting into it with somebody."

"Why didn't I know about this?" Kurt asked. He followed a line of cars past the showcase of shops.

"Because I was his get-out-of-jail-free card."

In elementary school, Kurt had known his stepfather to have a few mysterious disappearances, but his mother would always say he was out of town. It sounded plausible enough, especially given that he always reappeared a few days later. By the time Kurt was in high school, he spent as much time as possible away from home, so he didn't really keep up with his stepfather's comings and goings.

"I always covered for him, thinking that that's what a good Christian wife was supposed to do. For better or for worse, right?" She shook her head, the movement full of the same kind of self-condemnation Kurt had seen in his own mirror too often.

"What's the plan now?"

She lifted her gaze to her son. "God help him because I'm not covering up his dirt anymore."

Chapter 49

After his mother changed clothes and left to see about Val, Kurt strategically placed miniature audio recorders throughout the Burr Ridge mansion. He had bought them for his office back when cocaine was making him paranoid. Smaller than an everyday AA-battery, they were easily hidden. Melva had already shared with Kurt that she'd told Foster he would have to get home the best way he could, and Kurt wanted to hear with his own ears the tale he knew Foster would start weaving as soon as he saw Melva.

Roughly an hour after Melva got back from the hospital, Foster arrived home in a cab. Kurt was in the attic, where he told his mother he would be looking for his old baby things that she had put away. She wanted to join him, but he said he needed time to himself to process everything that was happening.

The earpiece he now wore made him feel like a Secret Service agent as he listened in on Foster and Melva's conversation.

"Can't he go somewhere so we can have some privacy?" Foster complained under his breath.

Melva matched his irritated tone. "We're down here; he's up in the attic. He can't hear anything."

Kurt moved a couple of boxes from here to there, making it sound like he was caught up in his chore.

"Fine then," Foster relented. "You know they're all lying on me." He was probably looking deep into Melva's eyes and caressing her hand as he tried to hypnotize her into agreement.

"Two women and a little girl say you raped or tried to rape them, but they're all lying?"

Kurt raised the volume on his earpiece.

"The police let me go, didn't they?"

"The investigating officer called and said you're still a person of interest."

"If you loved me like you say you do, you would believe me over anybody else."

Kurt smirked. *Classic line.*

"All you do is hurt people," Melva snapped. "And I kept my blinders on during our entire marriage." Her voice became raspy. "I prayed day and night that God would ... I don't know ... maybe snap His fingers and cause that … that … iceberg you call a heart to melt." Her stilted speech told Kurt that she was trying to hold back tears.

Foster got a syllable or two in, but she talked over him, something she didn't usually do.

"Your heart just got harder and harder. I saw it. But I couldn't bring myself to leave because I saw the wounded little boy inside of you and vowed I would never bring any hurt to you." She snorted out a sad laugh. "So I stayed. Even though you were cruel to me and my son."

Foster cut in, his voice unrepentant. "I never mistreated that boy! I made a man out of him. You kept him tied to your apron strings. The world is a hard place. I toughened him up and got him ready to face it."

Kurt stiffened, trying to keep his emotions in check.

"Toughened him up?" Melva taunted, her voice rising in pitch. "You tore him down every chance you got. Nothing he ever did was good enough for you. And you always made such a big difference between how you treated him and how you treated your precious Shannon," she spat. "But all the while, you were hurting her as much as—maybe even more than—you were hurting Kurt."

There was a sniffle, and when she spoke again, her sadness traveled through the earpiece. "My mistake was being so concerned about not hurting the little boy inside of you, that I didn't shield my own little boy from your hatred."

Kurt wished he could rush down to comfort his mother.

"I have to live with that fact every day of my life," she confessed. "And so does Kurt. He's half the man he should be because I wasn't one-hundred percent the mother that I should have been. And to think, I chose a man so flawed. You *knew* Val was your child and you let Kurt marry her."

Normally his stepfather would be full of fire. Evidently, that impulse was momentarily doused by raw truth. Foster wasn't about to confirm her assessment of the situation. He eventually said, "Let's put all that behind us. I don't want you to be mad. You're all I have, Melva. I love you."

Kurt frowned at Foster's peacemaker tone.

"You don't love me. You love the way I love you, but you're incapable of giving love to someone else. You're mean-spirited, and there's an evil lurking in your soul that I'll never be able to understand."

Silence. Kurt wished he had X-ray vision that could penetrate through the floor and into the dining room so he could see the look on Foster's face.

"Just tell me how to make things right with you," he said in a voice so low that Kurt almost missed it.

"You want to make things right? You can start by taking that money that's just sitting in the bank and setting up trust funds for Shannon, Kurt, Francesca, Dwayne, Val and the baby."

"But nothing's gonna be left for me," Foster complained. Kurt didn't have to see Foster's face to know that it was scrunched up like a Pug.

"It's always about you, isn't it? If you want any chance to make things right with me, you'd better start changing how you treat people—especially family."

"You would leave me? Over them?" He blew out a rattling breath.

Kurt held his own breath, wondering just how far his mother's new bravado would take her. The silence that followed was killing him. Then she spoke up.

"I stood by for too many years watching you hurt people. I can't do it anymore."

Kurt wanted to applaud and stick his fingers in his mouth to let out a loud whistle. But he remained quiet as his mother added, "I might not be able to stop you from mistreating folks, but I sure don't have to stick around and be a part of it."

Her footsteps were light as powder falling on a wooden floor. When he heard Foster's heavier steps, Kurt braced himself, ready to swoop to the rescue if his stepfather made a wrong move.

Reflex almost made him streak out of the attic door and down the stairs when he heard a loud clunk. But he stayed put after hearing his mother's exacerbated voice order, "Get up off your knees, Foster."

"Melva, all my life, I ain't had nobody to love me but you. Not my mama. Not my daddy. Just you."

Kurt wondered if his mother was rolling her eyes or if her eyes were filling with tears. He hoped to God it was the first one.

"Dry your eyes and quit slobbering all over my hands," she ordered.

A trumpet sounded when Foster blew his nose. "You're all I have. I'll do whatever you want. Just please say you're not leaving."

Kurt tensed as the seconds ticked by. When she said, "I'm not," his head dropped to his chest as if the disappointment had snapped his spine in two. But then she said, "*You* are."

Kurt threw a victory punch in the air.

"Don't try to hug me, Foster. This isn't a lovey-dovey moment. You're not welcome back in this house until you can prove to me that you set those trusts up."

"Melva, I'm … uh … I'm gonna take care of that. You … uh … wait and see." Stuttering was what he did when he was either telling a lie or thinking of a lie to tell. "Course now … that might … uh … take some time. Gotta get … uh … lawyers involved and what not. But I'm … uh … gonna do it," Foster promised in a tone nowhere near as controlling as it normally would have been. "I swear to God I will."

"Don't you bring God into this," Melva warned with pure venom. "You wouldn't recognize God if He came in here and showed you His i.d. card."

Kurt couldn't help but smile. *That's right, Mom. Keep your foot in his ass.*

Chapter 50

December 3, 2011

"Why are you here, Kurt?" Val's tone was hot as Tabasco, but Kurt expected no less.

"May I come in?" he asked from the porch, shivering from the icy wind.

Val forced out a breath, gripping the doorknob as though she might tie him up and beat him if she didn't give her hands something else to do. She cracked the door to let him in. As he stepped inside, took off his hat and brushed the few snowflakes off, a soft sigh from the bassinette by the couch caught his attention. Val's eyes softened and she went to pull a wriggly bundle out. Love flowed from her face when she looked down at the baby in her arms. But a cold front blew in when Kurt said, "Can I see him?"

She glared at him and sat on the couch.

He tilted his head to the ceiling and squeezed his eyes shut, searching for the right words. "I came to see if we can try to be a family. Me, you and the baby."

"You mean the baby you wanted me to abort? Or the baby you threatened to get sole custody of?" she snapped. "Why would we want you in our lives?"

Before he could stop himself, he blurted, "Because I don't want to end up like my stepfather, a fool who has nobody to love him."

Owning up to that fear left a knot in the pit of his stomach. How much more vulnerable would he feel before this was all over? He'd been working an inordinate amount of time to pay the people and companies he owed. He'd been taking the steps to recovery a lot more seriously. And he was helping his mother navigate these new changes in her life. All of it had taken a toll on him. But the one thing he realized he couldn't avoid any longer was making things right with Val and his son.

"May I sit down?" he asked while motioning toward the love seat. With a wary nod from his wife, he shrugged off his coat, hanging it and his hat on a hook near the door. "I'm not good at expressing my feelings," he said as he took his seat. "I know I haven't done everything right." Droplets of sweat formed under his arms. "But I'm asking if we can give our marriage another try. I don't want a divorce."

The caustic look she gave ate a hole in him. "You've got some nerve coming here with that. What happened? Things didn't work out with Whitley, so now you come running back to me?"

Whitley's marital problems had been all over the news. So-called friends went to the tabloids when Whitley bragged in Facebook posts about how she still had lovers on the side because her millionaire husband couldn't satisfy her in bed. Zhang Cái got the marriage annulled and petitioned the court for sole custody of their son. An ironclad prenup left Whitley penniless.

"Look," he said, holding his hands up in concession. "I don't want this discussion to go this way. I want to earn your trust again. And your respect."

Caleb let out a little peep, and she looked down at him. "Is it time to eat?" she cooed. One tiny fist poked out of the blanket. Val kissed the little hand and wrapped it back up in the blanket when he fretted. "Whatever you have to say," she said to Kurt, "make it quick. I've got things to do." She slipped a pacifier between the tiny puckered lips.

"I don't want to argue," he said. "Please let me see the baby. Let me touch him. He's almost a month old now, and you've kept him away from me."

She tightened her grip on Caleb.

"Don't be like that," Kurt pleaded. Part of him wished he could force her to resuscitate their marriage. But maybe it was too late. They both would just have to stand by and watch it choke to death on mistakes, hostility and unforgiveness.

"I brought something for you." He searched the inside pocket of his coat, bringing out a sealed envelope and stretching across the arm of the loveseat to hand it to her.

Giving him the side eye and balancing Caleb in one arm, Val took it. She slipped her nail under the flap and slit the envelope open. Flipping through the pages quickly, she said, "You're kidding me, right?"

He felt his forehead crease. "No, it's real. Foster set up two million in a trust for Caleb."

"Guilt money?" She swept the papers onto the floor. "Now I see why you want to come back. You don't need a divorce to get more money from your stepfather. You can just live off of the baby's trust fund."

"No, I want to come home because I love you," Kurt defended. "He gave me my own three-million dollar trust fund—*without* me having to get a divorce," he hastened to add. "I can take care of my family now— if you'll let me."

She cradled Caleb tighter in her arms. "If I remember correctly, when you thought you had to divorce me to get your money, you were more than ready to do that." The force of her voice startled Caleb. He began to cry. She rocked him and spoke softly to him until he settled down.

Kurt was mindful of his volume and tone as well. "But it's not like that anymore." He picked up the paperwork and sat it on the arm of the couch.

"We already had more problems than most marriages can survive," she said. "Then we found out that my father-in-law is also my father." She shivered. "That means that my husband is some pseudo-half-stepbrother to me. It's all too much. I can't live with that." Her eyes pointed the way to the door. "It's time to stay out of our lives, Kurt. Those papers you had the sheriff serve me with two weeks ago? I already signed them and took them back to the attorney. I'm giving you that divorce you've been begging for, and I'm getting the freedom that I need."

"Right," Kurt shot back, wounded beyond all belief. "Because you already got what you wanted."

Val wouldn't even look him in the eye to acknowledge that statement.

"But what about him?" Kurt said, gesturing to Caleb. "I want to be in my son's life."

Val looked up at the ceiling, weighing her next words before saying, "Kurt, there's no reason to come back to us. There is no us, and this isn't your child."

"So you slept around on me?!" Anger and vindication fought to take the driver's seat. "After all you put me through?"

"I slept with someone long before I met you. This is his child."

Her answer threw him for several loops.

"This is Hunter's child. Carries his DNA and mine. I was impregnated with our embryos." She cocked an eyebrow. "You didn't want any children, remember? Well, you got your wish."

Kurt slumped back in the loveseat.

"I truly am sorry it ended up this way," she said. "And for deceiving you."

"That doesn't matter, Val." And truly, it didn't. He was ready to be the man he was supposed to be and the father he'd never had.

"Kurt, the truth of the matter is … I don't love you nearly enough. I still had too much of Hunter in my heart when you and I started dating. And that wasn't fair to me or to you. So, as many mistakes as you've made in this marriage, I've made my share too."

"And I can forgive you for that."

"No, sweetheart. We aren't good *for* each other or *to* each other. We haven't been good for a while." She stood. After laying Caleb down in the bassinette, she said, "I'm still grieving for a man who's no longer

alive. So you were batting a negative five hundred from day one."
Getting Kurt's hat and coat off of the hook, she held the front door open.
"All you can be is Kurt Timmons. You're not Hunter and never will be.
It took me three years to figure that out and realize that I need to truly
let go of Hunter and find my own best self before I can fully give my
heart to another man."

Chapter 51

Thursday, December 15, 2011

A size two woman in a size six dress sat behind a reception desk as Uncle Bubba and Francesca entered the office of Gerald Penn, Esquire. The woman's austere, straight-laced look reminded him of Jane Hathaway from *The Beverly Hillbillies*. He gave a broad smile and extended his arm to shake her skeletal hand.

"I'm Paul Burgess, and this is my niece Francesca Harper. We're here to see Mr. Penn."

She drew her hand back and began clicking her fingers on the keyboard. Taking her glasses out of her hair and putting them on her face, she squinted at the computer screen. "Ah yes, you're his nine o'clock appointment. Won't you have a seat?"

Brushing a hand over her French roll, she tucked a few stray hairs into place, then touched a button on her phone. A buzz was followed by a male voice coming through the speakerphone. "Yeah, Erin."

"Mr. Penn, Mr. Burgess and Ms. Harper are here."

The phone crackled. "Give me a couple minutes to finish dictating this letter." His voice was in stereo, coming in Uncle Bubba's left ear from the speakerphone on the desk and in his right ear from a nearby open door.

Uncle Bubba gave Francesca a reassuring pat on her knee. She laid a hand on his, dropping the envelope she held. He bent to pick it up, noticing where the ink was smeared.

Poor thing is so nervous that her hands are melting the words off of the paper. She had come out of prison determined to make a nice clean life for herself. She hadn't asked for handouts from anyone and had taken great pride in getting herself on the right path. But this unexpected money was a welcome blessing, like God's way of showing her that He was proud of her efforts. Foster taking it back would probably make her feel powerless again, like when he raped her. "We'll get it sorted out," Uncle Bubba promised.

He opened the envelope, took out the folded letter inside and flapped it twice in the air to make the sheet of paper straighten out. He scanned over it once again, still not able to comprehend how one person could be so cruel.

> *I hope you enjoyed that first monthly allotment from the trust I set up for you. But effective immediately, I'm revoking the trust. The night my wife made me promise to set up the trust funds, she said she was leaving me. So I gave you the money because I thought she would stay with me if I did what she asked. She stayed, but things aren't the same. She's never shut me out like this.*

> *So take a good look at what I stapled to this letter. Just like I sent you a copy of the papers from me opening up the trust fund, I'm sending you this copy of papers showing that I closed your trust.*

> *Say goodbye to my money. I would say it was good while it lasted, but you haven't had it long enough to get much use out of it. Too bad. You know what they say: easy come, easy go.*

> *Bottom line—if I can't win, I sure as hell won't let*

you win.

Erin was all business as she said to Uncle Bubba, "Okay, Mr. Penn just emailed me. He's ready to see you. First door down that hall," she said, pointing the way.

He stood and helped Francesca to her feet.

Lord, please work this out in my niece's favor.

Gerald Penn waved them into his office, spoke a few more words into a Dictaphone, then hit his intercom button. "Erin, why don't you come get this tape so you can start transcribing it while I meet with these good people?" Like the Wizard of Oz, Gerald Penn had a booming voice and a small stature.

While Erin came and left, he stood and shook hands with Uncle Bubba and Francesca, each stating their name.

"So, my assistant tells me you have a trust issue." Penn cracked a smile. "Not trust issues as in you're afraid to trust people. But a trust issue as in an issue with your trust fund."

Francesca's lips pulled into a frown.

Uncle Bubba smiled back, but only out of courtesy. He nodded his head toward Francesca. "She *hopes* it's still her trust account."

"Hmmm." The wizard took small, quick steps back to his huge solid maple desk and sat down in a chair so huge that Uncle Bubba wondered if his legs were swinging in the air. "Tell me a little about what's going on, Mr. Burgess," the attorney said.

"Call me Bubba."

"Okay, Bubba. Call me Gerry."

Francesca motioned with her eyes to the piece of mail in her uncle's hand. He leaned over and placed it on the attorney's desk. Gerry examined the certified mail label and the return receipt. He read the letter aloud, although Uncle Bubba had memorized it by now. When the lawyer got to the part about the papers attached to the letter, he stopped reading aloud, but his mouth moved as his eyes went through the pages. By the time he reached the last page and his eyes and mouth became still, he wore his concern like a Halloween mask.

"That bad, huh?" Uncle Bubba ventured. He didn't chance a look at his niece, telling himself that he would put Foster out of his misery for hurting her again.

Gerry sat the paperwork on his desk. "One thing I know is that this Foster character clearly thought hiring a lawyer was a waste of time and money."

"What makes you say that?" Francesca asked. Uncle Bubba guessed that her mechanical tone served as a dam to keep her emotions from spilling out.

"Well, this revocation is signed and notarized. But there's no attorney or law firm listed."

Uncle Bubba reached over and flipped through the pages. "You're right."

"So it's not binding?" Francesca asked, pulling herself to the edge of her seat.

Gerry copied his client's posture. "In today's do-it-yourself world, any Joe Blow can get these forms online, and as long as they're filled out correctly, they are legal." He turned his apologetic eyes first to Uncle Bubba then to Francesca. "And unfortunately, these are done correctly. I'm sorry, but it does look like the trust he established in your name has been revoked."

Both clients sank back into their chairs, speechless.

"But," Gerry added, holding a finger up in the air. "I can't be a hundred percent sure without seeing how the trust was initially set up. When can you bring me that paperwork?"

"Right now." Francesca opened her purse and rummaged around in it. At the sound of crumpling paper, she pulled out a manila envelope and passed it to Gerry. "Here," she said. "I brought it just in case."

Uncle Bubba beamed his approval. "Girl, you're worth a dime with a hole in it!"

Francesca grinned, and Uncle Bubba clasped hands with her, both of them as nervous as turkeys on Thanksgiving Day.

After the lawyer opened the envelope and read a bit, his eyes crinkled around the edges and he inhaled so deeply that Uncle Bubba swore the man had swallowed his tongue.

Oh, Lord, it's so bad that it's giving him a seizure!

Then Gerry slapped the desk with his palm and roared with laughter at the top of his lungs, barely able to catch his breath between chortles and snorts.

"What's so funny?" Uncle Bubba challenged. "We might want to laugh too," he said, not the least bit amused.

Gerry wiped tears from his eyes, snatched a tissue from a box on his credenza and blew his nose before being able to compose himself enough to speak. "This friend of yours—or your enemy or whatever he is—drew up the trust himself, without a lawyer involved." He let go of a couple more chuckles. "Have you heard Abraham Lincoln's saying, 'He who represents himself has a fool for a client'?" he asked his baffled guests.

Uncle Bubba turned a wary eye on him. "I might've heard it in passin'. What about it?"

"Well, this Foster person is definitely a fool."

"Everybody knows that," Uncle Bubba said with a dismissive wave. "The ducks and the geese know that. What's your point?"

Gerry's index finger beckoned for them to move closer. They both leaned in as he whispered, "He can't revoke the trust."

"Come again," Uncle Bubba said.

"The trust that he set up is an *irrevocable* trust," Gerry said, barely able to get the words out around his smile.

"And?" Francesca asked, taking the word out of Uncle Bubba's mouth.

"And ... irrevocable trusts can't be revoked." Gerry bent over backward laughing. "That's why people need lawyers. Even the dumbest attorney would have been able to tell him the difference between a *revocable* trust and an *irrevocable* trust."

"Why don't you tell us the difference?" Uncle Bubba asked, trying to find humor in the situation.

Gerry nodded, still snorting his laughter as he passed the papers back to Francesca. "A revocable trust is the kind that the person can revoke ... close out ... take back. But an irrevocable trust is final unless the person puts some kind of stipulation in it and the person who gets the trust violates that stipulation. There's no stipulation in this one."

Seconds ticked by as Uncle Bubba mulled that over. "Foster done double-crossed his own damn self," he said, chuckling.

Another nod, then Gerry collected himself and said, "If he set up trusts for anybody else that you know of, you might want to mention this to them if you think he's going to try to revoke theirs too."

"If?" Uncle Bubba scoffed. "He will," he added, rising from his seat and helping Francesca out of hers. "But now we know that we get the last laugh." He reached in his back pocket and pulled out his wallet. "The girl at the front desk told us on the phone that the consultation was free, but the news you gave us is so great that I feel like I need to pay you somethin'."

Gerry shook his head. "Put your money away." He cruised over to a metal file cabinet and opened a drawer, flipping through several files. He pulled one out, laid it on the cabinet and motioned for Uncle Bubba and Francesca to join him.

He gestured to the file. "This is an agenda we're preparing for an upcoming meeting of the local Bar Association." He pointed a stubby finger at the third name from the top. "I'm one of the speakers that day. I'd like to open up by telling them what happened here today—without putting your names in my story, of course."

"Knock yourself out," Uncle Bubba replied.

Gerry closed the file. "They're gonna crack up. People like Foster think they're putting lawyers out of business, but they're guaranteeing our job security."

With that, Gerry gave Uncle Bubba a slap on the back, shook Francesca's hand and escorted them to the waiting area. "I just hate that I can't be there to see that man's face when he finds out that he can't get his money back."

בּ בּ בּ

"In all the years I spent in prison, not once did I run into anybody as wicked as Foster," Francesca said in the hallway as she put the paperwork back in her purse.

"I know," Uncle Bubba said, hooking his arm in his niece's. "I done asked God a time or two to just wash Foster clean from his sins, then take him on to glory to get him outta our hair."

They stopped at the elevator bank. "And what was His answer?" Francesca asked.

The door opened, they got in, and Uncle Bubba pushed the button for the ground floor. "He said He already had to throw one devil outta heaven and He ain't 'bout to go through that no mo'." Their laughter filled the elevator shaft.

Once in the lobby, Uncle Bubba pulled out his old flip phone and dialed. He had called Melva four days ago when Francesca received Foster's cruel letter. Though he would have preferred giving Foster another beat-down, Melva convinced him to go talk to a lawyer, then to give her a callback.

He held up the give-me-a-minute finger to Francesca. "Melva? It's Bubba."

The response was, "Bubba? Shoot!"

"This ain't a good time to call?" he asked.

"No, it is. I can talk. Just let me put this hot cobbler on the counter before I drop it."

Steaming, sweet, juicy peaches. Flaky, buttery crust with a dusting of sugar. Her cobblers were what Uncle Bubba called "slap yo' mama" good.

"I'm back," she said. "Am I going to need to sit down to hear the news?"

"Naw, because everything worked out for Francesca." She listened without interruption as he gave her all the details, then she gave him a rundown of things that had happened on her end. When she finished, he said, "God sure takes care of His own, don't He?"

After he snapped the phone shut, Francesca said, "There's a special place in hell for a man as evil as Foster."

"He's in hell right now," Uncle Bubba said with a lopsided grin.

"You remember I told you that when we got arrested last month, the police questioned him about trying to molest a little girl in the library in Chicago? And then several more people said a man looking like him tried it at other libraries nearby? Well, Melva just told me that he was worried sick that the girl's family might stick him up for some money. So to make sure he could cry broke if they came after him with a lawsuit, on the same day he set up these trust accounts, he turned right around and put all the rest of his money in Melva's name."

"I'd expect him to take all the money and get out of Dodge." Francesca said. "He had enough to stay hidden for the rest of his life."

"Funny you said that because that's what I thought too. But Melva told me just now that Foster thought that staying would make him look innocent in the eyes of the law, like he had nothing to hide. But that didn't work. Chicago Police has his butt locked up right now on the molestation charge."

"And Melva controls all the money now?" Francesca asked.

Uncle Bubba nodded. "They say God looks after babies and fools, but they didn't say nothin' about assholes."

Francesca busted up laughing.

Chapter 52

July 2012

"Are you ready to see your uncles and your Granny Fran?" Val said as she stood Caleb on her lap and pulled a onesie over his head. He gave a bashful grin and raised up on his tiptoes, gripping a fistful of her collar and pulling it toward his open mouth. She laid him on the couch, even though at eight months old he no longer liked to sit still or lie down.

When she finished putting on his shorts and shirt, she took him by the hands. He instinctively pulled himself up into a standing position, his pudgy feet sinking into the sofa cushion time and again as he lifted then lowered each foot in his excitement. He stuck a fist in his mouth, mumbling his happiness.

"Guess what, boo boo?" she said.

Caleb lowered his fist and got quiet, as though Val was about to divulge a classified government secret.

"I love you." She nuzzled his little neck and Caleb threw his head back, letting out a loud laugh. When he reached for her nose, she kissed the tip of his finger. "Come on, let's get going."

ת ת ת

Uncle Bubba and Francesca were enjoying the evening sun on the second-floor patio of his Richton Park townhome. Val's car pulled up, and as soon as she opened the back door and got Caleb out, Uncle Bubba leaned over the railing and called out his name. To his delight, Caleb bounced in Val's arms, tilting his head up to follow the sound of Uncle Bubba's voice.

Val adjusted Caleb on her hip and slung the diaper bag over her other shoulder.

Dwayne stepped out of his adjoining townhome just as she made it to Uncle Bubba's door. "Hey, you two," he said, giving Val a peck on the cheek and tickling Caleb's stomach until he got a giggle out of him.

Caleb reached for Uncle Bubba the minute he saw him. The old man kissed his niece and took the youngster in his arms. "Come on over here, ol' man," he said as Caleb did baby jumping jacks, his legs kicking in the air.

When they made it to the patio door, Caleb instantly clamored to get out of Uncle Bubba's arms and into Francesca's embrace.

"That always happens," Uncle Bubba proclaimed. "As soon as he sees his Granny Fran or his Gran'ma Melva, he unfriends me. Ain't that the way y'all young people say it, Dwayne?"

Dwayne smiled and nodded as Uncle Bubba passed Caleb to Francesca.

"How's Granny Fran's baby?" she asked, cuddling him to her. Caleb's delight bubbled out in a squeal. He bumped his lips against her cheek in his version of a hello kiss. He pulled his head back and they smiled widely at each other.

Studying the exchange, Val nudged Dwayne. "Every time these two get together they act like online daters who just met in person for the first time." She leaned down to give her mother a hug.

Uncle Bubba grinned at them and started humming the old gospel tune "He May Not Come When You Want Him, but He's Right on Time." He had prayed for years for Francesca and her children to come together, and he was so grateful that he had lived to see it happen.

The landline in the living room began to ring. As he got up to answer, Uncle Bubba said, "The meat Dwayne grilled is in the kitchen. There's baked beans, cole slaw and potato salad. Y'all come on in and fix your plates while I get the phone." This time of day, it was probably those bothersome telemarketers. "Hello," he said in an impatient voice.

"Hello? Paul Burgess?" The line was full of static, and the voice was heavily accented.

"You got him. How can I help you?"

"I ... we ... oh, what word is right word?" the nearly inaudible female voice said. "Hunter Pierce ... he ... he here ... need money."

"Who is this?" Uncle Bubba demanded in a harsh tone. "Don't call my house no mo'," he said, slamming the phone down. It seemed like every day some new phone scam aimed at stealing the life savings of elderly people popped up. A few years back, someone had called and said Uncle Bubba had to wire five thousand dollars immediately because Dwayne had gotten robbed and beaten in Mexico. But Dwayne had just left Uncle Bubba's townhouse two minutes earlier. The only way he could have made it eighteen hundred miles away that fast was if Scotty from *Star Trek* had beamed him up.

The phone rang again. Uncle Bubba walked to the kitchen where the rest of the family was.

"You want me to get that?" Francesca asked.

"Don't bother," he answered, eyeing the plate that she had made and put on his spot at the table. "Dwayne, ain't there some number I can call to report one of those senior citizen telephone scams?"

"Yeah, but we have to say what number the call came from. Since you're the only person alive who has a landline with no caller i.d., that's going to be kind of hard," Dwayne teased.

"Well, whoever it is, they ain't givin' up. That doggone phone ain't stopped ringin' yet."

Dwayne got up. "Let me handle it." He picked up the phone. "Listen, if you don't take my uncle's number off of your call list, I'll report—" His face blanched. "Wait, wait. Hold on a minute." Covering the mouthpiece, he looked at Uncle Bubba and said, "Go pick the line up in the living room."

When Uncle Bubba was on the other extension, he said, "What's goin' on here?" First he heard the crackle and hum in the line that he'd heard on the last call. Then a voice that seemed to carry across eternity said, "It's me, Uncle Bubba. It's Hunter. Hunter Pierce."

The old man's legs almost gave out. He reached his hand out to hold onto a high-back chair until he could steady himself. "Can this be true?" he whispered to himself. The man sounded just the way he remembered.

"Whatever you do, please don't hang up," the voice on the phone pleaded.

Dwayne jumped back in the conversation. "Do you have something to write with?" he asked the caller. "Good. Now take this number down and call me back in five minutes." He gave out his cell number. "Five minutes," he reiterated, then hung up and walked into the living room to take the phone out of his stunned uncle's hand. "Come with me," Dwayne commanded.

As he led the way to the front door, he called out to Val and Francesca, "We're running to my place for a sec. We'll be right back."

נו נו נו

As soon as they walked into Dwayne's townhome, he told Uncle Bubba to sit tight while he booted up his laptop. The computer screen came to life just when the man claiming to be Hunter called back. Dwayne put the phone on speaker.

"Hunter, that you?" Uncle Bubba asked. The connection wasn't any clearer than it had been on Uncle Bubba's landline. But this time they at least had the advantage of caller i.d. "Hold on a second," Uncle Bubba said into the phone.

Dwayne clicked the keys on the laptop. When he pointed to something on the screen, Uncle Bubba took his glasses out of his shirt pocket and bent over to squint at it. It was a Google search of the caller's phone number. It said that 62, the first two digits of the phone number, was the country code for Indonesia. The next two numbers, 21, was the city code for Jakarta, the capital of Indonesia.

"We're back," Dwayne said to the man on the phone. "I gotta tell you, you sound just like Hunter. But Hunter's been dead almost twelve years now."

"No, no, it's me." The man breathed desperation through the phone. "I wasn't dead. For all these years, I suffered from amnesia after the doctors I was with got attacked in the jungle."

"That's not telling us anything," Dwayne countered. "Anybody could know about those murders. It was all over the national news how Hunter and his other doctor friends had been killed by a group of rebels while on a humanitarian medical trip to Indonesia. The government over there never found Hunter's body. He was pronounced dead after so many years passed by without him surfacing."

Uncle Bubba leaned closer to the phone. "So what are you? One of those people who steal dead folks' identities?"

"I know how this must sound," the caller said, patiently. "I got the same reaction while trying to prove my identity to the Consulate. But just hear me out. Please."

Uncle Bubba and Dwayne listened intently as the man gave them the details of the last twelve years of his life. He told them everything from being found by Kepala and Toma, his path to being the next chief, creating the coalition of tribes that brought the Setan to its knees, and everything in between. He ended by recounting the day he realized who he was. More importantly, *whose* he was. "For three years of my life, I was blessed with the love of the most phenomenal woman I have ever known—Val. My only wish is to find her again. I don't want to turn her life upside down, but … do you think I could just see her? Talk to her?"

"Well, Val got married again," Uncle Bubba said protectively. "And she got a little boy now."

"But her divorce was finalized a month ago," Dwayne volunteered.

Uncle Bubba shot his eyes at his nephew. Frowning, he whispered, "He don't need to know all that."

The man on the phone gave a despairing sigh. "Ask me anything at all if you don't believe I am who I say I am."

"Okay," Uncle Bubba demanded. "Tell me something about Val that nobody but the family would know."

The newfound smile in the man's voice seemed to seep through the phone. "For starters, anytime she finishes eating something sweet, she has to follow it with a bit of something salty because she doesn't like having a sweet taste left in her mouth. Let's see … what else? She brushes her teeth with toothpaste in the morning and with baking soda at night. She hates liver but loves meatloaf. She can't stand to get caught in the rain but will run out and play in the snow at the drop of a hat. She wore braces until she was seventeen. She—"

"Well tell me this," Uncle Bubba butted in. "What advice did I give you on your wedding day?"

The man didn't miss a beat. "You pulled me aside and said, 'No matter how much I respect you—and I do respect you—givin' my little girl to you feels like givin' a diamond to a gorilla. You better treat her right, or it's yo' ass.'"

The phone slipped from Uncle Bubba's hand. The cane followed the same path to the carpet.

Chapter 53

August 2013

As a Boeing 747 coming in for a landing soared so close to the Kennedy Expressway that it looked like its belly would touch the roof of Dwayne's new Escalade, Uncle Bubba craned his head around to look at Val in the back seat. "You okay?" he asked.

She gave him a reassuring nod.

Caleb was strapped in his car seat between Val and Francesca, eating Gold Fish out of a baggie that his Granny Fran held. Each time he put a handful in his mouth, he would kick his legs up and grin.

Val was so nervous that it almost made her nauseous. After Dwayne and Uncle Bubba had confirmed from Hunter's initial contact that he was the real thing, Val had spoken with Hunter on the phone several times during the thirteen months that it took for the two governments to confirm his identity and for him to speak to people in the United Nations about the genocide the tribes had suffered.

Still, the thought of seeing him again felt surreal to her. Until today. Dwayne's SUV had made the lap around O'Hare's enormous

International Terminal three times already.

"Maybe he changed his mind," she said, wondering if she'd survive her heartbreak if that were the case.

Caleb, who was mesmerized by *Despicable Me 2* playing on a DVD screen, sang the chorus of "Happy" with Pharrell Williams, bobbing his head and trying to snap his little fingers. Val ruffled his curly hair. *Maybe we can be a happy family after all, Caleb.*

Dwayne was lucky enough to find a spot in front of the terminal large enough to pull the huge truck into without having to do the back-and-forward dance of parallel parking. Val sat sideways in her seat, the perfect vantage point from which to look out of the back window.

She squinted at a man who walked with a familiar gait. When he headed in their direction, Uncle Bubba and Dwayne stepped out of the truck and went to meet him.

Val agreed ahead of time to let them talk with the man before he came to the truck. Every butterfly in Val's stomach stopped flapping its wings when Dwayne and the man shook hands, the handshake flowing into what Val called a "man hug." Uncle Bubba stepped up and gave the man a handshake and a hearty clap on the shoulder.

Hunter.

My God, it truly is my Hunter.

נ נ נ

Dwayne came around to Val's side of the SUV. He opened the door, helped her out and led her around the back of the vehicle. She held her breath as Uncle Bubba stepped up with Hunter.

"Val ... baby, it's me," Hunter said with a voice forever etched in her memory.

She wanted to reach out and touch him, but she was so afraid that the mirage would fade away if she did. He extended his hand a little toward her, his expression reflecting the same fear that she felt. She stood planted in place and watched his hand get closer and closer. Then she felt his touch.

And he did not disappear.

This is real.

Her pent-up breath and tears flowed at the same time. Hunter inched closer, and she allowed him to pull her into the safety and comfort of his arms.

"I'm home, baby." He swayed with her in his embrace, like a palm tree in the gentle sea breeze.

Not even the noise from all the cars driving by or all the planes taking off and landing could dampen the sound of his heartbeat as Val closed her eyes and rested her head against his powerful chest. When she finally opened her eyes and glanced over his shoulder, Uncle Bubba said, "Y'all come on over here. There's some folks you need to meet, Hunter."

Francesca was standing next to the open back door of the truck with Dwayne. Her eyes were glistening with tears.

As Uncle Bubba unstrapped Caleb from his car seat, Val took Francesca's hand and placed it in Hunter's.

"This is me and Dwayne's mother Francesca Harper," she said, her voice cracking with emotion. "God brought her back to us just like He brought you back."

Hunter welcomed his mother-in-law into his embrace as Val shed tears of joy for her two lost treasures.

Uncle Bubba walked up with Caleb in his arms. The tot's eyes pored over his great uncle's features. Reaching up, he squeezed the old man's cheeks between his chubby hands. "Don' cwy, Uncca Bubba. Sing wit' me." He serenaded Uncle Bubba with a few words from the chorus of "Happy," then looked at him in confusion when he didn't join in as he usually did. Wiping Uncle Bubba's face, he said again, "Don' cwy."

"We'll sing in a minute, partner, but somebody wants to meet you." He waited until Francesca pulled from Hunter's embrace, then put Caleb in her arms.

"Gwanny Fwaaaaan," Caleb happily chanted. "Mommy! Uncca 'wayne!" he added with a big wide grin.

"Caleb," Val said, smiling at the apple of her eye while pointing at

Hunter. "This is your daddy. Can you say hello?"

"Heh-wo Da-da!"

"Daddy?" Hunter's head snapped back and forth from Val to Caleb. The man's face looked like an astonished child who opens a gift on Christmas day and finds something he had always wanted but never thought he'd get. "He's … my son?"

"Sure is," Uncle Bubba said, beaming. "Came from those scrambled eggs y'all had at that clinic."

As the family laughed, the twinkle in Hunter's eyes told Val that he recalled everything.

Slowly nodding he said, "Our embryos."

"Embryos, scrambled eggs, omelets—whatever," Uncle Bubba said. He took Caleb's hand and wiggled it as he added, "Ain't that right, boy?"

"Sing wit' me," Caleb said, stretching his arms out to Hunter.

And for the first time, Hunter held his son.

Happy. Hunter. Infinite possibilities. Yes, indeed, happiness was within Val's reach.

Cayenne

NATIONAL BESTSELLING AUTHOR

JANICE M. ALLEN

EXCERPT FROM *CAYENNE*

Michael raised the trunk and gazed at his ex-girlfriend's unconscious body. Nia was blindfolded, her wrists and ankles bloodied by the thick rope binding them. He had to play his cards right if he intended to get her out of this alive.

"You sure nobody saw you snatch her?" Michael asked Lee as the self-proclaimed pretty boy and wannabe gangster got out of his car.

"Positive." Lee leaned over to admire himself in the mirror.

Michael swore that he would make things right with Nia, make her his wife—as soon as he could free her from her captors.

"Before Angelique kills sleeping beauty," Lee said, "I'm gonna break her off some of what the women beg me for." He gave a wicked sneer that set Michael's nerves on edge.

Though his fists were aching to have a conversation with Lee's face, Michael chomped down on his anger. *Months of undercover work will go down the drain if you lose your cool.*

"You'd better get in the car and go meet up with your sister like she told you to," Michael warned. "People get antsy in this kind of deal." He glanced at his watch. "Keep them waiting, and they'll get cold feet. Then there won't be a baby to sell. Angelique will be pissed if that happens."

"Maaan, you think I'm scared of that chick?" Lee's chest was stuck out like a rooster in a cock fight, but his voice sounded more like a hen with its neck on the chopping block. "My sister don't run things. I do."

The only thing Lee ran was his mouth. None of the informants Michael had encountered in ten years of undercover work divulged as much information as Lee belched out while bragging about his power, prowess, prosperity, and plans—none of which he possessed. Angelique was the brains behind everything they did.

Michael raised his hands in mock surrender. "Since you call the shots, how about I look after her"—he nodded toward Nia—"until you get back?"

Cursing under his breath, Lee motioned for Michael to remove Nia from his black 2018 Lexus RX.

Michael gathered her slender body in his arms.

Lee slammed the trunk, gave a two-finger wave, and sped off into the night.

Nia never flinched. Her breathing remained slow and steady as the garage door closed, shutting her off from the outside world.

Not knowing when Lee and Angelina would return, getting Nia out of that place was Michael's priority. But concerns about Nia being unconscious for three hours trumped that. Michael carried her to his Cadillac CTS and gently laid her across the back seat.

Her natural beauty mesmerized him. Baby-soft butterscotch-colored skin. Eyebrows that framed her brown eyes like they were works of art. Thick black hair that created a halo around her face.

He placed a feather-light kiss on her lips. In a fairy tale, she would awaken with undying gratitude. But he feared that no magic kisses or potions could ever make her regard him favorably again.

He got the smelling salts from the first aid kit in the car. Getting in the driver's seat, he turned toward her and waved the bottle several inches away from her nose.

She wrenched away from the acrid smell of ammonia. Convulsing with coughs, she thrashed around, probably hoping to free her hands, take the blindfold off, and make a run for it.

Putting a hand to her chest, he gently held her in place. The heartbeat that was faint as he held her against his chest a minute ago now pounded against his palm like a battering ram.

"Shhh," he whispered.

Her head darted around to follow his hushed tone, then to take in other sounds in the space: a dog barking nearby; the hum of the furnace in the adjoining utility room; his ragged breathing as the fear of losing her to killers subsided.

Michael braced himself, knowing that once he said something, she would recognize him. "I'm going to take off your blindfold."

She gasped, cringed, and craned her head toward the sound of his voice.

He untied the black bandana that covered her eyes and let it slip off.

Light spilling from the dome light over Nia's head made her squint, but when she fully opened her eyes, she honed in on Michael's face. Her expression transformed from bewilderment to horror, giving voice to everything she couldn't vocalize.

Why did you do this to me?!

Also by Janice M. Allen:

About the author

JANICE M. ALLEN

was a sought-after developmental, content and line editor before she began writing. She edited for several National Bestselling Authors and Independently-published authors. Some of her editing projects sold to traditional publishers such as Brown Girls Publishing/Brown Girls Books and Harlequin/Kimani Press. Five of her edited works hit the Top 10 in AALBC's 2014 National Bestseller List.

A proud member of NK Promo Partners, a spin-off of the former M-LAS (Macro Literary All-Stars), she made her writing debut as a co-contributor to *Baring It All: The Ins and Outs of Publishing*, which the group released in 2014. *No Right Way to do a Wrong Thing* was her first work of fiction. She released her first Christian inspirational book *Growth: God's Extraordinary Lessons from Ordinary Occurrences* in 2021.

Janice is happily married to Pastor Sammie Lee Allen.

Join Janice M. Allen's mailing list at www.janicemallen.com

Like Janice's Facebook page at
https://www.facebook.com/Author Janice M. Allen